Koan Khmer

Koan Khmer

A Novel

Bunkong Tuon

Curbstone Books
Northwestern University Press
Evanston, Illinois

Curbstone Books
Northwestern University Press
www.nupress.northwestern.edu

Printed in the United States of America

10   9   8   7   6   5   4   3   2   1

This is a work of fiction. Characters, places, and events are the product of the
author's imagination or are used fictitiously and do not represent actual people,
places, or events.

Library of Congress Cataloging-in-Publication Data

Names: Tuon, Bunkong, 1972– author.
Title: Koan Khmer : a novel / Bunkong Tuon.
Description: Evanston : Curbstone Books/Northwestern University Press, 2024.
Identifiers: LCCN 2024002012 | ISBN 9780810147430 (paperback) |
    ISBN 9780810147447 (ebook)
Subjects: LCGFT: Novels.
Classification: LCC PS3620.U63 K63 2024 | DDC 813.6—dc23/eng/20240117
LC record available at https://lccn.loc.gov/2024002012

For April and David

Always for Yoeum Preng (my "Lok-Yeay")

Contents

PART III. **A Portrait of the Artist as a
        Young Cambodian American**

PART 1

A Cambodian Family Portrait

Under the Tamarind Tree

"What was my mother like?" I asked my aunts and grandmother one Saturday afternoon in our family's home in Massachusetts.

Ming Bonavy and Ming Narin sat on the couch with my grandmother, Lok-Yeay, between them. I lay on my belly looking up from the floor. The tape recorder whirred under an old lamp on the corner table. Ming Narin was quiet, staring into the distance.

Ming Bonavy said, "She was the most beautiful woman I had ever known."

"She was a good daughter. She helped around the kitchen and was always taking care of her younger brother and sisters," Lok-Yeay said.

According to my grandmother and aunts, my mother had a natural proclivity for learning. As a young girl, after completing her chores, she would escape into the world of books, sitting under a mango tree in the backyard reading everything from Cambodian folktales and romance novels to books on history, philosophy, and politics. Ming Narin added, "She always had a book in her hands. And she was strict with us. If we did something wrong, she would call us over, explain why it was wrong and, with a branch from one of our coconut trees, hit us."

Ming Bonavy continued, "I was a tomboy. I played marbles and kicked the cans with the boys in our village. I loved flying kites. One day, as I was building a kite, your Pu Ly, who wasn't your uncle then, saw me sitting in the dirt, my legs splayed unladylike, my lips pursed in concentration. He went to your mother and said, 'Bong Pheap, I saw Poan Bonavy making a kite. She's been playing with the boys a lot these days.' When I got home, your mother called me over and said that Pu Ly had paid her a visit. She then explained that girls shouldn't play with boys. She told me not to embarrass our family again, as her hand reached for a switch."

This was before my mother's marriage to my father, before the Khmer Rouge takeover, before Pol Pot times when she got sick from a lack of food and medicine. My aunts and Lok-Yeay grew quiet. Ming Bonavy closed her eyes and smiled. Ming Narin raised her right hand and playfully tapped her younger sister's head with her knuckles. "Continue with your story," she said. "The boy needs to know."

"When your mother was on her deathbed, she told many Cambodian fables and proverbs to teach me, her youngest sister, how to be a proper Cambodian woman. Even when she was dying, she thought of us, her family. She asked, 'How is the wound on my leg, Poan Bonavy? Does it fester with maggots and pus? When you finish dressing my wound, I will tell you a story about the old tiger with a wound on his head and the young girl who dresses that creature's wound.'"

Ming Bonavy explained, "Although she was strict, she was a good sister to us. Your mother would tell me tales about tigers and crocodiles, about Judge Rabbit and Snake Geangong. I was young then and knew nothing. After her death, I returned to work at the children's labor camp. Those tales helped me survive the Khmer Rouge, especially stories about Judge Rabbit, who outwits his bigger and stronger enemies." Tears in her eyes, she continued, "Of all the people in my life, I took care of your mother the most, more than I have taken care of my own mother, Lok-Yeay. I washed your mother's tiny, frail body, hunted eels when she craved them, skinned frogs when she was hungry for them. But no matter how much she ate, her body just withered. There was nothing we could do. We felt helpless, watching her slip away before our eyes."

"What about doctors and nurses? Why didn't you take my mother to the hospital?"

Ming Narin answered, "There were no doctors and nurses under Pol Pot. They were all killed during the first month the Khmer Rouge took over our village. The Khmer Rouge doctors and nurses were peasants like us. They offered barks dipped in honey for patients to suck on. We chewed on them for the sweetness that was lacking in our lives."

Ming Bonavy continued, "Your mother was brave. Her spirit was high, and she was constantly reassuring us that things would turn out as they should. She believed in karma, in fate. Her mind was clearer than ours. We were still in the Khmer Rouge world, but she was no longer among us. She was an angel. A tavedah."

A muffled choke escaped from Ming Narin. When my mother passed away, Ming Narin asked her maekong, the brigade leader, if she could attend her sister's burial, but the maekong refused. To this day, Ming Narin carries guilt for not being able to care for her older sister and say goodbye to her.

The afternoon sun came through the window to rest on the floor next to me. Ming Bonavy looked at the sunlight pouring into the room and said, "They loved one another very much, you know, your mother and father. Of all the marriages I've seen, theirs was the purest. It was something I hoped for when I agreed to marry your uncle." She stopped retelling her stories then, and started sobbing. Lok-Yeay gently squeezed her youngest daughter's leg. Ming Bonavy looked up at Lok-Yeay and said, "I miss listening to her stories the most. I miss her very much."

Seeing the pain I had caused my aunts and grandmother, I apologized for asking them to revisit their past. Ming Bonavy said, "It's OK. You need to know this. You need to know where you came from."

I was a graduate student taking a seminar on cultural anthropology. The final assignment was a research project that required me to interview my surviving family members. But even before the seminar, I had always wanted to know my family's history. I'd been afraid to ask. My uncles and aunts, like many other Cambodian refugees, did not easily talk about the past, their lives in the refugee camps and the atrocities and barbarity they'd witnessed and endured under the Khmer Rouge regime. The assignment provided a good excuse for me to ask about my parents and, by extension, to learn how and in what ways Pol Pot had destroyed my family. Being required by a university professor added legitimacy to my arrival at our family's home armed with a booklet of questions and a tape recorder.

This was all I knew about my parents. My mother passed away when I was about three years old. My father stayed behind in Cambodia when my family left for the refugee camps in Thailand. I needed to know more than just these two facts. I needed to know who my parents were, what they'd thought and felt, their hopes and dreams, their thoughts about me, their first and only child. Their absence had always been a haunting presence in my life, becoming palpable when I saw my cousins interacting with their parents— how their mothers cooked for them, how their fathers asked them about school. It wasn't just what was said; it was the way my uncles and aunts spoke to their children that made me wonder about my own mother and father. What were my parents like? What would my father say to me if he were alive today? In what tone would my mother speak to me? Would I be a different person if I'd grown up with my parents? Would I be less self-conscious, more confident?

Lok-Yeay walked over to the cabinet we bought at the Salvation Army and took out a plastic grocery bag that contained family photographs. She handed me a black-and-white photograph. It was my parents' wedding picture. Duct tape held together the torn edges.

I studied the photo of my parents standing next to each other, family supporting them on either side. Lok-Yeay stood next to her daughter and my father's uncle next to him. My mother was dressed in a traditional Khmer wedding dress. She had big round eyes, with jewelry adorning her neck, wrists, and ankles. I was surprised at the way she smiled, so freely that her white teeth showed. She was the only one in the photograph who was smiling. This certainly wasn't the image I had of her; in my mind, my mother was perpetually dying from hunger and sickness, her body wasting away on a bamboo bed while Lok-Yeay went to work at the sahakgor, a communal dining hall, under the watchful eyes of the Khmer Rouge. I was glad to see my Lok-Mak happy and healthy in at least one moment of her life.

My fingers traced the outlines of my mother and father on the photograph. My mother looked like any other Cambodian woman. I couldn't see how I was related to her, but I accepted this woman as my mother because my aunts, uncles, and grandmother told me it was so. "You have her eyes and cheekbones," Ming Bonavy said. Lok-Yeay added, "You have her face." So I learned to adore her, this woman in the wedding picture. I learned to love her unconditionally, as any child should love his mother.

As for my father, I imagined wild stories about him. He was a rebel, a ladies' man, but he loved only his wife, my mother, and no one else. Their love was tender, honest, and mutual. That was the lesson I gleaned from Ming Bonavy's stories, so I believed it. I also needed to believe that my mother and father loved each other very much. It made me feel good about myself.

In the wedding photograph, my father looked serious standing next to my mother. He had high cheekbones and, as far as I could tell, there was no hint of a smile on his thin face. A glimmer of joy, I thought I detected, sparkled in his sunken eyes. With this photograph in my hand, I traced my fingers over my parents' faces, crossing land and sea, searching for another world, wanting desperately to know what they would say to me if they were alive.

I don't know if the memory I have of my mother's funeral is real or if I dreamed it up. Nevertheless, I return to it like a prayer. When this memory comes over me, I feel the hot afternoon sun of a Battambang summer with the wind caressing my wet cheeks.

I remember the glaring sun that stood between the tamarind tree and the house. I smell the burning incense and hear the hypnotic chanting of Buddhist monks coming from the house, where my mother lay in a white shroud.

I was sitting on the lap of a young girl. We were under the tamarind tree.

I wanted so much to go to her, my mother who was sleeping so peacefully, so deeply. Each time I heard a Buddhist prayer coming from the house, I cried. Each time I cried, the young girl pinched my left thigh with her fingers. The louder I cried, the harder she pinched.

I didn't understand why I wasn't allowed to be with my mother. I found the old people, these strangers in our house, to be rude, inconsiderate, and disrespectful. "Why are they making such noise? How could they be so rude? Can't they see Lok-Mak is trying to sleep?" I asked the young girl. When she didn't say anything, I struggled to break free from her grip. She then answered my question with a pinch on my right thigh. Instead of sitting still and listening to what she had to say, I cried, "I want to be with Lok-Mak! Why can't I be with her? Where's Lok-Yeay? Go away from our house, go away, everyone, just go away. Lok-Mak is trying to sleep. I want to go and sleep with her."

The louder I cried, the harder the girl pinched me. It was a strange dance. In our different ways, we were dancing together to the hypnotic music of the Buddhist chants, dancing to the events in that house, dancing in the intolerable heat beyond the shade of the tamarind tree.

When I recounted to my aunts and Lok-Yeay this memory of someone pinching me under a tree, they began sobbing. Ming Bonavy said, "You were so young. How could you remember all of that? You wanted so much to see your mother, but they wouldn't let you. They were afraid the bad spirits might see you and possess you. So they asked me to take you out of the house. I'm sorry I pinched you. I was in pain too. I lost my beloved sister that day."

Birth

I don't know how old I actually am.

My aunts and uncles disagree over the year of my birth. I learned later, after talking to my family, that the immigration people had it all wrong. My social security card, my driver's license, and my school record all have my birth year listed as 1972. This year, along with my birthday, was chosen so that I would appear on paper closer in age to an uncle who'd lost both parents to the Khmer Rouge. His father was Lok-Yeay's youngest brother, Atid Meas, who disappeared during the Khmer Rouge's purge in early 1975. His crime was education. Our family, like most families from the Battambang Province, was dirt-poor. Around the age of ten, Atid Meas was sent to live and work at a monastery, where he was taught to read and write by the head monk. He memorized Khmer poetry, proverbs, Buddhist scriptures; he read works on Cambodian history and politics. He also picked up foreign languages, memorizing syllables and accents, vocabulary and verb conjugation in French, English, Việt, Thai, and Chinese.

"He was brilliant, a genius," Ming Bonavy said of her uncle.

Lok-Yeay chimed in, "The French really liked him. They took him wherever they went because he spoke so well and knew so much about Khmer history and culture." Atid Meas went to Siem Reap, where he ended up working as a translator and tour guide. According to Oum Seyha, wherever Atid Meas went, he made friends. He simply knew how to talk to people. It didn't matter if you were a farmer from the countryside or a general in the Lon Nol government, once he talked to you, you would feel that he was your long-lost best friend from childhood.

"His words opened doors," Oum Seyha said, smiling in admiration. "He knew exactly what people wanted before they even opened their mouths."

As a guide, Atid Meas was invaluable to the French-speaking and English-speaking tourists. He would dine with ambassadors and generals alike. When the Khmer Rouge came to power, he and his wife were seen as enemies of the state and were executed in the first month of the takeover. His children survived. In 1979, when the Khmer Regime collapsed, Pu Dara, Lok-Yeay's youngest son, went to Siem Reap to get two of Atid Meas's children, Vutha and Bopha. Their two older sisters were thought to have been killed. Pu Dara brought Vutha and Bopha back to our village in Battambang. When we were at a refugee camp in Thailand applying for sponsorship, Lok-Yeay said, "I have enough separation in this lifetime. I can't bear it anymore." Oum Seyha changed my last name to "Sok," his father's last name. He also changed our birthdates. He made me a few years older, closer to Vutha and Bopha in age. These changes were made so that, on paper, we were one big family, giving us a better chance of not getting separated.

That was how we became a family of blood and historical circumstances, where our names and birthdates changed during the immigration process. And over the years we learned to be kind and caring to one another, became a real family, because all we had was each other.

This is one of the reasons why I don't feel particularly special about my birthday. My birthday is a day invented for the immigration officers. After a while, I got tired of correcting people and telling them about the backstory of this date on my green card. I just got used to my fake birthday; it is the only birthday I have known. Back then, we didn't celebrate birthdays anyway. Birthday celebrations were an American thing. My uncles and aunts were too busy with work and trying to stay afloat to observe this "extravagant" tradition. They had no time for such trifles. And, since there were no birth certificates back then, they couldn't even agree on the year of my birth. Oum Seyha thought it was 1972; his wife disagreed. She was certain it was 1974, the year before the Khmer Rouge entered Phnom Penh and drenched Cambodia in blood, sadness, and grief. With the American War in Việt Nam raging to the east of us and the political turmoil and factional violence shaking up Cambodia at the time, my birthday was the least of their worries.

What Lok-Yeay remembered was the season. It must have been around harvest time, she said, because farmers were at home resting with their families and awaiting the fruits of their labor. People were gearing up for the New Year celebration. And everyone in the village was happy for the young newlywed couple expecting their first child. My father's relatives came by train from the southeastern part of Cambodia, which had just become part of Việt Nam. They bore fruits and spices from the Khmer Krom-Mekong Delta region. My mother's family prepared food to welcome guests. Lok-Yeay's sister was making tuk kroeung, a dipping sauce made from broiled fish, fermented fish, garlic, chilies, and lime. Lok-Yeay asked, "Shouldn't we also have something else for our guests? Our in-laws came all the way from the other side of the country. We should make something fancy, more opulent, befitting this special occasion." Tuk kroeung, a staple diet for Cambodian farmers in the countryside, was not enough for her in-laws, so my grandmother went to the local open market and bought chicken and beef. Relatives from surrounding villages came to help. The women sat in small circles telling stories and laughing. With mortars and pestles, they ground and smashed the garlic, chilies, and coriander pods. Others minced lemongrass, kaffir leaves, and green and red chilies. They were making chicken and beef curries. They were also making traditional peasant food, such as tuk kapik, a shrimp-paste dipping sauce, somlor srae, literally translated as peasant soup, larp, a kind of Cambodian beef salad, and bok lahong, Cambodian papaya salad.

When the in-laws arrived, my family greeted each other by pressing their hands together and smiling. They exchanged gifts and told stories about my mother and father when they were kids. As the two families became comfortable with one another, the men talked politics, how they'd begun seeing Vietnamese military presence in Khmer Krom and felt the pressure to join the South Vietnamese army. That was why my father and his uncle left and came to Battambang, the western part of Cambodia. My father married my mother, and his uncle married my mother's aunt, Lok-Yeay's sister, the one who was making tuk kroeung. They sat in large circles, ate stir-fried chicken and beef curry, told stories about their travels, drank homemade sweet rice wine, and laughed. One of the in-laws said that he liked best the tuk kroeung and prahouk that Lok-Yeay's sister made. Some nodded their heads in agreement; others cheered. They were farmers sitting together in large circles and eating peasant food, sharing stories of the rainy and harvest seasons, laughing and drinking away the hardships. Someone from Khmer Krom asked, "Have you decided on the baby's name?"

The laughter and chatting subsided, and heads turned to the expectant parents. With her left hand covering her mouth, my mother said, "We decided to call him 'Joam' in honor of everyone being here. It's a name befitting this special occasion." In Khmer, "Joam" meant "to come together" or "to be together." My father looked at his young wife and smiled proudly. Everyone laughed at the soon-to-be parents and began toasting to the future of the baby and the young couple. It was one of the happiest memories for Lok-Yeay who, with the help of her family and friends, was able to pull off such a celebration. Her husband had passed away from tuberculosis several years prior. The success of this family gathering and the birth of her first grandchild made all the sacrifices she had made over the years as a single mother worth it.

But the festive mood changed when I was born. I cried for three days and two nights. I refused my mother's milk and my father's soothing words. Whenever anyone tried to pick me up, I cried and cried as if someone or something was pinching my flesh. It got so bad that no one could sleep. Lok-Yeay was the one who stayed up all night and cared for me.

On the third day, Lok-Yeay left the house in search of a lok-kru, a shaman. The lok-kru told my grandmother that my spirit mother was missing me. She had been crying for her child to return to her in the spirit world. He said that monks must be invited for a renaming ceremony so that my spirit mother would not be able to find me. Lok-Yeay quickly visited the local wat and invited the monks; my parents and relatives called on friends and neighbors for help. A second gathering now took place at Lok-Yeay's home. Incense was burned; monks in brown and yellow robes chanted, with the lok-kru leading the ceremony. On that day, I was given a new name, "Samnang," which meant "luck" or "lucky" in Khmer.

After the name change, I stopped crying and accepted my mother's milk. The monks, the lok-kru, family, and friends were relieved. My parents rejoiced; they were happy to have their child back with them in this world. The neighbors were happy because now they could sleep. The monks returned to the wat and continued their monastic life. Friends and neighbors went back to their homes in nearby villages. Soon after, my father's family made the journey back to Khmer Krom. Before he left, the lok-kru said to my grandmother, "Like his birth, a difficult beginning awaits your grandson. But he will flourish. He will find peace and success later in life. He will be a leader of his people."

Despite U.S. military planes flying over their heads and news of the Khmer Rouge circling Phnom Penh, the people in my village were optimistic about the future. In a few weeks, there would be the New Year celebration. Families would bring food to monks at the temples. Children would chase each other around. Teenagers would throw colorful powder at each other, play tug-of-war, and flirt. There would be plenty of noms, sticky rice desserts, and coconut pastries for all to enjoy. There would be music and dancing. For now, there would be no hunger and starvation, no people sent to Angkar Leur and made to disappear, no friends becoming enemies, no children turning against parents, no Khmer Rouge in black clothes and with dark hearts.

My grandmother was happiest in this period of her life. She had all her children with her. And she was beaming with pride for her daughter and son-in-law. They were young, good, and hardworking people, and deserved this new beginning in their life together as husband and wife. She wished her own husband were alive to witness and experience this new happiness, where her very being overflowed and was reenergized with love. Such happiness had to do with this new word, this new identity she had taken upon my birth: Lok-Yeay.

Leaving Cambodia

I don't remember much about life under the Khmer Rouge. I was too little. I don't remember the hunger that I've read about in books and seen depicted in films like *The Killing Fields*. All I remember is the silence and the hot, dry sun and feeling like everyone was gone, left before sunrise to work somewhere, abandoning me. I was alone often. With a tree branch in hand, I walked around, looking for lizards and frogs. One time, a snake crawled out of a hole in the ground, and I jumped back and fell on my butt. I watched the snake slither away into the rice fields.

Years later, in graduate school, I asked my uncles and aunts what life was like when the Khmer Rouge took over Cambodia. They were quiet. Oum Seyha finally said, "It was a terrible time. People were starving and dying." After a pause, he added, "You don't need to know this stuff, Samnang. Focus on your studies and be a doctor or an engineer."

He pursed his lips when he saw me writing in a notebook. I reassured him, "The only people reading this essay will be me and my professor."

He said, "We're lucky to be here in America. U.S.A. is number one. Tell your professor that."

"I will. Don't worry. No government officials will be reading this," I told him.

He said, "Tell your professor that we are happy to be here. We hate communism. We hate Việt Nam. We hate China. We love only America. America is the number-one country in the world. Go ahead. Write it down, boy."

Not wanting to argue with my uncle about why we were in America in the first place, how Nixon's bombs helped to destroy Cambodia's countryside, mobilize support from farmers and the working class for the Khmer Rouge, and consequently disperse us from our motherland, I kept quiet. But still wanting to hear stories of our family past, I said, "Fine! Then tell me how we left Cambodia and arrived at the refugee camps in Thailand."

As for me, all I remember was being out in the rice field, looking for lizards and frogs. I remember running naked in the woods behind our hut. Everyone was so busy working for Angkar that they paid no attention to the naked boy in the woods. I remember how everything was alive. The trees moved their branches. The leaves shimmered. The wind whispered. Voices were everywhere. In the sky. In the trees and bushes. In the rice fields and streams. I felt loved, protected, and comforted. And I fell asleep as the world of nature sang sweet lullabies, surrounding me with great tenderness.

The rice stalks gathered around me and, whether in a dream or not I couldn't tell, voices spoke from everywhere. *Who is this child coming here each day to sleep at our feet? Does he have a name? Where are his parents? Look at how peacefully he sleeps at our feet! Look at his rib cage. Poor boy. He is such a sweet boy. We shall adopt him and make him our own.*

When I woke up, I felt rejuvenated and at peace. I walked home and, as soon as I saw Lok-Yeay, I ran to her. When she asked where I had been, I pointed to the rice field. She nodded and said, "Let's clean up, Samnang. I have some rice I saved for you."

It was late April 1979, four years after the Khmer Rouge had entered Phnom Penh and turned the once green and fertile fields of Cambodia into the blood-soaked killing fields that it is unfortunately known for today, with roughly a quarter of its population having lost their lives to executions, forced labor, starvation, and sickness. My uncle, Oum Piseth, and my great-uncle, Atid Meas, were the first to go because they were educated. My mother died from hunger and sickness in 1978, one year before the Vietnamese army invaded Cambodia, forcing the Khmer Rouge out of power and scurrying into the thick jungles near Thailand. According to those who came back from Thailand to trade goods with the Thai people, the U.N. had set up camp inside the Thai border, providing food and medicine for refugees from Việt Nam, Laos, and Cambodia. Many, including my family, took this opportunity and left our country for these camps. We didn't know there would be a sponsorship program that would deliver us to other parts of the world. We were hungry and scared; we went for food and protection.

Oum Seyha said to Lok-Yeay, "Lok-Mak, Việt Nam is communist, like the Khmer Rouge are communist. Cambodia under Việt Nam is the same as Cambodia under Pol Pot." Gritting his teeth, Oum Seyha added, "We have lived for four years under communist rule and look where that got us. We must leave while we still can!"

"But this is our home, Koan Seyha. Cambodia is all we know. We buried Sopheap here. I don't want to leave her all alone."

"Lok-Mak, she won't be alone. She has Bong Piseth and Oum Atid Meas." Oum Seyha was quiet but determined.

At the mention of her eldest son, Lok-Yeay's lips trembled. She repeated, "Cambodia is all I know. I don't want to be a refugee, someone without a home, someone who seeks shelter in another country."

Oum Seyha responded, "If we stay here, we'll starve. There's food at the camps. Lok-Mak, listen to me. We must leave for Samnang's sake. His mother would want it. There's a future for him there, away from here. There's no longer life here."

The next morning Lok-Yeay left her house, crossed the town square with its noodle shop, barbershop, and newsstand, passed the primary school and the Buddhist temple on the other side of the village, and walked on a narrow dirt path leading to my father's house. My father was sitting on the steps smoking cigarettes and listening to the radio. He looked up, smiled, and greeted my grandmother with his palms pressed high together to his chin to show respect for his mother-in-law. "Aroun sousdei, Lok-Mak," he said.

Lok-Yeay returned the greeting with her palms pressed together, "Aroun sousdei, Atid," and said, "I want to talk to you about Samnang."

"He's a good smart boy. Is there something wrong, Lok-Mak?" My father looked concerned.

"I know you have taken a woman. You are a man, and you have your needs. I understand, but I don't want my grandson to be someone's stepchild. You will marry this woman and have children with her. Samnang will be a second-class citizen in this new home."

"He is my firstborn, and I will take care of him." My father looked up at the blackbirds hopping from one branch to the next, chirping their meaningless songs.

Lok-Yeay continued, "A woman naturally loves her own children more than the children of another woman. That is normal. You can't blame her for that." Under the hot sun, silence stood between them. Lok-Yeay looked at my father, then said, "Listen, Atid. Samnang is all I have left of my daughter, and I want to take him with me when we leave for Thailand."

My father was not surprised at the news of Lok-Yeay and her family leaving. Many of the villagers had packed up their belongings, left their houses to friends and family members, and made the journey to Thailand. He was quiet at the mention of his wife. After the collapse of the Khmer Rouge regime, he took to drinking and staying up late at night with friends. My grandmother had been taking care of me ever since my mother became sick. When she went to the sahakgor to cook food for the entire village, she took me with her. She would put me on her hip and cook whatever fish stew the Khmer Rouge made her cook, cut whatever vegetables she was ordered to prepare, and clean whatever plates they had. Because she worked at the sahakgor, I never went hungry. She would hide a cup of gruel or a fish head for me to eat later in the evening.

My father finally said to Lok-Yeay, "Promise me that he will not be treated any differently from the other children and that you will protect him as best as you can."

Lok-Yeay nodded. "You have my word, Atid. He is, after all, my own flesh and blood."

A few days later, my father began showing up at Lok-Yeay's house looking for me. He took me to the noodle shop in the town square. We had rice noodles in beef broth with bean sprouts, mints, chilies, and lime. I remember my father trying to tell me something important, but the noodles tasted so good. I was also preoccupied with the small black-and-white television that hung high on the wall behind the counter. I was mesmerized by the images and sounds coming from that little box.

"Samnang, you will be leaving with Lok-Yeay in a few days. But this separation is only temporary. The Vietnamese have driven out the Khmer Rouge, and a new government will soon be installed. Plans are underway to rebuild our country. I speak Việt and I will be able to help when the time comes. There will be peace in Cambodia again. Our separation will not be long. Do you understand, Samnang?"

I sucked in the noodles and nodded. My father patted my head and said he loved me very much.

On the day before our departure, my father arrived early at Lok-Yeay's house and took me to an ice cream shop. He asked about my favorite flavor. I pointed to the rainbow-colored ice cream in a big round container because it looked so beautiful. When my father handed me a plastic cup of the ice cream, I licked the rainbow swirl as my father looked on and smiled. He kept telling me that we would be apart only for a while. We would see each other again. Then my father asked if I wanted some soda pop. I nodded eagerly.

After the soda pop, he took me to another store on the other side of the village square. Then he took me to see his friends.

When Lok-Yeay found out that my father had taken me out, she was furious. She walked to the village center and went from one stall to the next asking each owner about my father and me. A neighbor finally told her where she had seen us last.

My father and Lok-Yeay stood on the dirt road in front of the noodle shop talking to each other about me. I don't remember what they said. I remember hands moved me from my father's side to my grandmother's. I remember at one point they each held one of my hands. My father held tightly my left hand, while Lok-Yeay squeezed my right and pulled me to her side. My father let go of my hand once my mother's name was mentioned.

Looking back on that day, I remember it fondly. I had ice cream and soda pop and watched TV with my father. I spent the entire day with him. I felt immense love; I was my father's special boy. It was one of the happiest memories of my childhood in Cambodia.

Night had covered the sky with its bright starry blanket. Our path was illuminated by the stars and we felt protected, guided by nature's brilliance. Then, like the nights before, the gunfire pierced the night. The grounds trembled. The dark green leaves shook. The trees swayed and the mountains cried, and we heard people screaming, crying for help, begging Lord Buddha to intervene, and calling out for family and friends. Led by a guide, we had been walking and running in the forest for days now, corpses and body parts scattered along the sides of the jungle path. But we walked with a quiet determination and dreams of a safer world.

Later that night, the rain fell lightly over our heads. We trudged along the narrow path; our guide, a Thai-Khmer who grew up in Pailin, a town close to the border, walked in front of us. For his service, Lok-Yeay gave him my mother's wedding bracelet. I was on Lok-Yeay's back while Atid Meas's children, Vutha and Bopha, walked behind us, followed by Pu Dara. Lok-Ta, a former Buddhist monk who had married my grandmother, and Oum Seyha walked ahead of us, just behind the guide. Ming Narin, Pu Ly, and Ming Bonavy were already at the camp. They went ahead of us a week earlier, and seeing that it was relatively safe, Oum Seyha and Pu Dara came back for us.

Bopha, who was eleven at the time, looked up at the night sky and opened her mouth to receive the rainwater. Pu Dara yelled at her, "Hurry up, Koan. We cannot slow down. I'll give you water once we're at a safer place."

Bopha picked up her tiny feet to keep pace with the adults, but the mud was thick and heavy. I was on my grandmother's back, feet dangling from the kromar. "It isn't fair that the little brat gets to sit like a king on his grandmother's back," Bopha grumbled to herself. Angrily she stuck her tongue out in the darkness of the night.

Overwhelmed with exhaustion, she no longer had control over her eyelids, which got heavier with each mud-laden step. She caught herself and was momentarily awake. She tried to pick up her skinny legs and move them as quickly as she could. If she slowed down now, they would yell at her again. She could see nothing except the few feet ahead of her. She must move those legs of hers. This was her family now, she repeatedly told herself, and she must do everything in her power to make them like her. If they didn't like her, they could at least see that she was trying her best and take pity on her. But as she quickened her pace, her small legs gave in and she fell face first in the mud. She let out a small, helpless cry.

The guide stopped, turned around, and flashed a light on Bopha's face. Nothing could be seen except her round white eyes; her face was plastered with mud.

On my grandmother's back, I let out a laugh and said, "Look! A hungry ghost!" I then made funny faces. Lok-Yeay hit me across the head, and I kept quiet after that.

We walked on and on in the dark until we reached the top of a hill. "We're about a day away from the camp," the guide told us. "Be careful of Thai soldiers. They will kick you when they feel like it. Stay inside the camp and be around the United Nations people. Or else the Thai soldiers will put you in a truck and drop you off in the middle of a battlefield. You have the Thai to one side and the Khmer Rouge on the other. Don't leave the U.N. camp."

We saw other families pitching tents and building fires. The guide said we might as well camp there for the evening and gather our strength for the final stretch of the journey. Lok-Ta put down his bundle, and Lok-Yeay took out rice and dried salted fish from plastic bags. We huddled around her. Vutha, Bopha, and I ate rice and fish with Lok-Ta and Lok-Yeay, while Pu Dara, Pu Seyha, and the guide stood around smoking cigarettes and talking about the fighting between Khmer Rouge soldiers and Cambodia's Para commandos. After dinner, I rested my head on Lok-Yeay's lap and quickly fell asleep.

Later that night, we were awakened by gunfire. It was too dark to see anything. All we heard was a quick succession of gunshots and the sound of women and children crying. A man's voice yelled, "Give us all your gold and jewelry or we'll kill each and every one of you." Lok-Yeay picked me up and ran into the woods. Everything happened so quickly. Everyone left their belongings and ran into the woods. After the robbery, we came back to the campsite and found our bags ransacked. Our guide was nowhere to be found. Oum Seyha said, "We're not that far from the U.N. camp. I remember walking on this very trail last week." We packed up our pots and pans and left in the middle of the night. "Hurry, stay low and be quiet. We're almost there," Oum Seyha said, as he led with a flashlight. We walked all night and arrived at the camp the next morning. We crossed the dusty road to the registration center, a solitary building surrounded by tents.

Bopha noticed the sick watching us from their tents. Their sunken eyes stared with exhaustion, their lips dry and crusty. She saw a man being carried on a hammock toward a triage area near the registration center. He was cursing anyone who dared look at him. Then another man came by, dragging himself along with his arms; his legs had been amputated. The amputee frightened Bopha. She wanted to cry out but muffled her scream. She promised herself then that when she grew up, she would become a doctor. She would help the sick and needy. That night, she cried quietly in the corner of the hut. She could not erase from memory those sunken desperate eyes staring at her, the amputee moving toward her, and the scream of the man on the hammock.

At the registration center, Oum Seyha put down our names, birth dates, and the name of our home village; we were then given cans of food. We were told that a truck would come once a week to ration out rice, meats, and canned goods. Because everything was scarce, some of the refugees fought among themselves as they scrambled for food. The Thai soldiers stood watching as the U.N. staff unloaded bags of rice and canned goods. When the U.N. workers left, one soldier came over and kicked a young man in the stomach. The others watched and laughed.

Back at our tent, Pu Dara exclaimed, "Can you believe it? Fish in a tin can? You don't need to go to a river to fish. All you have to do is use this device and open this can here, and you get fish already marinated in tomato sauce! This is heaven!" He then began cutting the top of an aluminum can with a small silver can opener. Once it was opened, he passed around the can of mackerel in tomato sauce. We each took turns marveling at this tiny miracle.

In a quiet corner, Vutha sat and ate the canned fruit that was distributed by the U.N. staff. The sweet syrup felt like childhood on his tongue. It had been years since he'd had something this good, this sweet to eat. It was then prerevolutionary times, before the Khmer Rouge takeover of the country, when he was with his father on a trip to Pailin, near the Thai border. He had chek chien, bananas coated with flour and palm sugar and deep-fried in oil, and he associated that syrupy flavor with the tender ways of his father, Atid Meas. He sat in his little corner of the tent, chewing the sweet fruits and thinking of his Pok. Mucus mixed with tears slid down his chin as he spooned the syrupy pieces of pear, apple, and red grape into his dry mouth.

That evening, we sat together in a large circle and ate. The floor was hard, dry dirt. Oum Seyha, who always wanted to teach, talked about applying for a teaching certificate to teach Khmer to the children at the camp. Ming Bonavy hoped to work for the Red Cross's Save the Children program. She wanted to practice her English with the Americans and Australians. Ming Narin was pregnant with her first child. Her husband, Pu Ly, would begin working as a translator for the local clinic the next day. Vutha, Bopha, and I were going to enroll at the local school to learn English. The future seemed bright for us. The Khmer Rouge period was behind us now. Everything was possible.

Around four in the morning, we woke up to gunfire and explosions outside the camp. Then the sounds came closer. People were running. Someone yelled, "The Para soldiers and the Khmer Rouge are fighting again!" Women folded their hands to their chests and prayed to the Buddha and ancestors for help. We ran out of our tent and jumped into a large hole in the ground. When the stench reached us, we realized that we were hiding in a communal toilet, but it was too late by then. There was excrement everywhere: on our feet, our hands, our faces. I stopped crying for a second to realize that my body was shaking uncontrollably. My legs were kicking, my hands shaking, my teeth chattering. I felt a chill overtaking my tiny body.

Over our heads missiles whistled like old friends chatting excitedly on an evening stroll. Minutes later, an explosion lit up the night and crumbled one of the makeshift houses. I was trembling and crying. Pu Ly told Lok-Yeay to keep me quiet. "You don't want the Khmer Rouge soldiers to find us! Or we will be dead! They will cut off all our heads!"

Upon hearing this, I lost control of my bladder. Urine soaked my black pajama pants and bare feet.

We then saw a white man crouching in front of us. He had a camera around his neck. We'd seen him earlier that day; he was a journalist from the *New York Times*. Pu Ly whistled with his hands and made a gesture for him to join us. The photographer nodded his head and jumped into the pit. Together, covered in feces, we hid in the shithole: the American photographer and my Cambodian family.

Half an hour later, the fighting subsided. The smell of gunfire and fear was everywhere. We returned to our tent and washed the excrement off our hands, feet, and faces. I was told to go back to sleep on the dirt floor. Occasionally, we were alerted to the sounds of *tuk-tuk-tuk-tuk*, as if the Khmer Rouge were reminding us that they were still around and could take us away any minute. Then, silence again. No one slept much that first night at our new home.

The following day, Lok-Yeay met a neighbor from our village on her way to the registration center. The woman and her family left a few days after us. She said that on the night we left, my father came looking for me. But by that time, it was already too late. "We saw him the next morning," the neighbor said. "He was crying. I told him that if I saw you, I would tell you that he came for his son."

I wasn't told about this until some twenty years later, when I was in graduate school and started asking questions about my family history. Lok-Yeay said, "Your father came looking for you, but we were already at the refugee camp by then. It was too late for him."

My heart sank. What could I have said to her? And what could they have done at that time? Send me back to my father while the Khmer Rouge and Para soldiers were still fighting? And she was my grandmother, after all. I was what was left of her daughter.

Lok-Yeay and Her Children

Lok-Yeay had all of her remaining family members with her in the refugee camps in Thailand: Oum Seyha, Pu Dara, Ming Narin, and Ming Bonavy. Her oldest child, Oum Piseth, disappeared after the Khmer Rouge swept the country for enemies of Angkar. He was the son who joined the Lon Nol army after he failed the college entrance exam. He was living in Phnom Penh at the time. As a child of farmers, he didn't have the resources and connections needed to win favors from college and university officials and gain acceptance. Some said he joined the army because he was too embarrassed to return home. Others said he joined the army to impress the family of a city girl he had fallen in love with. No matter the reason he quit school and joined Lon Nol's army, everyone believed that Oum Piseth was dead, except Lok-Yeay who still sought a lok-kru for his whereabouts. Whenever she met someone, a lucky survivor from the Lon Nol army, she would ask him about her son, Piseth, the one who went to study in the big city and never came back.

Oum Seyha, her second child, became the head of the household when his father, Lok-Yeay's first husband, died from tuberculosis. In his teens, Oum Seyha dropped out of school to work on the land to pay off the family's debt so that his brothers and sisters could attend school. When asked if he ever regretted leaving school and not being able to pursue his dream of becoming a teacher, he said, "If I didn't do it, who else would have? Lok-Yeay was a single mother doing her best to feed all of us. We did what we had to do. I have no regrets."

My mother, Sopheap, was the third child, and the second to die under the Khmer Rouge regime.

Pu Dara was the fourth child, the youngest son. In his heyday, Pu Dara mimicked the fighting styles of Bruce Lee and made the same crying sounds as the legendary martial artist and actor. As part of his training, he even attempted to break coconuts with his bare knuckles and, in one story, his head. Once, under the influence of cannabis, he tried riding a moped up a palm tree. Many of the fathers in the village were weary of his exploits and kept close watch on their daughters.

The fifth child, Ming Narin, was known as the quiet one. Everyone knew to stay away when she got angry, but she was also the kindest and most loyal when you found yourself in her good graces.

Ming Bonavy was the youngest child. She was the aunt who cared for my mother when she was ill, who cooked eels when my mother craved eels, who hunted frogs when my mother craved frogs. She was the one who pinched my thighs to keep herself from screaming when they buried my mother.

These were Lok-Yeay's children. She did everything in her power to feed and protect them. After her husband's death, she and her eldest son worked the land in order to gain enough surplus to pay off the loan to the landowner whose money her husband borrowed to buy farming equipment. Between farming seasons, Lok-Yeay smuggled goods across the border between Thailand and Cambodia. As a young girl, she was taught Thai in school when Thailand occupied the northwestern part of Cambodia. Even to this day, she could sing Thailand's national anthem, "Phleng Chat Thai." She hid spices, salt, pepper, plates, sarongs, and even eels in her tightly lidded boxes. Once, she was trying to close the handle of the outside compartment when a piece of her clothing got caught on a nail as the train started moving. She was pregnant at the time with Ming Narin. Luckily, her friend Cheng saw what was happening, ran over, and helped her.

When smuggling was too dangerous, Lok-Yeay sold food to travelers, workers, and government officials at the train station in Battambang. At four in the morning, she got up to cook. By seven, with my mother Sopheap, she was at the station waiting for the train from Oakjrow. After the train left, she went to the market and bought what she needed for the next train arrival. She returned home and, with my mother's help, cooked again, a different dish from that morning.

Under the Khmer Rouge regime, she was given two choices: marry a recently defrocked monk or face execution. Lok-Yeay wasn't afraid of death, but she didn't want to leave her children alone in this brutal world. So she married this monk, my Lok-Ta, who had to learn the worldly ways of men and women. He had to learn to plow the land, work the fields, and dig dams. He had to learn how to love a woman and her family. Like her first husband, he was gentle. He never raised his voice at her or hit her.

Love, for Lok-Yeay, was getting up at the crack of dawn, blowing and fanning the embers under the heavy pots in order to cook the food to sell at the train station; it was smuggling eels and risking a beating, or worse, from the custom officials and the Thai police; it was taking a second husband not because she was lonely and needed a husband, but because she loved her children and didn't want them to be orphans. Love was walking up to my father that day and saying to him, "I don't want my grandson to be anyone's stepchild." It was also: "He is all that I have of my daughter."

Love did not come before marriage. Marriage was something you did when your parents said that the time had come. Love emerged from years of facing hardships alongside someone you were married to. You didn't know love until it hit you suddenly, as if by surprise, that you loved this man who had seen the worst of you and still stood by you, this man whom you were so afraid of on your wedding night, whose mother you couldn't stand, who took you away from your family, whose children you bore, whose bed and food you shared, whose frail body you cared for before it withered away and left you a widow in your late thirties to take care of your six children.

And then Lok-Yeay's children, my uncles and aunts, one by one, they got married. It was what people did when they came of age. Before we left for Thailand, Ming Narin married Pu Ly, a Chinese Cambodian from our village. In one of the refugee camps, Oum Seyha married a woman whose family was from a town outside of Phnom Penh. Pu Dara married a young Chinese Khmer woman from Preahnet Preah, also in Battambang province. Ming Bonavy was not yet of marriageable age. She was sixteen when we arrived in the first refugee camp in Thailand in 1979.

We were a family then. Though we lived in different sections of the camp, we were together. Lok-Yeay's and Lok-Ta's tent was the family center. That was where I slept. And this uncle or that aunt would drop by to check in on the grandparents. Sometimes we would gather for a large family dinner. Pu Dara and his wife brought somlor, Cambodian stew, with pork. Oum Seyha and his wife contributed fresh fish caught in the Gulf of Thailand. Pu Ly, who worked with Westerners, brought in beer and soda for the potluck. Lok-Yeay made tuk kroeung with fresh vegetables from her garden. We ate, drank, and talked about life at the camp. Being together and having so much food, someone, usually Ming Narin, mentioned how they had starved under the Khmer Rouge. "I prayed each night to Lord Buddha for just a few grains of white rice and salt. That was all my body needed, just rice and salt to keep it alive." And that got Ming Bonavy and Pu Dara to talk about friends whom they missed, those who were killed or died from hunger in those terrible times. It got quiet really quick after that. Lok-Ta finally said, "What happened is now in the past. Let's focus on what we have in the present: each other. We must pay attention to the now."

I remember one such gathering. We had rice and somlor made of vegetables from Lok-Yeay's garden. Pu Ly brought fried fish he received as a gift from a patient. At the time he was working as a medical interpreter at the U.N. clinic. He was a small, short muscular man, with a deep baritone. I was terrified of him.

After dinner, Bopha got up and left to play with her friends. This was unacceptable for Pu Ly. He recently married Ming Narin, and he needed to make his presence known in the family. "She is a girl, after all," he said in a deep voice that came from his small chest. "She must know her duties and wash the dishes without being reminded. Who would want to marry such a girl?" He looked at my uncles, aunts, and Lok-Ta as if everyone had failed Bopha by not raising her properly. I sat, listened, and watched Pu Ly's every move.

He got up from the dinner circle and called to her. When she poked her head in, Pu Ly yanked her arm, went behind her, and spanked her bottom with his hand.

"She is going to be someone's wife and someone's daughter-in-law someday. Her negligence will reflect badly on our family. This is unacceptable," he said to all of us.

He continued beating her. I felt so bad for Bopha, but I was also scared for myself. No one had ever beaten me before, but I knew this could happen to me too. We were both orphans with no one to protect us.

When Pu Dara tried to intervene, Pu Ly said, "This is for her own good. Such a thing must not happen again. She will remember to do the dishes from now on."

He reminded Bopha, "Neang eng keur jear srey!" *You are only a girl.*

He then asked if Bopha had learned from her mistake and would remember her duties as a young woman. But Bopha didn't answer him. So Pu Ly continued to beat her and remind her of her role. Bopha's brother, Vutha, sat in silence, eyes blinking, head bowing down to the dirty dishes in front of him. He was thirteen years old, and he couldn't do anything to help his little sister.

Instead of answering Pu Ly's questions, Bopha finally let out a piercing cry. The scream felt like it came from the bottom of her being, all those buried feelings—about her dead parents and missing sisters, about being one of the two known survivors in her family, about leaving her ancestral land—came rushing out. Pu Ly stopped momentarily, his hand yanked back, as if surprised by this daring girl.

As soon as she heard the cry, Lok-Yeay ran into the tent. She had been outside watering her vegetable garden. Lok-Yeay said, "You leave my niece alone. Whatever she did, you stop it. She's my little brother's daughter. She's all I have of him!"

Pu Ly stopped beating Bopha and backed away. If the children got out of hand, he warned Lok-Yeay, he would not be held responsible. The blame would fall upon every adult there. He had tried his best to discipline these unruly children. He left the tent in a storm of rage.

Bopha remained sitting on the ground sobbing. Her sarong was soaked with urine. Lok-Yeay told her to get up and wash herself. She did as she was told.

Bopha

Twenty-five years later, I still remember that night. Pu Ly hit Bopha, her little body turned this way and that with the force of each spanking. He asked repeatedly if she had learned from her mistake. She stood quietly until she could no longer hold it, then she let out a piercing cry and lost control of her bladder.

Bopha is now happily married to a white man. They live in Idaho, far from Massachusetts, too far away from us, her only family. Her husband works as a systems analyst for a communication firm in Twin Falls, and she is a dental hygienist after failing to get into medical school. I wonder if she ever thinks about that night, if she's ever told her husband about what she went through in Cambodia and the refugee camps in Thailand.

Bopha and I fought a lot when we were kids. She would tell me to sweep the floor, and I would tell her, "No. That's not my job. That's yours. You're the girl." I had a mouth back then, and I knew exactly what to say to fire her up. We fought like mortal enemies, like friends, like brother and sister. She overpowered me, threw me on the ground, and pinned me down with her knees. Afterward, I told Lok-Yeay, who then proceeded to scold Bopha, "You are older than Samnang. You are supposed to take care of him. You know better than this!"

But over the years we became close. We cared for each other. We were both orphans, and we belonged to that 1.5 generation of

Cambodian refugees who were born in Cambodia and came to the States when young. She was put into the ninth grade as soon as we got here, and I was put in the fourth grade. Her brother Vutha was placed in the tenth grade. I had no idea how he survived those high school years.

I called Bopha's home in rural Idaho and told her that I was writing my life story. "I was too young to remember what happened, but I need to know about my past. You can help me fill in the gap," I told her.

"I don't want to go back there again. It's too ugly," she said.

I told her how writing about it had helped me somewhat, how it helped explain why I felt so different and alienated, why I had so much anger and hate bottled up inside, and why at one point I wanted to end it all. That after I started writing, it felt like a boulder had been lifted from my chest and I could breathe again.

"There are things I wish I could un-remember," she told me.

"Bopha, I need to write this. It is something I have to do. I'm not sure if anyone will read our stories, but the urge to write, to speak, overwhelms me. It's all I can do to stop from going crazy."

After a long pause she said, "I'll tell you what. I'll jot down on paper what I remember and mail it to you." I thanked her profusely. Then she returned to our usual topic, "How's Lok Yeay? Is she still making prahouk for you?"

I laughed, then told her, "Lok-Yeay is physically fine, but you know how she is, she worries about everyone, about her children, grandchildren, and great-grandchildren. You should give her a call when you have a chance. That would brighten her day."

"Whenever I call, she always hands the phone to Oum Seyha or one of his daughters. You know how she is about talking on the phone. And anyway, I've forgotten some of my Khmer, so sometimes she doesn't understand me. As you know, there are no Cambodians where I live."

"And that's a problem, Bopha. You should move back to the East Coast when your husband retires. You are too far from your family."

This was a sore subject for us. She moved to Idaho because of her husband's job. I wonder if she was trying to get away from the bad memories that our very presence conjured up. We reminded her too much of a life she wished to forget. She said she missed speaking Khmer and eating Khmer food.

"Well, you can always buy a plane ticket and stay in Massachusetts for a week. I'll help pay for the ticket."

She laughed, "Save your money for your books." Then she added, "I'm really proud of you, you know. Are you going to be a writer or something?"

I answered, "Writers don't make money. We'll see where this PhD thing takes me. Hopefully, I will teach literature at some school not far from Lok-Yeay. If not, I can always shelve books at the local library in Malden."

It felt good, making Bopha laugh. Then we began talking about how lucky the young generations were. They knew American culture more than we did. If their parents were to raise a hand at them or if their fathers were to abuse their mothers, they would pick up the phone and call the police. Those who went to school in the 1990s had other Asian classmates in their classes. I wondered if they ever felt hopelessly alone, self-conscious, and alienated from the rest of their peers, as I had. I thought about us orphans: Vutha, Bopha, and me. Growing up without parents, we learned not to take things for granted, not to create troubles for our elders, not to expect too much from anybody. We learned to be independent, to keep things to ourselves.

Bopha's letter arrived a few weeks after our phone conversation. I sat down on the futon in the living room of my studio apartment and read it quickly. I went to the refrigerator, got a glass of water, and drank. The cold water soothed me. I went back to the living room, sat on the futon, and reread the letter. She glossed over everything. Descriptions were absent in her narrative, and I couldn't get a sense of what she truly felt. The letter was a two-page biographical sketch of her life: where and when she was born, who her parents were, how many siblings she had, her relocation from Siem Reap to Battambang, then from Thailand to the U.S. She ended her story with gratitude for Lok-Yeay and her family for taking care of her. It felt like a college application letter. But it seemed sincere enough. Maybe she didn't feel what I felt; maybe she wasn't traumatized by the beating as I had imagined it. Maybe she was more Cambodian than I was, accepting the beating as a necessary discipline, seeing it as an act of love, a kind of parental duty. Maybe she didn't want to be too close to the past, delve too deeply, digging up the things she wished she could un-remember. To this day, I still don't know how she truly felt about the terrible things that happened to her.

But I saw the fear and trembling that day when Pu Ly beat the piss out of Bopha. I felt the same thing when Thai soldiers beat up us refugees. The fear and trembling came out of an understanding that one human being could have so much power and control over another that the victim of such a beating became lesser, reduced to an animal in fear and acceptance, believing that she had done something to deserve such careless and cruel acts of violence. There was an absence of respect, a total disregard for the victim's humanity. I felt the same thing when I heard an awful story that spread like fire throughout the camp, about a mother who, in a moment of rage, pushed her daughter into the public toilet to drown her, so as to hurt her cheating husband. No one knew if the story was true, but it inspired the same fear and trembling in me. The fear sat like a giant black cat in the center of my being.

The lesson was this: anything could happen to me. My mother and father were not there to protect me. I started being watchful of everyone around me. With every action I took, I thought it over about a hundred times. To douse the flame of anxiety and paranoia, I reminded myself that I was Lok-Yeay's grandson and, if anything were to happen, she had the authority to demand the beating to stop—to protect me. After all, she'd hidden a few grains of rice from the Khmer Rouge to make barbor, rice gruel, for me. I was her blood.

I carried another memory of Bopha with me. I don't know if this memory came out of a real event, or if I made it up, or maybe a combination of both. It must have happened at the third refugee camp, Meirut, because I remember the sound of crashing waves and children laughing and Meirut was the only camp where we were allowed to go to the beach. Bopha stood on the shore with the wind caressing her dark bony face. She felt the sand gripping her feet. The waves crashed against the shore. Someone called out to her, but she didn't hear. She turned and ran with girls her own age. She splashed the water, laughing and running with other girls. She ran farther and farther away. Soon there was nothing but the lapping waves and cool summer breeze. And her laughter—carefree, beautiful, eternal laughter.

Yellow Bird

I woke up and found myself alone. Lok-Yeay was outside working in her garden next to our home. I stepped out of our one-room dwelling and immediately felt the hot sun burning my skin. The air was dry as the wind picked up dust and blew it all over the camp. The red dirt was hot on my bare feet. I hopped around until my feet adjusted to the heat. It was Sunday, the one day of the week when I didn't go to school. My uncles and aunts were already out; they were always busy working on some project or another, always helping a friend, a neighbor, or someone's family. A branch in hand, I walked around the camp looking for telltale signs of lizards and snakes. I poked holes in the red clay dirt with my branch. Still, no creatures came out on such a blistering day. But I continued walking, stopping, bending down and poking the ground with my little tree branch.

I stopped at a small dirt field to watch a group of young men play soccer. They were running, chasing and kicking the white ball, yelling in different languages. One team was made up of Khmer, and the other Vietnamese. They were pointing and yelling at their teammates as the ball flew from one side of the field to the other, bouncing closer to the goal. A player with possession of the ball tripped and fell. He sat up and grabbed one of his knees. Players from both teams swarmed around him, then a fist was thrown, and a kick, and then more fists and kicks followed. Whistles were blown when the Thai police finally showed up, hitting the young men with rifle butts. Those who could run did, while the injured lay on the ground, protecting their heads as rifle butts rained down on their shoulders, backs, and stomachs. It didn't matter which team they were on, whether they were Vietnamese or Cambodian, they were all refugees in the eyes of the Thai soldiers, and that meant they were so poor that they didn't have a home, that they were living in someone else's country, and that the soldiers could do as they pleased with them. That is the unofficial law that refugees acknowledge and must abide by.

My heart ached when I saw Thai soldiers beating the soccer players. Such violence terrified me. I didn't like the idea of anyone getting hurt. Gripping my branch, I ran away from the yelling and crying in different languages, bodies being kicked repeatedly, and refugee bones breaking. I slowed down once I reached a hill near the perimeter of the camp. I walked around poking at the red clay beneath my bare feet, when I heard a low chirping from a nearby bush. Under the shade of a tree was a small yellow bird with a red beak. I crouched down and crawled on my hands and knees, gripping the branch in my hand. I got closer to the bird, and it hopped feebly. I moved quickly and cupped the bird with both hands. I slowly opened my palms, leaving enough opening to see the yellow bird lying still in the middle of my hands. The top of its left wing was torn. There was a smidge of red under its left wing.

I put the yellow bird in my pants pocket and half-ran, half-walked home. Lok-Yeay and Lok-Ta were sitting on the dirt floor, eating bai and tuk kroeung. They dipped slices of cucumber from Lok-Yeay's garden into tuk kroeung.

"Come join us for lunch, Samnang," Lok-Ta said.

"Go wash your hands and feet first," Lok-Yeay ordered.

I went outside, washed my hands and feet with the water from the teang, a large clay pot that Lok-Yeay used to water her garden. I reached inside my pocket and felt the warm little bird. I took it out and whispered, "You will be safe here, my little friend. Don't worry, I'll take care of you like I was taken care of in the rice fields when we were in Cambodia." I hid the yellow bird behind the teang and went inside to have lunch with my grandparents. Lok-Ta asked where I had been, and I told them about the soccer match. Lok-Yeay told me to stay away from young men, especially when they talked about politics.

"Don't get involved in politics," said Lok-Yeay. "It never amounts to anything good. Look where politics has taken us," she said.

"But they were just playing soccer, Lok-Yeay," I pointed out.

"Because of politicians, I lost my children and brother. It's why we are like dust, scattered all over the place. The Thai police can do whatever they want to us. They know we don't have a country and so we are less than human in their eyes," Lok-Yeay answered back.

Lok-Ta said, "Leave the boy alone. He's probably hungry. Let Samnang eat in peace."

After lunch, I went back to the yellow bird, built a nest for it with leaves and tiny branches, and when I was about to dig the earth looking for worms, Lok-Ta called me for our weekly ritual. Every Sunday after lunch, I would recite the lessons I had learned from the previous week to him. Now, I went inside our home, sat on the bamboo bed, and recited the Khmer alphabet: Srak-aw, srak-ah, srak-aek, srak-aye, srak-ouk, srak-o . . .

Lok-Ta smiled as I sang the Khmer alphabet. He asked me to repeat my alphabet song, and I did. He showed me how to combine the sounds to make real words. I was so excited to finally learn how to read! Years later, after his passing, Lok-Yeay told me how proud my grandfather was of me. Because he was a Buddhist monk for most of his life, he never had any children. I was his first grandchild. He told Lok-Yeay that I was a serious student and, even more impressive, I had a fascination with words. "That meant a lot coming from him," Lok-Yeay said. "He was the head monk at his temple before the Khmer Rouge takeover. He was a true scholar. He knew Khmer history and literature, world history and international politics, in addition to his expertise in Buddhist scriptures. And when he said how proud he was of you, I was so happy. You know how we Khmer people are. Compared to Americans, we're not that affectionate. We're not open with our feelings. I knew then he was going to be a good father and grandfather to all of you."

While I was sounding out the word "garden," Pu Ly and Pu Dara ran into our home carrying Oum Seyha on a stretcher, followed by Ming Narin and Ming Bonavy. Oum Seyha's face was bruised, his left eye swollen shut and his lips busted up. Pu Dara told Lok-Yeay that Oum Seyha was caught outside the camp by the Thai police late at night. They held him in their makeshift cell. It was Pu Ly who went with Pu Dara to the police after his colleagues from the clinic told him that they'd seen his brother-in-law tied up and kicked by Thai police officers. Lok-Yeay cried when she saw Oum Seyha's face. Angrily, she said, "I told him not to leave the camp. We don't need any more fish. It's too risky to go out there at night to fish."

"What's done is done. I'm grateful that he's alive and back with us. Thank Buddha." Lok-Ta said.

That evening, we sat in our circle and ate in silence. We had bai, tuk kroeung made from canned fish we received for that week, cucumber and boiled green from Lok-Yeay's garden. After supper, I went out to wash my feet in preparation for bed. I went behind the teang to check on my yellow bird. I bent down to pick up my beautiful friend, but it was not moving. I cupped the tiny, feathered thing in my hand, brought it to the dim light, and saw the blood was crusty and dry beneath its broken wing.

The Old Man
and the Mermaid

We lived in several camps before we found out that we would be going to the States. Our first camp was Khao-I-Dang, then came Sa Kaeo I and Sa Kaeo II, and, finally, Meirut. The living conditions improved with each camp—from the dirt floor of Khao-I-Dang to the back-aching bamboo beds of Meirut, from the thatched roof in Khao-I-Dang to the metallic roofs of Sa Kaeo I and Sa Kaeo II, where you felt like your brain was being fried by the heat in your home. No matter which camp, there was a heavy sadness and desperation in the air, fear mixed with the stench of sweat and humiliation. Somewhere in this thick fog was a glimmer of hope that we refugees placed on the future, and on America. The camps were quickly assembled and heavily populated. The communal toilets were a large ditch: privacy was not on the minds of the builders when they were built. You squatted over the edge of the plank and, before you had time to take in the stench and filth, did your business and left.

We were thus excited when we received an official letter of intent from the U.S sponsorship program. Richard Langer of Massachusetts was the only sponsor willing to take in such a large family as ours. But before we were allowed to leave, we had to pass a medical exam.

The next morning, we all got up early and walked over to the clinic. We gave our paperwork to the Thai nurse at the desk and waited with other families in the hallway. Lok-Ta and Lok-Yeay sat on a bench, while my uncles and aunts stood around them and Bopha sat on the floor looking sleepy. I too was bored, so I decided to mill around the other side of the hallway, where a group of young men were talking and laughing.

One of them said, "You get naked like a baby in there. They want to see *all* of you before they let you in the U.S. of A."

"We get it easy. The women, especially the ones that the Thai doctors fancy, are asked to turn around several times and bend over before they are allowed to put their clothes back on."

"It is not enough that the Thais take our land but they also take our women. Have you heard about the girl who was pregnant after a Thai soldier raped her? She felt so ashamed afterward that she hung herself."

"I heard about that story, too!" The guys continued talking until they noticed me standing around and kicking dirt. Feeling their stares, I walked back to my family and waited in line with Lok-Yeay and Lok-Ta.

An hour later, the men and women in my family were separated into two groups and sent to different rooms. I found myself standing in line with other men and boys from the camp. An elderly man was ahead of me. When his name was called, I watched him walk with determination to the desk where a partition wall had been erected for privacy. When it was my turn, I walked with my head down. Behind the white partition, I was told by a translator to take off my clothes. I did what I was told and stood with my hands covering my privates. I was told to move my hands and I did. There I stood, completely naked, in front of three adults: a Khmer translator and two Thai men, one of whom must have been a doctor because he was the one talking while the other took notes on a clipboard.

I was asked to cough, breathe slowly in and slowly out, then turn around, while they looked at my little naked body. I had never felt such embarrassment. I was vulnerable, so helpless, completely naked, as the three men looked up and down at me, gazing at my nakedness and talking about my malnourished body. One even touched me, pressing his fingers on my stomach and chest. I was then told to put my clothes back on. I walked out of that make-shift office carrying shame in my heart. When I heard laughter in the hallway, I thought everybody was laughing at me. Then I saw him: the old man. He was prancing around naked in the hallway, his brown penis swinging left and right. The men cheered, and the women were red-faced, hands covering their faces. In our culture of modesty, the only people who saw us naked were our parents and the spouses who cared for us in old age.

One of the young men asked, "Why are you walking around like that, Ta Cheourt?"

He smiled, "You know, no one likes to be stared at. And these people have no shame. They look at you all over and poke around some. So, I got angry and started thinking that since they wanted to see me naked, I might as well walk around like this for everyone else to see me naked too. That will teach the Thai a lesson."

Everyone laughed and smiled. The young men hit each other and bellowed with laugher. The women covered their mouths and hid their faces. In our communal laughter, we momentarily forgot about what had happened to us earlier, the embarrassment and shame, the lack of control we had over our own bodies.

After being properly documented and physically examined, we were placed on a bus and transported to a waiting station. It was our first time outside the camp. Like tourists staring at this strange new bright world, my uncles, aunts, grandparents and the other families gawked at the city outside our bus windows. Bangkok was bustling, bright, and noisy. People everywhere, moving around, talking, laughing, eating. There were families eating at plastic tables outside of restaurants and people dancing and singing along to music. They were oblivious to us refugees—dirt on our faces, hunger in our stomachs, and memories in our aching hearts.

After the excitement died down, Lok-Yeay started vomiting into a plastic bag. One hand on my shoulder, she told me to sit in my seat. I sat back down and, minutes later, felt queasy from the moving bus and the stench of vomit. I told her I needed to look out the window again. Lok-Ta said, "Let the boy look out the window if it helps him." All the way to our waiting station I was on my knees looking out the window as we traveled farther away from Cambodia. I knew we were leaving the place of my birth, where my mother and ancestors had come to rest, where my father was left behind, so I looked out the window and tried to see Cambodia one last time, muttering goodbyes to my parents, to the land, trees, sky, and water ways of my country.

A storm was brewing on the horizon as we boarded a small boat leaving for Indonesia, where we would be taught English and U.S. culture before coming to America. The people who came after us later said that they thought we were going to drown. All they saw was our dinghy diving into and disappearing under big waves. They whispered prayers for our safe crossing.

My family, along with other refugees, was on the main deck. The adults sat, their heads in their hands, worried looks on their faces, while the children cried, sprawled out around the adults, frightened by the flashes of lightning in the sky and the crashing of thunder outside the boat. We were all scared as the dark waves rocked our tiny boat. Lok-Yeay vomited and prayed to Lord Buddha for safe passing. Lok-Ta sat, legs crossed and eyes closed, his lips moving. The Thai sailors were running around yelling at us to stay calm and remain seated.

While everyone was stricken with horror, crying and praying, I got up and stood near the railing, staring at the raging storm. I wasn't sure where we were or where we were going. I knew that we were leaving Cambodia, that I might not see the place of my birth again, so I tried to remember my mother and father. I remembered sitting with my father in the café eating ice cream and watching the small black-and-white TV hanging over the counter. My father grew quiet. But I was not sad. I was happy, eating that bright rainbow ice cream and watching that small television. Next, I tried to remember my mother. I saw her lying in bed. Her cheeks hollow, eyes sunken, lips pale and dried. I remembered those pale, dried lips of hers trembling as if she needed to tell me something important, but no words tumbled out. Then I remembered the smell. It was a death smell, a smell of in-between worlds. Her lips quivered when she saw me. She motioned to me to come closer. As I moved closer and closer to her, my skinny body began to shake.

In that moment of remembering my parents, I began to feel the warm kindness of the cosmos all around me and I believed that things would turn out all right. I was not afraid or sad as I stood on the deck looking out, while everyone else was crying and praying. Nothing was different from the norm. Life was life, and it was meant to be for all of us. Some arrived later and left sooner than others. I accepted what fate lay before me, and I felt love radiating from everywhere.

The waves slammed against the small boat, drenching me in saltwater, as I calmly looked out and into the screaming storm. I was surprised no one yanked me away from the railing. Then I saw something that couldn't be explained by the rational mind: a woman rising up with the waves. She saw me and smiled. Her right arm waved at me. I smiled and waved in return. Then she dove headfirst into the water. I saw her rainbow fishtail rising and falling, flapping among the waves, as she disappeared into the water.

Our world became completely dark then. Only the flashes of lightning were visible in the distance. Thunderclaps boomed overhead, and people cried, vomited, and prayed on the floor of the main deck. The captain and sailors continued screaming at the refugees and at each other. Some of the refugees lost control of their bladders.

But I remained calm as I observed the suffering around me. I walked back to the main deck, where my family looked terrified. I took refuge in Lok-Yeay's tearstained arms. I wanted to tell her what I had seen, but I was afraid that it would be interpreted as a bad omen. I cuddled in her warm arms and kept quiet. Still, I remembered the mermaid's face. She was beautiful, gentle, and caring. I didn't know why or how, but deep down, I knew we would be fine. I felt the warm presence of my mother with me. She was trying to tell me that everything would be OK, that the journey would turn out fine, that I need not worry. She would always be watching over me, protecting me, her only son.

Somehow, we made it through the rough waters and arrived safely on one of the islands of Indonesia.

PART II

Surviving in America

Dust from the Sky

1982. Night. The plane circled above Logan International Airport. I looked out the window at the blinking lights below. Red. Green. Yellow. America at night was lit like a Christmas tree. Lok-Yeay sat next to me vomiting in a plastic bag. I looked around. We had never been on a plane before. Everyone leaned against the seats in front of them, heads resting on their forearms, groaning. I heard the captain's voice on the intercom: "Ladies and gentlemen, welcome to Logan Airport. The local time is 11:45 P.M. and the temperature is 39 degrees Fahrenheit. For your safety and comfort . . ."

Weighed down by fatigue and lack of sleep, we filed slowly out of the airplane, with Oum Seyha keeping an eye out for our family's sponsor. Tall light-skinned people were everywhere, moving fast and certain of where they were going. Ming Bonavy exclaimed, "Everyone is so white like milk, so clean. And everyone here walks so fast, with such purpose. What a strange world we've landed in."

A bearded man holding a placard with our family name on it waved to us. It was him: our sponsor, Richard Langer, standing in his blue puffy winter jacket, gray pants and black shoes, flashing a welcoming smile at us. Oum Seyha said, "Hello, Richard Langer. I am happy to be in America. My family and I thank you very much," and extended his right hand. Richard Langer held Oum Seyha's hand in both of his and said, "Welcome to America, Mr.

Sok." He then began firing rapid English at us. Oum Seyha said, "Sorry, I don't understand. Please slow talk. Thank you very much."

Richard Langer smiled again, pointed toward a revolving door, and said, "Let's go home."

Once we stepped out of the airport, we felt the cold in our chests as we breathed in the November air. Our bodies shook, our teeth clattered. Richard apologized for the cold, pointed to the parking lot on the other side of the street, and said that was where he'd parked his van. We half-walked and half-ran, fearful of the blinking taxis, as Richard laughed and told us to follow him.

In our sponsor's van, Oum Seyha sat in the front passenger seat, again thanking Richard in his broken English while we sat in the back, smiling and nodding in agreement. We were all transfixed by the newness of America: the lights blinking at every corner; the streets crisscrossing and tunneling underground; cars changing lanes with blinking lights; our sponsor's strange beard, so full and wild, like a nest of bees hanging from his face. I told Lok-Yeay, "He looks like the Son of God in that movie we saw in Meirut. Jesus Christ!" Richard looked in the rearview mirror and smiled.

Lok-Yeah told me, "Be quiet, child. Let them speak and we just nod our heads and smile."

Oum Seyha looked worried. The sponsor found it difficult to understand what my uncle was trying to say except the words "Thank you very much," which he uttered with every other sentence. To Oum Seyha, the English in America was too fast, had too many shortcuts, so different from the English he learned in the camps.

Twenty minutes later, the van pulled into a garage next to a two-story white colonial house on Main Street in Malden, a city north of Boston. We stumbled into the bright house, were shown our two bedrooms and the living room where Oum Seyha and Pu Dara would sleep. But none of us could sleep that night. We were restless, anxious, worried. The beds and pillows were too soft. The room was cold. The floor was cold. The noises coming from the lights and machines downstairs hummed throughout the night. We ended up lying on the rug together, trying for a few hours of rest.

The next morning, we were given a tour of the house by Richard and his wife, Shelly. Shelly had long brown hair, milky skin, and blue eyes. When she smiled, we could see her sparkling, perfectly aligned white teeth. Richard and Shelly showed us the refrigerator, the stove and oven, and the dishwasher, explaining how to operate each appliance. We stood terrified in front of the shiny machines. Everything was new, different, magical. There was a machine that washed our clothes. We wouldn't have to walk to the stream, bathe in it, then change into dry clothes and wash our wet ones in the stream. Bopha couldn't believe there was a machine that washed your dishes while you were sleeping and the next day, like magic, the dishes were squeaky clean. We didn't have to go out and search for kindling if we needed fire; all we had to do was turn one of the knobs on the stove and a blue flame miraculously appeared. My uncles, aunts, and grandparents looked at each other. "This must be heaven on earth," they whispered quietly to one another.

Oum Seyha was terrified by the newness of this country. He was the head of our family—the one who'd filled out the Application for Sponsorship forms and wrote letters to the United States government; the one who'd put down our names and birthdates at the registration center in Camp Khao-I-Dang; the one who'd decided we should leave Cambodia for the U.N. camps; the one who'd quit school so his brothers and sisters could get an education; the one who'd sent money to his older brother, Oum Piseth, in Phnom Penh; the one who worked on the family farm when his father died from tuberculosis—he was responsible for us all. While everyone was excited by the newness and strangeness of this world, Oum Seyha kept quiet. For the first few weeks in America, he didn't sleep much. His mind wandered: *There's no dirt, no water anywhere. No rivers and lakes. Where do I fish? I don't see any farmland. Only concrete sidewalks and streets and skyscrapers everywhere. Where do I find work? Oh, Lord Buddha, how will I feed my family? How will I take care of my loved ones? In this strange new land, how will we survive?*

At first, Ming Bonavy thought that dust was falling from the roof. As she sat by the window and wondered, the dust particles kept falling and accumulating into a white fluffy blanket covering the ground, the porch, the roof, the sidewalk, the streets—everywhere. She didn't know what to do, so she ran to the bedrooms and woke her family. Everyone trundled down the stairs and gathered around the living room windows. Oum Seyha slipped into his shoes and went out of the house to learn more about this heaven on earth. He reached for the dust and grabbed a handful of it. He brought it to his nose and tongue as we watched anxiously from the window.

He walked back into the house. Shivering, he opened his palm to show the white dust in his hand. "It's cold, like ice." I reached for his hand, and feeling the icy dust, quickly pulled my hand back. We all laughed.

Awakened by the commotion, our sponsor came down the stairs and calmly explained to us: "It's just snow. It comes down from the sky. It is like rain, except it's fluffier. It falls from the sky when it is really cold, like this morning." Richard smiled, then asked, "Do you understand me?" We nodded, "Yes, understand," then burst out laughing.

We didn't understand him, of course, but we felt that the way he smiled as he spoke told us what we needed to know. The white flakes were harmless, normal in this strange and wonderful land called America. America was the land of magic, the land where anything was possible. We felt like we were in some Bollywood film where the hero climbs to the top of the Himalayas and attains supernatural power. Anything was possible, even for us.

Over the course of our first week in America, Richard and Shelly took us shopping at a supermarket near Route 1, a department store in Malden Square, and an Asian store in Revere, a city that borders Malden. We were amazed by the cleanliness and organization, the bountiful meats and produce within, how the meats were clean and packaged, ready to be used. Richard also took us to the government center in Revere to help us apply for social security and government welfare. He helped my uncles and aunts find jobs. Richard was a pastor at his church in North Revere. On Sundays, our family went to this church, congregated with his flock, and prayed. Even Lok-Ta, a former monk, went along. He said he was curious about religion in America and did not want to be seen as ungrateful to Richard and Shelly, who'd brought us to America with their kindness and generosity, who welcomed us to their home with open arms, who showed us the way of life in this new place.

On these mornings, we sat in pews and repeated the holy words along with the congregation. I didn't understand the meaning behind the words or why, an hour later, we all stood up to sing. This new language tasted funny in my mouth; it was fast and slippery, sliding this way and that, difficult to control, frightening and untrustworthy.

On these mornings, I felt two different worlds colliding on my Cambodian tongue. First, the world of the Buddha; the world of my grandparents, uncles, and aunts; the world of smelly prahouk; the world of the Khmer Rouge, killings, and hunger; the world of leaving home and being tossed around like dirt by war and history; the world of my father, mother, and that mermaid in the Gulf of Thailand, so full of kindness and love. Then, there was the pastor's world, our sponsor's world, the American world: the world of cleanliness, machinery, precision; the world of newness and modern technology; the world of televisions, refrigerators, dishwashers, stoves, and ovens; the world of linoleum floors and sit-down toilets and soft toilet paper; the world of history books, the *Encyclopedia Britannica*, the American War in Việt Nam, Henry Kissinger, the Nixon Doctrine, and the Bible. There was Buddha on one side and Christ on the other. I felt pulled in two directions by my love of this stranger who had both rescued us from the refugee camps and torn me away from my Cambodian world, from my memories of my mother and father. I moved my lips along to the prayers and hymns, mimicking the worshippers in the church. But the words that flowed out of my prahouk mouth were not holy: they were Khmer curse words. A-chkourt! A-khdor!

Our sponsor looked in my direction and, seeing my lips rapidly moving along, as if in rapture, he smiled. He was pleased with me, this refugee boy who had no parents, who was raised by his grandparents, uncles, and aunts. After the sermon, he told Oum Seyha, who interpreted the sponsor's praise to Lok-Yeay, that I was a good boy and that I learned things quickly and that I would do well in America. "Tell your mother not to worry about her grandson. God looks after his flock," he told my uncle. Lok-Yeay nodded and smiled; Lok-Ta tousled my hair.

There was pleasure in all of this. Early on I discovered the freedom and power in a foreign language. No one could accuse me of my crime of swearing, since they did not understand the language and thus were not aware of any wrongdoing on my part. Such liberation was that much more rebellious and meaningful because the transgression occurred in the church.

After the service, we congregated in the church lobby and had donuts and coffee. Richard and Shelly introduced us to their friends. Vutha and I loved honey-glazed and Boston cream donuts. We grabbed one each, went outside, sat on a bench, and ate. It was the only part of attending Sunday service that we looked forward to. It was our reward for getting up so early, for singing strange words we didn't understand.

At the Langer house, Thursday night was TV night, and for me, it was the most exciting and most liberating of nights. On our first Thursday with them, we sat in the living room to watch *The Greatest American Hero* with Richard and Shelly. It was the first time I tasted popcorn. We stood around the popcorn machine together waiting for the kernels to pop. I jumped back when I heard the popping sounds begin. Richard and Shelly laughed, and everyone followed suit. I wasn't trying to be funny. The noise really had scared me; it reminded me of those nights when the Para soldiers and the Khmer Rouge fought as we made our way through the jungles of Cambodia, and then later, as we slept inside the refugee camps. I didn't understand this until years later, when my therapist explained PTSD to me, how such sounds triggered my memories of the war.

On those Thursday evenings, I lay on the carpeted floor of the Langer living room, hands under my chin, mesmerized by the black-and-white television. I learned about America from the American sounds and images coming from that twenty-five-inch box. William Katt, star of *The Greatest American Hero,* had curly blond hair, a set of pearly white teeth, and could fly. His students were beautiful, young, and strong. Everyone spoke English; everyone seemed happy. When the theme song came on at the beginning of each episode, I imitated it in my new, still-broken English: "Believe me Ma, I walking on air. I never think I be free." Everyone burst out laughing. I looked over my shoulder and saw Lok-Ta smiling at me. I waved to him. Lok-Ta was proud of me for learning English so fast.

We watched other television shows, too, like *The Dukes of Hazzard* and *CHiPS.* On *Dukes of Hazzard,* those American boys in the red car with a giant Confederate flag on top were handsome and happy. Their teeth, like Katt's, were also pearly white as they smiled and laughed, outrunning and outsmarting the authorities, seeming to have a good time doing it. On *CHiPS,* the two cops riding their silver motorcycles were likewise handsome and brave, their smiles contagious—especially the shorter and dark-skinned officer. In fact, his skin color was closer to my own, and he seemed to have all the luck with the ladies. I felt everything was possible in America. If this cop, whose complexion resembled mine, was accepted into this American world, then why not me?

During the opening credits to *CHiPS,* we stared in awe at the bird's-eye view of the Californian highway, its roads intertwining and overlapping one another, a technological breakthrough, with cars, trucks, and motorcycles driving every which way, under and above, a modern maze of magic and technological wonder. By the end of each episode, the cops had defeated the bad guys, law and justice was upheld, and everyone smiled and laughed in a series of freeze-frames playing to upbeat, early-1980s music. This was the America I saw on television: young, strong, clean, healthy, free, modern, happy, and just. I felt optimistic and hopeful about America. According to the television shows I watched, the American dream was real. I felt fortunate to be part of it.

After one month of living with the Langers, we had to move out. Richard and Shelly were sponsoring other refugees from Southeast Asia. It was part of their service to their God. They'd tried to bring us to Christ, their Lord and Savior, but Lok-Yeay said, with Oum Seyha translating, "We will always be grateful to you and your family. We respect your God but we have ours. Thank you for bringing us to America, Richard, and for giving us your home to stay. We will always be grateful to you and Shelly." Lok-Yeay was clasping Richard's hands, and then Shelly's, and looking into their eyes. Richard kept quiet while Oum Seyha translated. Oum Seyha concluded by speaking for himself, "Thank you very much for what you've done for me and my family. Please keep in touch."

Richard nodded and said, "I understand." He hugged each one of us, and then we climbed into his van and he drove us to Revere. He dropped us off at the stoop of a red brick apartment building where he and Oum Seyha had found a unit for us to rent a few weeks earlier. That was the last time I saw Richard Langer.

Lucky

In the early 1980s, Southeast Asian refugees began arriving en masse in Revere, Lynn, and Chelsea, and by the mid '80s we spread into neighboring cities. The Italians, who arrived in the area nearly a century before us, weren't too happy with us refugees showing up and living alongside them. Fights over turf exploded in back alleys and parking lots. Car windows were smashed; tires slashed. Police were called, but the officers had grown up in the same neighborhoods and knew the vandals, so there were rarely consequences. They came in their flashing vehicles, asked questions, jotted down what we told them, and then drove away, leaving us Cambodian refugees helpless and alone.

Later, as a graduate student, I returned to Revere, visited its museum on Beach Street, and studied the black-and-white pictures of the city back in the day. In the 1950s and '60s, Revere was a place where inlanders took their families and friends to vacation during the summer. Restaurants, bars, arcades, concerts, and ice cream parlors adorned the shoreline. Then we Cambodians arrived. We looked different, ate different foods, spoke a different language, and practiced a different religion. We dressed as if we were still in the 1970s, with our brightly colorful clothing sourced from donation bins in the basements of our sponsors' churches. Our presence changed the look and feel of Revere, the cultural landscape of this city beside the sea.

And we'd never learned to rest. Given our reality in Cambodia under the Khmer Rouge, we counted ourselves lucky to be alive, and from the moment we arrived in America, everything was about survival. We never went to eat in restaurants. We didn't visit department stores to buy clothes. We wore the hand-me-downs given to us by our sponsors and their church groups until the sleeves were torn and the buttons dropped off. We fried leftover rice with scrambled egg or Chinese sausages. Nothing was wasted: not money, not time, not even the weekend. On Saturdays and Sundays, we went to the beach—not to swim or sunbathe like normal Americans, but to collect empty cans and bottles left by swimmers and sunbathers. There was no time to relax and enjoy what my young cousins would later call "quality time" with family. We saved money and food because we'd known poverty and hunger most of our lives and we wouldn't go back to that life if we could help it.

At the beach, Lok-Yeay and I carried grocery bags we'd saved from Foodmaster and walked the shoreline looking for soda cans and beer bottles. Like scavengers, we searched inside trash bins; we checked the public bathrooms. When our grocery bags were filled, we poured the cans and bottles into larger black plastic bags and brought them to the local liquor store near the beach. We waited in line at the cash register. The young woman with long blonde hair rolled her eyes and called the manager, who winced when he saw us. He brought a few trays and asked us to line up the cans along the dotted lines. When the trays were filled, he gave us money. Sometimes we made as much as twenty dollars. Lok-Yeay saved the money to be sent to her sister in Cambodia.

Even at that age, I was self-conscious, embarrassed of our visible differences. Instead of wearing swimming trunks and bathing suits, we wore pants and long-sleeved shirts in the summer, carrying our plastic bags and a shovel to dig for oysters and clams while beachgoers watched us curiously, inquisitively, and sometimes with annoyance. But a Khmer neighbor, Mrs. Nhim, returned those rude gazes, saying out loud to Ming Bonavy in a language that was as foreign as our brown skin, black hair, and rolled-up bell-bottomed pants, "Look at those American women. Nothing is left to the imagination. They should be ashamed of themselves." I trailed behind them, my head down, my eyes diverting the stares. I was nine. We were heading to the other side of the beach where, according to Mrs. Nhim, oysters and mussels adorned the rocks on the ocean surface. Wearing a wide-brimmed hat, Mrs. Nhim carried her shovel proudly on her shoulder, as I trailed along with a plastic pail and its tiny shovel.

In those days, we lived in a red brick apartment complex on Centennial Avenue, a few blocks from the beach. We could see the blue Atlantic Ocean from our third-floor apartment. There were about thirty apartments in that three-story brick building; most of the tenants were Cambodian refugees. A white woman in her thirties managed the property. We knew her as "Chrissie." Chrissie had tattoos covering her arms. During the weekends, when Lok-Yeay and I returned from the beach carrying our bags of soda cans and beer bottles, we would see Chrissie chain-smoking and listening to hard rock music on her back porch, singing along to lyrics like, "Yeah, you, you shook me all night long," or "Come on feel the noise, girls rock your boys." Because English was still new to me then, I thought the singer was screaming, "Girls, fuck your boys." I was horrified at the words and embarrassed for Chrissie, who seemed to have a new boyfriend visiting her apartment every other month.

Chrissie also had an American terrier named Lucky, who was always chained to the back porch. When Lok-Yeay and I returned from the beach we decided to take a shortcut and entered the backyard, empty cans rattling in our plastic bags. Lucky, ears pricked up, ran toward us until the dog's body was yanked backward by the chain. Lucky barked and barked, frantically pulling the chain, jumping up and down at us, mouth dripping with saliva. The chain rattled viciously as Lucky's weight pulled this way and that. I froze. The plastic bag of empty cans fell from my hands, which incited the dog's anger even more. Lok-Yeay turned around, "Samnang, that dog is chained to the fence. Just walk around it and you will be fine." I couldn't move my legs. "I can't do it, Lok-Yeay. Its teeth are big and white. And its barking is so loud. I'm scared, Lok-Yeay. Help me!" Seeing my trembling legs and tear-stained face, Lok-Yeay walked over to me and held me in her arms. Together we walked out of the backyard, went around the apartment complex, and entered the front door.

Dawn

I don't remember when or how I learned English. I just remember being put into the fourth grade in Garfield Elementary School, where I had a few regular classes with the American students, but most of the time, I was in ESL classes with other Cambodian kids. In the regular classes, I sat at my desk and didn't say a word. Everybody was so different from me, and I was afraid to say anything that might attract my peers' attention. The ESL classes were taught by Ms. Souza. I was fascinated with Ms. Souza's blonde curly hair. It reminded me of William Katt, the actor who starred in *The Greatest American Hero* television series. *Maybe Ms. Souza is his sister*, I thought. *Maybe she's a superhero during lunch break or when school is out.* I learned later that she'd participated in protests during the war in Việt Nam and had traveled to D.C. in protest of the U.S. secret bombings of Cambodia. She told us that it was her duty to take care of us Southeast Asian refugees after what her government did to our countries and people. We didn't know what all of this meant; most of us were just happy to be in the classroom together with other Asian students.

Ms. Souza was often seen chatting in the hallway with Mr. Berg, the sixth-grade math teacher with a moustache and big shoulders. All of us boys were afraid of Mr. Berg. But we knew Ms. Souza was sweet, so we took advantage of her gentle nature. We flew paper airplanes and talked among ourselves while she was trying to teach us English words. When she looked in our direction, we stopped our chattering and airplane flying and remained quiet until she turned back around and resumed writing on the blackboard. The Cambodian girls were always well behaved. They did their homework, listened to teachers, and paid attention to what was said in class; they raised their hands and volunteered answers to questions that were beyond my comprehension. They sat next to me, but they didn't want anything to do with me. They probably thought I wouldn't amount to anything good.

And they were right. I had difficulty paying attention, understanding Ms. Souza, and following her directions. I was always daydreaming about life in the refugee camps and the times I spent with my father in Cambodia. I missed the freedom I'd had, walking barefooted with a branch in hand, looking for crickets, frogs, and snakes; I couldn't do that in America. I missed my father taking me around to food and ice cream stands, showing me off to his buddies. I was now beginning to forget the flavor of the ice cream I had on our last day together. I only remembered its bright rainbow color and the sensation of having my father with me, the feeling of having him pay complete attention to me, of him being proud of me. My heart ached. Those days were long gone. I sat in my seat and watched Ms. Souza gesture like a broken bird and sound out English words for us to repeat.

When the bell rang, I realized with disappointment where I was. Following other kids, I ran out of Ms. Souza's classroom, down the hall, and into the cafeteria. It was noisy, crowded, and exciting as I caught up with other Cambodian kids I knew from the apartment and waited in line for food. During this period of my life, I rarely felt uncomfortable with myself. It was always us Cambodians against them Americans—I knew who I was and where I belonged.

One day, I was caught staring at a girl named Dawn Chilton by my friend Samit, who lived in the same apartment complex as I did. Dawn wore her hair short, and I had never seen her in a dress. She played soccer with boys on the playground. I was fascinated by her.

In Khmer, Samit asked, "Do you like her, Samnang?"

"Who?"

"Dawn. The girl who is always hanging out with boys."

"No," I replied quickly. Embarrassed, I blurted out in English, "I just think she's interesting. She's like a boy. Look at her hair!"

I thought the matter settled but, during lunch, another friend leaned across the table and asked, "Hey, I hear you like Dawn?"

"No. Who told you that?"

"That's what everyone's been saying."

"Wait . . . what? Who? Everybody?"

Then I saw her. Dawn was walking with a bunch of her friends toward where I was sitting. I looked up, frightened of what would happen next.

She leaned over the table and looked down at me, "So what did you call me, China Boy?" Her friends laughed. I tried to smile. Dawn moved closer. She was a few inches taller than me, and had a reputation of beating boys up and publicly humiliating them. I felt her warm breath in my face. She asked, "You call me a 'boy,' China Boy?"

I looked around the cafeteria. Kids were clustered in groups, laughing and talking. Dawn repeated herself: "I asked if you called me a 'boy,' China Boy?"

"No, no boy. I like you," I blurted out.

Dawn pushed me with her hands, and I fell back against my seat. Other kids surrounded us, hollering and screaming. There was no way I could escape. Finally, Mr. Berg and a few other teachers arrived and ordered everyone to return to their seats. Dawn was told to wait outside the cafeteria for Mr. Burns, the vice principal, and we were both given detention. Before she walked away, she smiled at me, then said, "I guess we have ourselves a date. I'll see you after school, China Boy."

When the bell rang, I ran out of the classroom, down the hallway, and out the back door, past the playground, across the green field next to the school, not looking back. Cars drove by as I ran with my red backpack, straight jet-black hair bouncing on my little head. I kept thinking to myself, *I didn't do anything to Dawn. I just thought she was cute. The words didn't come out right when I told Samit. English is a wild language that I have yet to tame. I don't like fighting. I never like fighting. I don't want to hurt anyone, especially Dawn!*

I ran as fast as my feet could carry me until I reached our apartment building. I rang the doorbell again and again, but neither Lok-Yeay nor Lok-Ta came down the stairs to open the door. I was panting, sweating, even though it was cold outside. I banged on the door again, but still no one answered. Finally, I decided to walk around the apartment and try the back gate. I figured that the bell was broken and my grandparents were probably in the kitchen at the back of the unit. They would see me walking up.

As soon as I entered the back gate, Lucky started barking ferociously at me. The dog's white fangs dripped with saliva, eyes possessed by some demon spirit. The chain rattled against the porch, as the dog lunged itself at me again and again. I was afraid the chain would break. I stood paralyzed with fear. Then I began to cry. I didn't know where to go, what to do. No one came to my rescue. I just stood there, my body shaking, and I cried.

We Were Refugees

At 6:30 A.M. Lok-Yeay called from the kitchen, "Wake up, Sam-nang. It's time to get ready for school. It's almost seven!" The apartment felt quiet and empty. Lok-Ta was already out for his morning walk; he liked to explore the city and learn about this new world called America. Like in our refugee camp days, my uncles and aunts were already out the door by six. Ming Bonavy found work at a plant in Revere, where she stood in an assembly line all day, putting boxes together. Oum Seyha had a job in Chelsea. To save bus fare, he walked from where we lived, close to the beach in Revere, to downtown Chelsea. Pu Ly and his wife, Ming Narin, had been talking about taking Vutha and Bopha to Philadelphia to work for the summer. They learned from a friend that there were farms in Pennsylvania that needed seasonal farmhands to pick fruits and produce. The work was backbreaking, but the pay was in cash. We could save money and finally buy a car for our family.

We refugees sought every opportunity available to us. In comparison to what we'd gone through in Cambodia and Thailand, life in America was good. We had jobs. We rented two apartments for the fifteen of us, with Ming Narin's baby on the way, our first American-born family member. We were relatively safe, no bullets or bombs threatening our lives, no Thai soldiers beating us. We had plenty of food; we bought frozen chicken, beef, and pork from Foodmaster and stored them in two refrigerators filled to the brim.

We had actual doctors and nurses who prescribed actual medicine, unlike those peasant Khmer Rouge doctors and nurses who gave us tree bark and leaves mixed with honey. Bopha, Vutha, and I had actual teachers; we attended schools in actual buildings with doors, desks, blackboards, and chalk. Life was good, as good as it could get for refugees who'd fled their native country and had to learn how to make a life in their new country.

Still, there were things that we had to endure as new immigrants in America, as survivors of the Cambodian genocide, and as war orphans.

I remember one time Ming Narin came home crying. She was riding the subway on her way to Chinatown in Boston to buy rice, fish, soy sauce, and Asian vegetables when someone reached into her purse and stole money from her. She slumped down on the living room couch and cried, "That was most of last month's work, now gone!"

Her husband, Pu Ly said, "Lucky for you, you had enough change to buy a ticket home."

She didn't say anything, so he continued. "Serves you right. You've been stupid for trusting these Americans. America is no land of opportunities; its citizens are no angels. Americans are thieves and their government is warmongering. We are here because of their government."

For the past couple of months, Pu Ly had been seeing a psychiatrist for PTSD. He had awful nightmares. In Pol Pot's time, he was responsible for transporting the dead to ditches and unmarked graves. He had a recurring dream about one of the dead whom he cradled to his chest and carried to the wagon, where other corpses laid waiting in a twisted pile like kindling waiting for a funeral pyre. In the dream, the dead man opened his eyes and cried out to Pu Ly, "I'm not dead yet. Please don't bury me, sir. I'm not dead yet. You're the one who is dead!" Pu Ly woke up each time screaming, "I'm not dead. I'm not dead." Ming Narin tried to console him, and once, he hit her. When my aunt sported a bruised face the next morning, Lok-Yeay and Oum Seyha didn't say anything. After all, Pu Ly was the head of his family and Ming Narin was his wife.

Pu Ly also got into fights with his coworkers and boss. Unhappy with his work of packaging clothes and toys all night at a local department store, Pu Ly criticized his coworkers and boss for being "so stupid." He told us, "These people, they don't think for themselves. They simply do what is asked of them." When he came back from seeing his psychiatrist, he complained of the doctor's method: "The so-called doctor asked me to close my eyes and pretend I'm at this place called 'the Caribbean.' He wanted me to relax and find peace. But what is this 'Caribbean' thing he was talking about? And how can I find peace if all I do is stand around all night and make sure which pile of clothes belongs to which bin? Everybody here is stupid. I thought America was the land of opportunity. But in reality, it's the land where people don't think. Everyone is a zombie! I've got this brainless job where I'm asked to do silly things."

We learned not to say anything when Pu Ly was on one of his tirades. We sat and listened to him complain about our lot in America, about his dream of working in the medical field, about his wife and us children—orphans who should realize how lucky we were that he brought us to America. He said to Vutha and Bopha one day, "There's a summer job in Philadelphia picking fruits at the local farm. It's good for you. It will teach you the value of hard work."

With no one to speak up for them, Vutha and Bopha didn't have much of a choice. That summer, a friend of Pu Ly's drove them to Philadelphia, where they shared a two-bedroom apartment with ten other Cambodian workers. Bopha hated sharing the bathroom with others, especially strangers who also happened to be young men. But she didn't say anything. She knew better than to disagree with Pu Ly. What Vutha and Bopha remembered most about Philadelphia that summer was that it was always dark. They got up at three in the morning and waited for the van to pick them up and drive them to a farm over an hour away from the city, where they picked blueberries, filling little baskets with them. Then they arranged those baskets on a tray and handed it to the Pennsylvanian Dutch woman, who gave them a ticket in return for each tray of blueberries. At the end of day, they took their tickets to the cashier and cashed them, two dollars for each ticket of grueling work under the hot summer sun. At seven in the evening, they were driven back to Philadelphia, where they took turns washing up, ate food prepared by the woman who ran the place, and slept in their own sleeping bags on the floor next to each other. Vutha and Bopha didn't complain. At least they had each other. They knew they were lucky; they weren't digging a dam with a Khmer Rouge maekong looking over their shoulders, or lying face down in a ditch among other corpses, with vultures circling in the sky above. They knew they should be grateful. Happy, even.

So it was with all of us. We were refugees and we should be grateful to be in the United States. Physically, we were safe. We weren't starving like we had under the Khmer Rouge regime. All of our surviving family members were accounted for, housed together in one apartment building. But after some time passed, we knew we didn't feel truly welcome in America.

The first couple of months in the States were great. The morning we discovered snow. The early weeks when Richard Langer and his wife brought us to the grocery store, the bank, the government center, to Boston Commons, where I got to ride one of the swan boats with Ming Bonavy while Lok-Yeay carefully watched us from the land. America was magical then, and we felt anything was possible. But the magic wore off. We had to go to school, factories, the supermarkets, the government center, and we didn't feel welcome or wanted there. We were refugees, and to make it worse, we were from Southeast Asia. We were ghostly reminders of the shameful war in Việt Nam, an embarrassing blemish in a nearly flawless record of American military victories.

But we weren't in America to remind people of the war in Southeast Asia or to taunt the American people with Vietnamese victory. There are no victors in war, only losers. And we lost. We lost big. We lost our homes, the people we loved, and eventually our cultures and languages. We wore the dust of history on our listless faces and carried painful memories of what we'd witnessed and survived. We were here, in America, because we wanted to make new homes for our families. Most of us were haunted by the unimaginable atrocities committed by the Khmer Rouge, the ghosts and memories of victims, the dark and screaming jungles of Cambodia, the powerlessness and embarrassment of life in refugee camps. Here, in America, we were simply seeking a home.

Tom and Jerry

That first fall season in America, I was fascinated with the cartoon show *Tom and Jerry*. I loved the way the small mouse used his wit to outsmart the big cat; it reminded me of the stories of Judge Rabbit in Cambodian folklore. One of the smallest kids in class, I found hope and inspiration in such stories. I remember one afternoon, Lok-Ta and I were watching *Tom and Jerry* in the living room—the room that, at night, we transformed into a bedroom by pulling the sofa out into the bed where I slept with my grandparents, Bopha and Ming Bonavy wrapped in blankets on the floor. We were laughing at Tom being tricked by Jerry to eat his own tail when we heard the key turning the lock on the apartment's door and Bopha came in carrying a big plastic bag over her shoulder. She was returning from the laundromat on Shirley Avenue, a few blocks away. Lok-Ta and I looked up. Egg yolk plastered Bopha's long black hair. Broken eggshells clung to her jacket. Tears stained her eyes. She looked like a sad ghost lost in the concrete jungle of America.

Lok-Ta asked, "What happened, Jeow Bopha?"

"I was pushing the shopping cart with my laundry bag in it when suddenly eggs came flying in my direction. Some hit me, some missed. When I looked up, I saw kids in the second-floor window laughing at me. I ran as fast as I could." Breaking into sobs, Bopha hid her face in her hands. "I hate this place. People here don't like us. I want to leave here! Can we move somewhere else? Can we move back to the camps?"

Lok-Ta answered calmly, "We can't move back to the refugee camps in Thailand. Oum Seyha still owes the American government money for the plane tickets. Besides, moving to another place will not help." Lok-Ta spoke in a tone that was both understanding and irrefutably certain. "The problem will follow us wherever we go, Bopha. Remember, we are not in Cambodia anymore. We are refugees. The sooner we learn to accept this fact, the better it will be."

Bopha stared silently at the floor. I looked up at Lok-Ta, waiting for his words to comfort and guide us.

Lok-Ta finally said, "There are good and bad people everywhere. That's life. Give this place a chance, and soon you will find good people who are nice and caring, who will help you."

Bopha looked up at the television screen. Jerry had managed to trick Tom into cutting himself in half with an electric saw. Blood spewed everywhere as the teeth of the saw hit Tom's body.

"Listen," added Lok-Ta. "I'm sorry that this had to happen to you. Go wash up now. I will ask Lok-Yeay to cook your favorite dish, somlor srae."

Bopha went into the bathroom and closed the door behind her. Her quiet sob was like a sad violin song that cut through the wacky world of *Tom and Jerry* and went straight into my spine. I couldn't hear anything but her muffled cries. Lok-Ta pursed his lips and shook his head.

The next morning, Lok-Yeay called from the kitchen, "Wake up, Samnang. It's seven o'clock!" I didn't know how long she had been calling my name. I sat up, opened my eyes, closed them, and fell back to sleep. Minutes later, Lok-Yeay came into the living room and shook me awake. I looked at the clock and, to my dismay, it was 7:20 in the morning. I hated getting up for school, especially when it was cold the previous night because my uncles and aunts were saving money by not turning up the heat, the apartment just warm enough to keep the pipes from bursting so that we didn't have to call our landlady, Chrissie. I got up begrudgingly, washed my face, had rice gruel and salted fish for breakfast.

Outside the snow was a soft white blanket covering the streets and rooftops of Revere. Dressed in a maroon winter jacket given to me by Richard Langer's congregation, I stepped out of the red brick apartment on Centennial Avenue and headed for school.

It was an unusually quiet morning. *Strange, no one is around,* I thought. *No mothers walking with their children. No school buses. No kids throwing snowballs at me. It must be the cold.*

My K-Mart sneakers sank completely into the snow, soaking my socks and numbing my feet with cold dampness. I crossed the empty field near Garfield and saw the vast whiteness around me. Again, I thought to myself, *Where is everyone? Lok-Yeay must have misread the clock again. That's why nobody is around. No school buses or crossing guards. No parents, no adults in sight. No children chasing each other, screaming and laughing. Only me, alone on this cold school morning.*

I reached the school's main entrance and tried to open the doors, but they were locked. I peered inside one of the windows; the school was empty. The building stood quiet and still as snowflakes fell gently around me. I wiped my nose on the back of my sleeve, looked around, and began crossing the field next to the school.

I stopped in the middle of the field and studied my surroundings. Empty. I looked up at the dim sky and felt the snow falling onto my face. Silence surrounded me. I felt such immense pleasure at this strange solitude that I let my body fall backward into the snow. Lying motionless, I watched as soft, cold flakes fell from the sky. The white flakes gathered, forming colonies over parts of my body. I felt the snow touching my face. I licked the snow off my lips. The snow silenced the world. I was slowly being buried by its whiteness. I was now part of the snow.

For some unknown reason, I let out a primal scream. I expected voices to holler back in response, but no one was around. I screamed again and again. Then, I started to laugh. A kind of joy overtook me, as I laughed and laughed. I didn't want to be anywhere but here, underneath the snow, where there was peace and quiet. Where I could hear my own laughter. Where no one could hurt me.

American Dream

Every evening, about a quarter to eight, we gathered in the living room, eyes glued to the television, waiting for the Massachusetts Lottery program to come on. Pu Dara and Ming Bonavy were particularly excited when the numbers were announced, their fingers gripping lottery tickets. Ming Bonavy was the lucky one in the family. She usually got three or four of the six numbers. Those winning numbers often came to her in dreams. Not the numbers themselves, but stories that somehow had numerical significance, according to Ming Bonavy, who interpreted their meanings and converted them into numbers. After the numbers were announced, she raised her right arm, hand clutching the winning ticket. She jumped up and down screaming, and we all laughed along with her. It was contagious; even Lok-Ta joined in the fun. He thought the frivolity was something we all could use after what had happened to Bopha on her walk home from the laundromat.

Then Pu Dara came up with this crazy idea of buying the winning ticket as soon as the winning numbers were announced on the television. Because the liquor store sat right across from our apartment on Centennial Avenue, he reasoned, we had a chance of beating the computer and winning the lottery. We were too high on the idea of winning the lottery to question the ridiculousness of such a plan. We declared it brilliant. When the numbers were announced on television, Pu Dara quickly put down the winning numbers on the playslip, gave me money for the lottery and some change for candy, and I ran down the stairs, jumped over the threshold, and landed at the bottom of the steps. I crossed the intersection of Centennial Avenue and North Shore Road, where the convenience store sat with its blinking lights. I ran in and stood behind a few people, some of whom were carrying boxes of Budweiser or Miller Light. I was a bit anxious, waiting behind them. When it was my turn, I handed the store clerk the playslip with the already-winning numbers marked and gave him a one-dollar bill. The store clerk, a big man with beer belly and mustache, didn't look at it. He simply put the slip into a slot in the machine, pushed some buttons, and with scratchy noise the lottery ticket came out. I smiled, put the ticket in my pocket, and ran out the door.

Outside the store, a bunch of kids from school were hanging around on their bikes, smoking cigarettes. They were older, in the sixth grade; I knew I was in trouble. As soon as they saw me, they got up and moved toward me, swarming around me. One kid said, "Why don't you go back to where you came from? We don't want your kind here." Another kid spat at me, as if I was not worthy of his words. The saliva hit my hair. They laughed. "You stink! Go back to Vietnam, Ching Chong!" What they said was predictable and unimaginative, but I knew I was being humiliated and that hurt me. I ran back to the store, deciding to wait the bullies out. I didn't want to get beaten up. The cashier at the register saw me, panting, with spit in my hair and panic in my eyes, but he didn't say anything. As though I weren't worth his trouble, he went back to the Red Sox game on the small black-and-white television hanging on the wall.

I took my time roaming each aisle, pretending I was looking for items to buy. I lingered in the candy and the magazine aisles. I picked up *Flex* magazine and turned its glossy pages. There was a photo of Arnold Schwarzenegger, dressed as Conan in his leather headgear, holding up a sword and flexing his muscles. I had never seen anyone so big, so muscular, so confident. I wished I could be someone like that—Samnang the Savage—and take my sword from its sheath, wipe out those sixth graders with a single swing of my blade. I looked out the store's window. The kids were still milling about, puffing on their cigarettes and laughing. I went through one magazine after another, paging through *Transworld Motocross* and *BMX Plus!* as though I were fascinated by their contents.

I put the BMX magazine back on its rack and returned to the window. This time, I saw no one. Relief came over me. I went back to the candy aisle, picked out a Twix and Lok-Ta's favorite, a Snickers. Each was thirty-five cents. I counted the coins from my pockets and went up to the counter. The clerk seemed annoyed that I was interrupting his baseball game, and I avoided making eye contact as I placed the coins on the counter. With the two candy bars, I walked out into the cool evening breeze. It was eight fifteen. I crossed the intersection, went over to Centennial Avenue, and walked along the street, rubbing my eyes and wiping any trace of spit from my hair. I felt weak, embarrassed, but I was determined not to let my family know what had happened. I walked up the stairs, blew my nose one last time, and knocked on the apartment door. Ming Narin opened the door and let me in. Pu Dara asked, "What took you so long, Samnang?"

"Sorry, Lok-Pu Dara. I went back to the store after remembering that Lok-Ta always likes Snickers. But the line was longer this second time. And I was waiting behind this elderly lady who took a really long time getting money from her purse." I walked over to Pu Dara, "Here's the lottery ticket, Pu."

I then excused myself, went to the bathroom, looked at myself in the mirror, and wept quietly.

I was angry at those older kids for ganging up on me; I was angry at Pu Dara for his stupid dream. I was angry at myself for not telling my uncles and aunts the truth. The truth was I was ashamed of being a victim, of being humiliated so openly, so publicly, so easily. I was most angry at the store clerk. He'd seen what was happening, but he hadn't bothered to help me at all. He could have told those kids to leave me alone; he was an adult, the store's owner, an authority figure. They would've listened to him, but he didn't even try to intervene on my behalf. Instead, he turned and looked up at the television screen. I was a nuisance, an interruption to his Red Sox game. The incident reminded me that I was insignificant, a nobody, a refugee child—an orphan, all over again.

A couple of summers after we moved to Revere, I witnessed the aftermath of a motorcycle accident on one of the hottest nights, the kind when all the windows were open and we could hear our neighbors screaming and yelling at each other, smell the garlic pork from the neighboring apartment, and hear Chrissie rocking out to her music while Lucky barked at some kids playing in the yard. It was a little after midnight when there was a loud crash. We woke up, looked at each other, and instinctively stumbled to the apartment's front windows. We saw a man lying in the street, about fifteen feet away from his motorcycle. We went outside to see if there was anything we could do to help him. I was surprised that I wasn't told to stay inside; we were all shocked by what we saw, even the adults. The man was on his back in a pool of black liquid. He grimaced in pain. In a torn leather jacket and blood-soaked bandana, he kept screaming at us, "Fuck you, gooks. What are you staring at? Get away from me, motherfuckers. I thought I killed all of you in 'Nam." He must have been frightened to see us coming out of the red brick apartment, surrounding him, staring at him and speaking in our foreign language. I felt sorry for him. He was alone, none of his people coming to his rescue.

It took some time for the ambulance and fire trucks to arrive. When they did, the man was lifted onto a stretcher and rolled into an ambulance. He was still cursing at us when they shut the ambulance door. The officers asked us to return to our building. Walking back to our red brick apartment, we were flushed with excitement, making sleep difficult for most of us.

On the night of the lottery ticket incident, I locked myself in the bathroom and studied my face in the mirror, examining my otherness—my dark skin, my flat nose, my round eyes and big upper lips. I thought about the Vietnam veteran lying on the street, his vulnerability exposed for the world to see, and I cried for the both of us. He and I were alike. He fought on the American side of the war—a war that my family had no role in—but we were both victims to forces outside of our control. We were both hurt by war, by life; we were both helpless, publicly humiliated, afraid, and, in our individual moments, deeply alone.

Lok-Ta

On weekends, Lok-Ta and I took long walks together. The doctor said it was good for his health; the exercise helped with his blood pressure and cholesterol. We went out, sometimes around the neighborhood and sometimes to the beach, where we sat on a bench and watched people ride their bikes along the boardwalk or swim in the ocean. I knew from Lok-Yeay that Lok-Ta was once the head monk at a monastery in Battambang, before the Khmer Rouge desecrated the temple and forced him to marry her. Every Khmer person we met showed him respect by pressing their hands together and bowing to him. Whenever we were together, Lok-Ta always asked how I was doing at school. "OK," was my usual answer.

Sitting on a bench at the beach one afternoon, looking at the Americans waiting in a long line that wrapped around the ice cream shop on Revere Beach Boulevard, Lok-Ta said, "You have to do more than 'OK,' Samnang. Befitting your name, you are lucky to be here in America. You have free education here." Sensing that he was about to dive into a speech, I kept quiet. Lok-Ta continued, "When I was your age, my family was dirt poor. Both my mother and father were farmers, like their parents before them. And the harder they worked, the more money they owed the landowner. The only way for me to get an education was to go to the temple and become a novice monk. And I did. I read everything I could get my hands on, from Buddhist prayers and epic poetry to Khmer history and politics. Remember, thieves may steal your material possessions but they cannot take away your knowledge. Knowledge will always be yours. It's the key for you to make something of yourself."

"I know, Lok-Ta. You've told me that many times before. But the Americans don't like us. They don't want us here. It's difficult to concentrate on schoolwork when you are made to feel bad about yourself, when you feel inferior, unworthy."

"Don't pay them any attention, Samnang. They know not what they do. They speak in ignorance and act in fear. Some are hurt by the war in Việt Nam. You have to find compassion, learn to forgive them. It's the only way to stay strong," he said.

We sat on the bench in silence and watched people walk by. Lok-Ta turned to me, "And you will be strong, Samnang. You will survive all of this and make something of yourself. You will do more than 'OK.' And when you do, don't forget who you are, where you came from. Know that our people have a long rich history. Our great king Jayavarman II announced independence from the Java Empire some nine hundred years before this country declared its independence. The Khmer Rouge are just ants, an annoyance, pests in the context of this great history, and we will rise again from the ashes of war. Never forget this: you are and will always be a child of Cambodia, our Koan Khmer. Be proud of who you are."

I had never seen Lok-Ta so animated before. It was as if he had been bottling up these thoughts and feelings and was now unleashing them onto me. He turned to look at the waves crashing, then got up from the bench. I followed him.

We walked along Shirley Avenue, past the laundromat, Khmer grocery store, and video rental store until we saw a giant tree stump on the sidewalk. Lok-Ta stopped and looked at the recently cut tree, its inner whiteness exposed. "That's the way of this place. They cut down everything that is natural. Everywhere there is concrete; there are more buildings and houses than trees." Lok-Ta looked at me, "Samnang, everything in this world is alive, including trees and plants. This giant oak tree is still alive. I can feel its presence, but its voice is weak. Behind all that we can see with our eyes, there is the other world. You have to pay attention to it, to listen for its guidance."

I knew that other world Lok-Ta spoke of, but I hadn't felt its presence in a long time. Beyond the noise that was life in America, there was only silence. I couldn't feel or hear anything but my isolated beating heart. I told Lok-Ta, "I miss Cambodia, its trees, its waters, its mud on my bare feet. I miss catching lizards and grasshoppers."

"I know, Jeow Samnang. I miss Srok Khmer too." He turned to me, "No matter where you are, you can always return to it. It's always here waiting for you. The trees, the sky, the birds, the living creatures all around us, the things we see and don't see with our naked eyes." He pointed to the natural world around us. "Remember this, Jeow ."

At the end of Shirley Avenue, we turned left and walked up a hill, heading westward past the Khmer neighborhood and into a part of the city that was new to us. I noticed Lok-Ta slowed his pace. Ahead of us, kids were playing in the front yard of a three-story white colonial home. Two adults sat on the front porch, watching them. Lok-Ta kept walking, and I walked next to him. A skinny kid around my age saw us, came up to the fence, and spat. His saliva nearly hit my feet. Lok-Ta stopped, looked up at the porch, and made eye contact with one of the adults there. A woman in a wicker chair cradled an infant child. The man sitting next to her got up, put his hands on the porch's white railing, and stared at us.

My cheeks flushed and I looked away. "Lok-Ta, we're not supposed to be out this far. Let's turn around and go back home." And we did. We crossed the street, turned around, and walked back home. We heard laughter coming from the porch. Lok-Ta and I didn't say anything afterward. We walked in silence. We didn't mention the incident again, to anyone else or to each other.

Lok-Ta never recovered from our walk that day. I would ask him to come out of the apartment, plead with him, but he would say he was tired. "I'm too old for this world, Samnang. You go outside and play with your friends."

"You're not old," I argued, but he wouldn't budge. Lok-Yeay said to leave him alone and show some respect to my elders.

He never left the apartment to go walking with me again. I didn't know what had hurt him more: the kid spitting at us or the adults watching it happen and doing nothing about it. What I knew was that I couldn't understand the ways of this American world, how alienated from the spirit and natural world we were, how we disrespected elders and disregarded strangers, how the value system was different from what I felt in my bones. The more I thought about Lok-Ta, the more I became angry at those adults on the porch. I feared them more than I feared the kid who'd spat at us. Try as I might, I couldn't find the compassion for these adults that Lok-Ta had asked of me.

Lok-Ta's health began to decline in the months following this incident. Several times he was taken to the hospital due to shortness of breath. Once, while we were watching *Mighty Mouse*, he collapsed on the living room floor, clutching his chest and complaining of pain. It was Chrissie, our landlady, who called for an ambulance. The EMTs placed Lok-Ta on a gurney and wheeled him down the stairs. Lok-Yeay got in the back of the ambulance with him, and Chrissie drove me to the hospital in her beat-up Chrysler. Inside the hospital, we were led to a room where Lok-Yeay and I were informed by a doctor that Lok-Ta had died before arriving, from a clot in his heart. I wrapped my arms around Lok-Yeay's waist and wept uncontrollably. The doctor said, "These things happen. Your grandfather was very old, and his heart just gave out."

Friends

After Lok-Ta's death, I began to stay away from the apartment. I wasn't afraid of his ghost. In fact, I wish Lok-Ta had haunted us, so that I would have him with me again. The apartment reminded me too much of Lok-Ta and what happened on our walk that summer afternoon. This was in 1985, and I was now a sixth grader at Garfield Elementary School. I had a few friends, but none I was close to. Sometimes you become friends with those you have little in common with. Certain forces—mostly situational, some cultural—draw you together. Sometimes you have friends who shape you in one way or another, but you don't know it then, only much later, when you are in your forties and start looking back at your childhood with fondness. Sometimes you find yourself in disbelief at the silly things you did with your friends when you were young.

First, there was Samit. He lived with his family on the second floor, on the side of the apartment building facing the convenience store. His skin was darker than mine. His hair was coarse and thick. He looked like one of the ancient warriors on the Bayon Temple walls. He was the one who told people that I liked Dawn Chilton. I never asked why he did what he did. I was afraid of him because he was much bigger than I was.

One day, while playing marbles with the rest of the neighborhood kids in the backyard, I noticed Samit reading something on his apartment balcony. I thought it was strange that Samit was reading, he wasn't the type to be interested in books. He got me in trouble many times by talking to me in class, so much so that Ms. Souza asked me to switch seats with another student. That day, out of curiosity, I walked over to Samit. He saw me coming and said, "Hey Samnang, come over here. I have something to show you."

I walked over, made sure to avoid Lucky, and climbed up the steps to his balcony. When I reached the top, Samit stood facing me, his hands behind his back, grinning.

"What are you reading, Samit?" I asked.

"Come closer" was his reply. When I did, he showed me what he had been staring at. It was a dirty magazine. He flipped the glossy pages, found what he liked, and said, "Here. Look at this!"

It was a picture of a woman lying naked on a bed, her eyes closed, her lips making a red "O" shape, her legs spread to reveal her pink self. I was shocked, horrified.

"She has hair in that area?" I said.

"All women have hair in their crotches. All adults do. You will have it, too."

Then Samit turned another page. It was a picture of a naked man surrounded by two nurses, one a redhead and the other a blonde. The redheaded nurse was unwrapping bandages on the man's penis.

"That's gross, Samit. That's really yucky."

He laughed and said, "Suit yourself. Go play with your marbles and rubber bands. Collect them and see what you can do with them." He returned to his magazine as I backed away and quickly went back down the steps.

Then there was red-haired and freckled Robert Darling. His mother worked as a stripper at the Squire, a gentlemen's club in north Revere. Robert never knew his father. Every day after school, he begged me to visit him at his home, which was a few blocks from my apartment. I didn't have anything better to do one day and I really didn't want to hang out with Samit and look at pictures of naked women, so I walked with Robert up the hill to his house, which sat on top of Franklin Avenue, overlooking Route 1A.

It was a two-bedroom apartment on the ground floor of a ranch house. The apartment smelled of tuna fish, and there were clothes flung all over the sofa and living room floor. Robert went to the kitchen and got us each a can of Coke. A note on the refrigerator's door read: "Sweetie. Warm up pasta for dinner. Will be home late this evening. Love, Mom." A heart followed the scribble.

Robert took the note, crumpled it into a ball, and not even bothering to look, threw it at a trash can. It missed, but he seemed not to care that the crumpled paper was on the floor.

We went to the living room, sat on the sofa, and drank Coke. He turned to me and said, "Let's watch wrestling." Before I had time to answer, Robert got up and put a VHS tape into the VCR. We watched Hulk Hogan do his finishing signature move, a leg drop, on Rowdy Roddy Piper. Robert turned again, and said, "Hey, let's wrestle." Before I said anything, he began clearing the coffee table, told me to get on my hands and knees, and then proceeded to headlock me with his legs. Once he had my head between his legs, Robert got to his feet, jumped, and drove my head right into the floor. My head slammed into the rug and twisted with Robert's weight. I got dizzy, stars in a sky of darkness swirling in my head. I felt like I was about to heave. But Robert said, "Get up. Come on. That was fun. Let's do it again."

After the pile-driver, I lay still on the rug. When I came to, I saw above me Robert's legs high in the air. I coughed after his legs slammed into my chest. I crawled on my hands and knees on the living room floor for a few seconds. I finally got up, found my backpack, and stumbled toward the door.

"Hey, where are you going? We're playing wrestling. You can do the moves on me next."

As I ran out the door, I heard Robert crying, "Come back, please. Don't leave me. You can do a leg drop on me anytime. I promise. Just don't leave me here."

I ran down the street as fast as my legs could carry me. My backpack bounced on my back. I looked back to see Robert walking back inside his apartment and slamming the front door behind him.

Boran, whose name refers to the classical style of Khmer architecture and art, was the most interesting of the people I knew in Revere. His family arrived in the States in 1984, two years after ours. Tall and thin, he had on a white T-shirt with the letters "UNESCO" in blue across it when I met him. He was a few years older than Samit and me but he was placed in the sixth grade.

Armed with a No. 2 pencil, Boran sat at a table during recess while the other kids chased each other around on the playground. Using white lined papers, he drew all sort of things that reminded us of Cambodia. A house standing on stilts a few feet above ground during rainy season. A bright sun shining over farmers bending low to plant rice seedlings in the field. Mountains with birds flying in a V-shape across a Cambodian landscape. A man waist-deep in water casting a fishing net, above him birds flying in a clear blue sky. A woman in a sarong bathing in the pond. She had a champa flower in her long black hair.

We couldn't wait to see what Boran would draw next as we huddled around him. Samit said, "Boran, draw us a boy riding a buffalo across rice paddies." I too remembered those rice paddies. I used to chase wild birds in those fields and fall asleep under a tree afterward.

Another kid, who was older than most of us but was also placed into the sixth grade because of his rudimentary English, said, "Draw boun joul chnum thmey. I miss our New Year celebration. Have the kids throw powder at each other with the parents looking on."

"Better yet, draw us nom-ah-som," I suggested, thinking about those steamed glutinous rice cakes wrapped in banana leaves. It had been some time since I ate nom-ah-som. Lok-Yeay used to make and sell them in the refugee camps. Everyone laughed but I knew we all longed for the same thing: a life we'd left behind.

One afternoon, Boran and I were walking home from school and we got to talking. I asked, "How did you learn how to draw like that?"

"I don't know. I just picked up a stick one day and started to draw on the dirt in the refugee camps. I had this fear that I might forget Cambodia. I had to draw it to remember it and make it real. I want to feel Cambodia wherever I go."

"Well, it's certainly real to us. Your drawings remind us of the Cambodia we knew and felt." Then, like the other Cambodian kids, I asked him to draw something for me. "Hey, Boran, can you draw a family in the village in the late afternoon, with the mother watering her vegetables, the father returning from the field and the children running up to him?"

He laughed. "Samnang, you always seem to know exactly what you want. Why don't you draw it yourself?" We both laughed. Then he said to me, "You know I won't always be here, Samnang. You'll have to learn how to draw and tell your own stories."

I grew quiet as I tried to take in what Boran was saying, when a group of kids walked toward us. The leader was Robert, the kid who "played wrestling" with me. He stepped forward and said to Boran, "What are you doing hanging around with this faggot? He was at my house the other day and tried to kiss me. Unless you're a faggot too, faggot!" Boran dropped his backpack to the ground. Standing face-to-face with Robert, Boran was an inch or two taller. Robert stared at Boran, then spat at his face.

Boran jumped up and gave a roundhouse kick to Robert, who staggered to the side and fell. On the ground, Robert grabbed ahold of one of Boran's legs. Boran got down on the ground, wrapped his legs around Robert's neck, then squeezed. Robert's friends yelled, "Get up, Robert. Get up and give him a beat down!" But Robert was foaming around the mouth, his freckled face reddening and his eyes bulging white.

I screamed, "Boran, you're going to kill him if you don't stop. He's turning red. He's not worth it. Let's get out of here before someone calls the police."

Boran loosened his legs, got up, and looked down at his opponent sprawling on the cement sidewalk. He kicked Robert on the side.

Sadly for me, that was Boran's last year at Garfield. He moved to California with his parents that summer. Rumor had it that there were more Cambodians in California than anywhere else in

America. Boran and his family simply packed up and left, without telling anyone. Even Mr. Keo, our Khmer community liaison at the school, didn't know; he was as baffled and sad as we were at Boran's leaving.

With Boran gone, I was left with Samit to explore the streets of Revere. Living in the same apartment building, we saw each other every day. He was braver than me. We walked down to Shirley Avenue, where Cambodian grocery stores were starting to line the street, then climbed Highland Street where other Cambodian families lived. There was an apartment on Thornton Street that we visited. I didn't know how Samit knew the people there. The kids were older than us. They smoked, looked at dirty magazines, and fought each other in the backyard. Their parents must have worked on weekends because I never saw them.

Once one of the older kids came into the Thornton apartment, closed the door behind him, and put a videocassette into the VCR. It was an X-rated film. They all sat there, glued to the television screen, especially Samit. Then, one by one, they got up to use the restroom. I didn't understand what was going on, but I felt uncomfortable and told Samit, "Let's get out of here!" He brushed me off with his hand. I got up, left the apartment, and walked home by myself.

I'm not sure why Samit and I were friends. We had so little in common. He was interested in pushing boundaries, and I was no troublemaker. I feared our landlady's dog, Lucky, while Samit picked up a tree branch, taunted the dog with it, and when Lucky got close, he picked up a rock and threw it at the dog. I was afraid of Dawn, while Samit had no problems talking to girls, any girl. Maybe our friendship was based on me having never said no to any of his ideas. I just went along with whatever he suggested. One time, he decided we should ditch school, and we did. We were in Mr. Foley's gym class. A whistle around his neck, our gym teacher stood over six feet tall and weighed at least 225 pounds. Like most folks in Revere, he was a Celtics fan. He wore Celtics jerseys and hats, had posters of Larry Bird and Robert Parish in his office. I remembered one lesson he taught us. We were looking at two slides of Bird shooting a free throw. He asked, "What's the difference between these two slides?"

We looked at each other. No one said anything.

Mr. Foley answered his own question, "Look closer at the slide on the left. You see that player wearing jersey number seven? One of his feet touches the line. It doesn't matter if Bird shoots the ball in. It's automatic disqualification. So boys, remember to watch where your teammates stand." He looked at us as if he were imparting the kind of wisdom that would lead us to happiness for the rest of our lives.

Mr. Foley had a group of sixth graders who worshiped him and did everything he asked of them. They ran around the field, did jumping jacks and push-ups, climbed ropes. He didn't know what to do with Samit and me. I couldn't do push-ups and climb ropes; my jumping jack skills were below par. I was a skinny weakling with a protruding stomach. Samit either didn't understand what people said to him or simply refused to do what they asked of him. Mr. Foley ended up telling us to walk around the field next to the school.

As soon as we reached the basketball court, Samit said, "Let's get out of here." And we did. We took our shortcut—climbing fences and running through people's yards—to the local arcade, where no one was around except us. The proprietor saw us but didn't say anything. He was busy talking to someone on the phone. We used whatever quarters we had to play *Ms. Pac Man* and *Defender* until our stomachs growled. It was close to lunchtime. We decided to go apple picking. We climbed a hill, ran through people's yards, and found ourselves on Franklin Avenue. A car slowed down alongside us. It was Mrs. Katz, the school social worker, and Mr. Keo, who was the Cambodian liaison at Garfield. To our surprise, they didn't ask why we weren't at school. They simply wanted to know if we had seen Chen, the new kid who had arrived from the refugee camp a few weeks ago. He was quiet and didn't have any friends. We shook our heads, and Mrs. Katz thanked us. We watched the car crawl down Highland Street.

We kept walking until we saw the white house on the hill that overlooked Route 1A. We'd gone there a few times before. The house had a large apple tree in the backyard. We climbed up the tree and picked its small crab apples, the kind that Americans found sour on their tongues, when a woman emerged from the house, curlers in her hair, and screamed at us, "You kids, get down from there. Get out of my yard or I'll call the police." Frightened by her scream, I fell from the tree and had the air knocked out of me. Samit quickly jumped down the tree, threw a small apple at the woman's feet, and shook me until I came to, while the woman ran back into her house to call the police. With hollering laughter, we climbed up the fence, ran down the hill, and hid inside the arcade until it was three in the afternoon. We walked back home to our brick apartment complex on Centennial Avenue. I told Lok-Yeay that I had to stay after school to help my teacher and, busy taking care of my younger cousins, she didn't ask questions. She hadn't even noticed I was late coming home.

Pu Vaesnar

Ming Bonavy spoke into the receiver, "If you don't stop talking like that, I'm going to hang up!" Lok-Yeay and I could hear the man's voice over the phone. He sounded like he was pleading with her. I told Lok-Yeay that I felt sorry for the man.

"Goodbye now," Ming Bonavy hung up the phone.

"What does he want?" Lok-Yeay asked.

"He wants to take me out to the beach. I told him we're not husband and wife. I can't be seen with him in public."

"You know you're twenty-one. You are of a marriageable age."

The man continued to call. He got our number from Pu Ly, who went to Philadelphia to pick up Bopha and Vutha from their summer work picking fruits. He met this young man, Vaesnar, who'd lost both his parents to the Khmer Rouge. He had been living with a Cambodian family in Philadelphia since his arrival in 1983. He called them "Pok" and "Mak" and their children "Bong" and "Poan."

He was thin, dark-skinned, and had a friendly smile that showed his white teeth. Pu Ly told Lok-Yeay that Ming Bonavy should marry Vaesnar. If she got any older, no one would marry her. Now was the time, he warned her and us. Pu Ly gave Vaesnar a picture of my aunt wearing a white blouse and long black skirt, playing badminton at a cookout in Lynn. Oum Seyha had recently bought a used Oldsmobile, the Delta Royale, after saving enough money from working at a lumber company in New Hampshire. He organized a cookout and invited his friends from work. We drove in the burgundy Oldsmobile to a state park in Lynn, grilled curried chicken and steak, played volleyball and badminton, ate, drank, and laughed.

Ming Bonavy stared at the picture of the man in a gray cap, jeans, and white shirt. Behind him was a field of apple and cherry trees. He looked friendly enough. "That's him?" she asked, without waiting for an answer. "He looks African. You can't see anything but his teeth and eyes. And his hair is curly." Everybody laughed.

Pu Ly said, "He's hardworking. He will work hard and make lots of money for you. And in return, you can make lots of children for him."

Ming Bonavy turned to her mother for help, but Lok-Yeay said, "I was eighteen when I got married, and that was considered old back then."

With no one else to turn to, Ming Bonavy decided to give this guy with black curly hair and white teeth a chance and talked to him on the phone. She had had other Cambodian suitors visiting our home, talking to Lok-Yeay and taking every opportunity to glance and smile at Ming Bonavy when she came into the living room bearing a tray of fruits and drinks for her guests. But my aunt didn't say anything about them. For some reason, Vaesnar stood out in her mind. He was the most unattractive of her suitors. Maybe it was his voice or that she had never seen him in person. She later explained to me, when I interviewed her for my graduate research, "I thought, if I marry him, I know he won't cheat on me. What lady in her right mind would want to be with such an ugly man?"

That was the reason Ming Bonavy married Pu Vaesnar: he was so unattractive that there was little chance he could cheat on her. It was our family's first wedding in America. Lok-Yeay invited a monk from a Buddhist temple in Rhode Island to officiate. Oum Seyha woke up at four, drove to Providence, and brought the monk to perform the wedding ceremony at eight in the morning at our Centennial Avenue apartment. A picture of Lok-Ta at the altar with fruits and burning incense watched over the couple. Friends and neighbors clamored into the small apartment. About fifteen people sat in the living room, mostly adults, hands clasped, legs folded, and mouths chanting in Pali. The body heat and burning incense made the room quite unbearable. I went to the kitchen, where the women were preparing food. Samit's mother, a chubby woman in her late thirties, said, "She is such a beautiful bride. I don't know why she's marrying such a dark-skinned man. He's darker than Samit's father. You see his hair. His ancestors must be from Africa."

"It's better that he's dark than if he beats you," another woman answered.

"As long as he takes care of her and loves only her," someone else said.

"You know how men are. As soon as a woman smiles, and it doesn't even have to be at him, he swarms at her like a bee to honey," Samit's mother said.

"You don't trust these young women in America. They think that, now that they're in America, they can just toss off our Cambodian values." The women in the kitchen all nodded in agreement.

I walked out to the balcony in the back of our apartment. Chrissie stood outside, chain smoking. Her radio was playing Queen's "Crazy Little Thing Called Love." Chained to a post, Lucky was too busy chewing a bone to notice me.

Pu Vaesnar was a good uncle to me. If I asked him for money to buy Snickers and Twix, he gave me a couple of bucks. He never yelled at me. He was nice to me, maybe because he knew what it felt like to be an orphan. He never tried to spank me or said anything to belittle me. He was, as my cousins nowadays like to say, "pretty laid back." A year after their wedding, Ming Bonavy and Pu Vaesnar gave birth to their first child, Cindy, named after Cindy Brady from the sitcom *The Brady Bunch*. She was given an American name because she was born in the States. A few years later, after we moved to Malden, another child, a son named Ratana, was born. Oum Seyha and his wife had a second child too, another daughter, Christina, also born in Malden. She was named in honor of our sponsors' religious tradition. Her older sister, Chanthy, was born in Thailand. Pu Ly and Ming Narin had their third child in the States, a daughter named Chanda. Their other children were Raksmei, the oldest and only boy, and Leakena, a girl, both born in refugee camps in Thailand. And thus, after several years in the States, our family had finally put down roots and began sprouting different branches of the family tree.

To Lok-Yeay's sadness, Pu Dara and his wife decided to move to Southern California because they somehow got word that his wife's family was living there. Before he left, Lok-Yeay said to her youngest son, "Dara, you must not forget your family. If they mistreat you, come back to us. Your family is always here for you." Then she watched her son, his wife, and their daughter board the plane that would take them to Long Beach, California.

It was during this time that Oum Seyha, Pu Ly, and Pu Vaesnar pooled together their hard-earned savings and bought a three-story colonial house in Malden. The family was getting too big for our two-bedroom apartment. And Revere was getting too dangerous to raise kids, as each night we woke to car alarms and police sirens. One morning, we found our car windows smashed, tires slashed, and doors spray-painted with obscenities and warnings: "Gooks," "Go Back Home," "We Don't Want You Here." When we looked around to see who was responsible, we saw teenagers standing at the convenience store on the corner of Centennial Avenue and North Shore Street. They smoked, laughed, and waved. One gave us the middle finger. Our faces reddened; we were embarrassed and felt helpless to do anything in response.

Malden seemed, in comparison, like a quieter place to live and raise children. There were not many Asians or any other minorities living there at the time. Oum Seyha said, "There won't be any minorities where we will be, just white people. There'll be no more tires slashed and windows broken. People in Malden trust each other, say 'hi' to each other on the street. It's like that old TV show with the boy and Sheriff Andy. In Malden people have money, and when people have money, they have class. It doesn't matter if they are Black or white or Asian like us, rich people have class."

Enclosed Paradise

It was the summer of 1986, our first summer in Malden, and I was heading into the seventh grade at Browne Junior High School.

Oum Seyha was right. Malden was quiet. No one was vandalizing our cars. We were able to sleep through the night without fear of somebody trying to break into our home.

By this time, Pu Vaesnar had bought a used blue Buick LeSabre. He bought an American car because he believed in the quality of American-made automobiles. He also wanted to support the U.S. economy any way he could. After all, we were living in America and America had given us so much already. In only five years, my uncles had pooled their money and bought us a house with a silver chain-link fence around our property. It was a big three-story white colonial house, with each branch of the family having an entire floor to itself. Oum Seyha, his wife, and two daughters lived on the first floor. Lok-Yeay, Lok-Ta, Ming Bonavy, Pu Vaesnar, and I lived on the second floor. Pu Ly, Ming Narin, their three children, and Bopha lived on the third floor. Vutha had a room in the basement. It was crowded by most American standards, but it was home for us. And as Lok-Yeay often reminded us, "Better a crowded home than an unhappy one."

Our new home became a hot spot for parties every other weekend. My uncles and aunts invited friends from Revere, Chelsea, Lynn, and Lowell to come over, eat, drink, and forget. Pu Vaesnar grilled teriyaki chicken wings, lemongrass-flavored beef, and skewered shrimps. My aunts and their friends made somlor with beef and tripe and plear (thinly sliced beef cooked in lime, salt, pepper, and lemon grass). Lok-Yeay made her famous prahouk with minced garlic and pork. Oum Seyha raised a bottle of Heineken and said to his friends, "Brothers and sisters, thank you for the opportunity to celebrate with you on this day. We have come a long way. We survived hunger and escaped the killings under Pol Pot rule, avoided jungle pirates on our way to the refugee camps, and survived the Thai soldiers and military police. We left our friends and family back in Cambodia. We left our beloved motherland. But we are here now. We have jobs; we drive our own cars; we have plenty of food, as you can see here. Our children were born here. America is our home now. Raise whatever you're drinking and make a toast to our new home, to America!" Everyone cheered, "To America!" Amid the bounty of food, drink, and good spirit, everyone felt lifted, hopeful; our circumstances, if not transcended, were momentarily forgotten.

A karaoke machine was set up in the living room, where Ming Bonavy got up and sang with her brother-in-law, Pu Ly. After every song, someone got up, raised his or her glass, and toasted to new beginnings. Everyone cheered. The adults talked about life before the Khmer Rouge, when they were young and strong, when they had freedom to farm their own land and fish their own water, when their loved ones were still alive. By eleven in the evening, people began crying over family members or friends taken away by the Khmer Rouge. People started to leave, somber. By one in the morning, someone vomited at the bottom of our driveway.

For my cousins and for me, our new home was a self-enclosed paradise. I was scared to walk around the neighborhood, as people were rarely seen out on the sidewalks and streets. Unlike Revere, our new neighborhood was unusually quiet. I stayed inside the boundary of our chain-link fence, keeping to the land on either side of our house. There were apple and cherry trees on one side, and another apple tree and a huge willow on the other. A variety of pear trees and Concord grapevines adorned both sides of the driveway. I didn't have to go into people's yards and climb their trees for apples anymore. Now I simply walked out the back door and into our yard, climbed one of our apple trees, and held on to the highest branch of the tree, which was as high as the third story of the house, where Pu Ly and his family slept. Clutching the branch with my bare feet, I took out a grocery bag from my pocket, tied it around a nearby branch, and started putting apples into the bag. My little cousin, Raksmei, who was five at the time, saw what I was doing and began climbing up the tree after me. Ming Narin called out, "Raksmei, Raksmei! Get down from there this minute. Don't follow Samnang. You'll fall and break your neck." With disappointment, Raksmei climbed back down the apple tree.

Oum Seyha said he chose the house for its land, with a yard on all sides that covered half an acre. It reminded him of our family's farmland in Cambodia. For us kids, the yard became our jungle, where we climbed trees, played hide-and-seek, ran and chased each other, kicked around a soccer ball, and played whiffle ball. Late in the afternoon, when the sun began to set, I called to my little cousins: American-born Cindy, Christina, Ratana, and Chanda, and Thai-born Raksmei, Leakena, and Chanthy. Of the group, I was the only one born in Cambodia. I taught my cousins the rules of each game and separated them into two teams. They were to participate in our own summer Olympic games, where they ran relays carrying tree branches as batons around our new home and jumped across a patch of dirt. Using a stick, I drew a line in the dirt to mark the distance of each jump. Then, as a grand finale, they all lined up on one side of the yard and raced to the other side. One of the girls, Christina, fell and was left behind in the race. She began crying, tears streaming from her eyes and snot dripping from her nose. Lok-Yeay, who was tending to her vegetable garden, looked up from her rows of corn, basil, and green and red chilies. She called out, "Samnang, stop making them run. Go and help Christina. You're the oldest, you should know better!"

We had such freedom that summer. We were kids running around the yard, screaming and laughing, climbing trees, and throwing our bodies over and against the dirt and grass. We played until it was time to wash up and go to bed. One by one, my aunts called to their children, "It's time to come in and wash up." And one by one, my cousins went inside. The kitchen door slammed, and all was quiet.

I was left alone, standing in the yard all by myself. No one had called me in. I sat on the swing that hung from the willow tree. The breeze blew, rustling the leaves and making the willow tree weep in the late summer evening. I stayed out until it was too dark to see. Eventually I decided to hang it up and walked up the front stairs, opened the front door and went inside, washed up, and made my way to the bedroom that I shared with Lok-Yeay. I climbed into my bed and tried to sleep.

The Old Woman
and Her Dog

Each morning, an old woman walked past our house with her dog. And each afternoon, she returned with her dog, a Yorkshire terrier. She always stopped at the end of our driveway, where her dog barked. The little scruffy animal barked and barked, pulling its leash against its owner. That was how we knew the old woman was there. We stopped whatever we were playing, ran to the driveway, and waved. But the woman pulled on the leash and yanked her little creature away from us. The dog kept barking as the woman walked toward her house on the corner of the block, on the other side of our street.

We didn't think much about the old woman until the end of that first summer, when I was heading into the seventh grade at Browne Junior High School and my family decided to have another barbecue. Oum Seyha had accepted a new job working at a lumber company up north, somewhere in New Hampshire. He invited his friends over to celebrate the end of summer and his new job.

Food was prepared the previous night and finished early that morning. Visitors from Revere, Lynn, Chelsea, and Lowell were parked along public streets. Everyone was eating, laughing, and drinking. Pu Ly and his friends sang karaoke. My cousins and I played hide-and-seek in the yard. When we grew tired, we went to the grill and each got ourselves a plate of pork or spiced beef on a skewer and iced cans of Coke. Later in the day, when we got super hungry, we went inside the house and each of us got a bowl of rice soaked in somlor with chicken. We sat on the living room floor, watching the adults smoke and listening to their talk of politics, of how there were still Khmer Rouge in Cambodia's government and Hun Sen, the prime minister, was a former Khmer Rouge leader.

Then the doorbell rang.

When Ming Bonavy saw the policeman at the door, she burst into tears. With his dark uniform and a gun strapped to his waist, he was the authority figure, and for my aunt, authority meant Angkar, the Khmer Rouge government that took away her uncle and brother, starved her sister to death, and murdered her friends and neighbors. She ran out the back door, eyes wide, crying, and into the backyard, warning her family and guests that the police were at the door. Oum Seyha calmly went to the door, smiled, and nodded. He said politely, "Welcome to our house, officer."

The policeman explained his presence. "Dogs were reported missing in the neighborhood," he said. "I need to search the premises."

My uncle said, "Yes, OK. Come in, please. Thank you."

The policeman walked through the house. Smelling the tripe boiling in the big pot, he scrunched his nose and asked Oum Seyha, "What's that?"

"It's cow, sir. Stomach of a cow," my uncle explained.

The police officer went out the back door, walked around the yard, and checked the trash cans under the stairs. He found nothing. He walked down the driveway, got in his patrol car, and drove away. Our neighbors looked on from their yards even after the police cruiser left.

My uncles and aunts were embarrassed. They tried to resume their celebration, turning on the karaoke machine and having Ming Bonavy sing to entertain the guests, but it was too late. They had lost face in front of their friends and neighbors. Ming Bonavy sang like she was crying. Our guests stayed quiet and still, and everyone had sobered up. Our guests began leaving one by one while Ming Bonavy continued her singing-crying.

After the police crashed our party, I was nervous about going to school. I knew that things would be different now. There wouldn't be any Khmer students at this new school. No Samit and Boran to protect me. On my own, I'd have to figure out things fast and learn how to survive. That morning, I left the house at seven for an eight o'clock bell. I didn't want to be late on my first day. The streets I crossed were new to me, so I repeated their names in my head as I walked block after block, passing many New England colonial homes, the red fire station and the local library on Oliver Street, and the corner store near the school. There were kids around my age walking in groups and young children with their parents. They were talking and laughing. A mother held her child's hand as they crossed the street to the elementary school on the other side of the road.

When I arrived at Browne Junior High School, I noticed that its doors were closed; a chain wrapped around the door handles, with a big lock hanging from it. It was seven forty-five. I saw kids standing in a line along the side of the school building. I went to the back of the long line and waited with them. Unlike Garfield, Browne didn't have any other Asian students, never mind Cambodian students. My classmates were mostly white, with a few African Americans among us.

The September morning wind blew cool against my skin. My teeth chattered. A group of kids hanging around the steps took notice of me and came over.

A red-haired kid said to me, "Hey, what's up?"

I smiled.

"Are you new here?"

I nodded and smiled.

"Where are you from?"

"Cambodia."

"Oh yeah?" He paused, thought about something clever to say, and blurted, "Hey, do you know any kung fu?"

I said nothing.

"Show us some of your moves." The red-haired kid curled his fists, shook his fiery head, and made monkey noises. They laughed, and I laughed too. What else could I do? I didn't want trouble, especially on my first day.

Then a second kid asked, "Do they eat dogs where you come from?"

They all laughed, and the questions kept rolling.

"Do they use branches and leaves as toilet paper where you came from?"

"Do they dig holes for you to shit in?"

"Man, that's gross! Alan, where did you get this stuff?"

The redheaded kid answered, "My father fought in 'Nam. He told me all kinds of crazy stories. Crazy and gross all right, where this kid comes from."

"That ain't right. That's some backward shit, man. Pun intended."

Everyone laughed.

"My father also told me that they dig holes in the ground and live in the dark like rats. That's why they're called tunnel rats," Alan continued. "They killed us Americans too, but we got them back. We even got their little gook babies. Isn't that right, gook boy?"

I tried my best to smile. The other students waiting in line saw what was happening but they turned their backs and pretended not to notice. I looked at the school door, hoping to see someone inside coming over to unlock it. I stood there, hands in my coat pockets, teeth still chattering from the cold.

Finally, the eight o'clock bell rang and I was, briefly, rescued.

A Simple Misunderstanding

At my new school, I was taken out of social studies class in the third period and placed in a small windowless office, where I had a one-on-one session with Mr. Giuseppe Galanti, a tall, thin man in his early fifties, who wore wire-rimmed glasses and, always, a tie, a cardigan sweater, black slacks, and shoes. His hair was parted to the right, and his voice was gentle and caring. He was like Mr. Rogers, except he was an Italian who grew up in Argentina and came to the U.S. in his late teens, attended Boston Prep, and went on to study American history at Tufts University.

Mr. Galanti knocked on the classroom door, smiled, and Mr. Hill, our social studies teacher, looked in my direction. "Samnang, Mr. Galanti is here to see you." I got up, embarrassed, and could feel the other students watching me as I packed up my schoolbag. Once with Mr. Galanti, I was comfortable, relaxed, as there were no other students but me. I paid him respect and attention as I learned rudimentary English, read fifth-grade books, took dictation, and answered his questions about my life. He listened to me with fatherly concern. When my session was over, Mr. Galanti walked me back to my fourth-period class. I hated returning to the regular class because it meant the other students would be looking at me again.

I met with Mr. Galanti twice a week, on Tuesdays and Thursdays. The other days of the week he went to the high school, where he taught a class full of international students. I didn't mind these one-on-one ESL lessons; Mr. Galanti was the only adult who paid me any attention. The only problem I had was the anxiety I felt when I had to leave the class—the eyes of my classmates and teacher alike following me as I packed my bag and left the classroom. I already looked different from my peers, so why make it worse by having an official segregation from the rest of the student population?

Of course, it didn't help that I hadn't made any friends in the seventh grade. I was quiet, and no one came to talk to me. I shared a locker with Matt Searle, who pretty much left me alone. I had the top part of the locker, and he had the bottom. He was a nice kid, shy and quiet like me, but he didn't want to be associated with me for fear of dropping a rung or two on the social ladder of junior high school. And he already had his own group of friends that he'd known since kindergarten. Not wanting to hurt Matt's social standing, I kept to myself most of the time. Lunch period was painful; I sat alone at a table in the back of the cafeteria. In gym, we had to play dodgeball, a war game disguised as exercise for us kids. Under five feet tall and about a hundred pounds, with a haircut that looked like someone had put a coconut shell over my head and trimmed the sides, not only was I the smallest in school, but I was unmistakably the only fresh-off-the-boat Asian. This automatically meant that I was Chinese and knew kung fu and sometimes the kids confused Chinese with Vietnamese because of the American War in Việt Nam. At the beginning of dodgeball, my opponents usually left me alone, since I was no threat, and focused on tagging my teammates. Once they were out, the other players ganged up on me and, counting to three, threw their dodgeballs all at once.

It was a funny sight for them, this small Asian kid curled up like a centipede as they hurled ball after ball at him.

"Look at him curl like that! That's how they slide into their rat tunnels."

"This one is for you, Uncle Mike." A ball flew over my head, ricocheted off the wall, and hit my lower back.

Coach Fitzgerald was too busy in his office talking to another teacher to hear the yelling and laughing coming from his gymnasium.

"This is war. And we're dropping bombs on your chinky ass."

"Yeah, gook! Go home!"

One time, I was hit so hard on the left side of my head by a dodgeball that my ear buzzed for a few minutes. When I opened my eyes, the world spun and I fell to the ground, hands holding my head. Coach Fitzgerald came over, took me to his office, and gave me an ice pack. My left eye turned puffy and was bruised by the fourth period. Between classes, someone stopped me in the hallway and asked, "What happened?" I saw Alan and his buddies walk by and remembered what they did to me that first day of classes. I didn't say anything: just watched as Alan walked by. By the end of lunch, a rumor had spread across the cafeteria: a bully by the name of Alan Webb was responsible for my swollen eye. A few days later, Alan sported two black eyes of his own. He walked up to me while I was putting my books in the locker and apologized for something he actually didn't do. "Sorry about your eye, man. I'm sorry, OK?" By lunch, another rumor swirled in the cafeteria hall: the legendary B.K., upon learning what had purportedly happened to me at Alan's hands, felt sympathetic for this Asian kid and decided to set things right.

I didn't know what to say or do. Who was this B.K. guy, and where could I find him to explain in my limited English that there was a simple misunderstanding? It wasn't Alan Webb who did this to me. It was a bunch of kids playing dodgeball in the gym and reenacting their fathers' and uncles' war traumas. Sure, Alan was a bully who had said stupid things to me on my first day of school, but he wasn't responsible for my black eye. But apparently, not many students had ever seen B.K. in the hallway, classroom, or anywhere on school grounds. No one knew whether he was still in school or had dropped out. He was a mythic figure who haunted the hallways and schoolyard of Browne Junior High School. But from then on, the other kids left me further alone. At recess, lunch, gym, and even after school, they backed off.

With no one bothering me, I decided to take my studies seriously. I paid attention in class and did my homework. I never raised my hand to volunteer an answer, but I didn't give my teachers any trouble either. I did well that first quarter, making the honor roll. I got As in math and art, a B+ in English, and a few Bs in science and social studies. Math was the easiest subject for me. I didn't have to know English to excel. Art, too, had its universal language. But science was tough, especially during labs, where I had to follow directions in English. I didn't know what I was supposed to do or why. I ended up standing next to my lab partner and letting him cut open a dead frog.

And each day, when the seventh period bell rang, I packed up my books and went straight home. There wasn't anyone to hang out with after school.

The Doyles

Walking home from school one afternoon, I saw a group of boys forming a circle outside of Johnny's Convenience. Someone was crying, "Guys, come on." I couldn't see who he was and what was happening to him.

"Come on what, Fat Boy? What are you afraid of? Getting your ass kicked?"

I again heard the same feeble voice. "Stop it, please."

"It'll only hurt for a while. You should be used to this by now." This response got a few chuckles from the other bullies.

"Don't be a pussy! You're a big boy, fight back." There was silence, then another voice said, "Man, have some dignity. Defend yourself."

Inside the circle was a slightly overweight boy with a crew cut. His eyes were wet, bewildered, and sad. His cheeks were flushed. Out of desperation, he threw a wild punch, but the force of his punch was empty and, reaching no one, disappeared in thin air. The bullies laughed. The overweight boy stared at his hands in disbelief. He was pushed against the wall by one of the bullies, a short, muscular boy with a neck wider than his head. He was a few inches shorter than the overweight boy, but he was lean, fit, and had pimples around his mouth and forehead.

Other kids walked by us, but they pretended not to see or hear what was happening. Parents in their station wagons drove by, and like the children, they too paid no attention to what was happening in plain sight.

The short, muscular boy turned to me and said, "What are you looking at? Do you want some of it too?"

I stood there, not saying a word, but stared back at him.

"I said, 'What do you want? Do you want some of this too?'" He held up his fists.

The overweight boy avoided making eye contact with me. I was sorry that he felt embarrassed and humiliated. I had been this boy once; I remembered that night at the convenience store in Revere, when I was sent to buy a lottery ticket for Pu Dara. I recognized his bewildered, sad gaze pleading for help from the world. I remembered feeling helpless, disappointed that no one came to my rescue. And so, somehow, I found it in me to utter, "Leave him alone."

"What? What was that? Are you going to make me if I don't?" The leader said the last question slowly and loudly.

"You guys leave him alone."

"Beat it, kid. Go on, get out of here!"

But I stood my ground. I was filled with sympathy for the overweight kid. Like me, he was an outcast.

One of the bullies said, "Isn't he that new kid who got Alan Webb beaten up? Yeah, that's him all right."

The leader paused for a second, then turned to the overweight boy and said, "You're lucky this time. Next time, we're going to sweep your ass on the concrete floor." Then, they left.

The overweight boy stood still in disbelief. We both watched the group of boys walk away. Then he walked over and extended his hand to me. "My name's Jeff Doyle."

I told him my name. He asked me to repeat it, and then he tried to say my name. He asked where I was from. I said, "Cambodia. It's in Asia."

"That's near Vietnam, right? My mom and dad had a foster kid from Vietnam. He's studying to be a priest now." Jeff shook my hand, and we both smiled.

I took a liking to Jeff right away. With his weight and height, he was an easy target for kids who hungered for a certain sort of reputation at the school. All they had to do was beat up Jeff, a bigger kid who couldn't throw a punch to save his life, and they would get the respect they felt they needed from their peers.

The two of us walked home together. He lived on Oliver Street, a few blocks from my family's home. He had a younger sister, Sarah, and a younger brother, Anthony, the youngest of the siblings. Jeff's mother came over to the dining table and shook my hand, "Hi, I'm Maura." She had short hair, like Mary Tyler Moore in the 1960s and '70s, but I was too shocked that an adult had introduced herself to me by her first name to be surprised by her haircut.

"Nice to meet you, Mrs. Doyle."

She went back to the kitchen and asked if she could offer me something to drink. "There's juice, tonic, and water," she said, looking into the fridge.

I politely asked for a glass of water and thanked her.

Sitting at the kitchen table, I drank a glass of iced water and ate a slice of banana bread that Mrs. Doyle put in front of me. It was delicious! The sweet scent of banana, vanilla extract, sugar, and butter perfumed the Doyles' kitchen. I felt like I was in an episode of *The Brady Bunch* and that here, in this room, was the America that I'd always wanted: warm, friendly, welcoming to strangers and outsiders.

Anthony went upstairs to his room and came back down with his GI Joe and Hulk Hogan action figures. I had only seen those toys advertised on TV. I wanted one badly, but Lok-Yeay would never allow such frivolous spending. Money was for necessities: food and clothing for school and temple. I asked Anthony if I could draw his action figures. Sarah brought a pencil and paper for me to draw. I sat drawing at the kitchen table while the family stood around me.

I had learned how to draw from Boran. The Doyles liked what I made, and Anthony asked if I could draw another. It was around five o'clock when Jeff's father returned from work. He was tall, medium-build, with thin, light hair. He smiled, shook my hand, and introduced himself as Christopher. Then he excused himself and went upstairs to get ready for supper. Mrs. Doyle asked if I would like to stay. I nodded.

That afternoon, we had meatloaf, mashed potatoes, and apple pie. The food was delicious, and the company was warm.

I said to her, "American food is delicious! Thank you, Mrs. Doyle."

Mrs. Doyle looked over to Anthony and said, "See, not everybody can't stand my cooking."

Anthony rolled his eyes, while Sarah and Jeff laughed.

"You know, there are starving kids in Africa, China, Cambodia, who would be grateful for the bounty we have here at this table," said Mrs. Doyle.

There was silence. Then Mr. Doyle asked me, "How do you like Malden?"

I told them about my classes and Mr. Galanti, and then I told them about the police paying a visit to our home, looking for missing dogs.

Mrs. Doyle was visibly upset. She shook her head and said she couldn't believe that such a thing had happened in her neighborhood in 1986. She asked, "Why didn't they visit the other houses on your block? They knew you didn't know the law. They knew you didn't know that you have the right to ask for a search warrant. I'm sorry that happened to you and your family, Samnang."

Jeff asked his parents, "Is there anything we can do for them?"

Mrs. Doyle said, "I will call city hall and the police station tomorrow."

And the next day, she called the station and complained over the telephone. But the police said they didn't know anything about it. The folks at city hall said they would make an inquiry. Of course nothing ever came of it. But it was important for me to know that someone was willing to stand up for us, that someone cared for us and would try and make sure that from now on, we were protected by the law.

Maybe Lok-Ta was right when he said to Bopha a couple of years ago, "Not everyone is bad. There are good and bad people everywhere, of every race, creed, and class. You must have patience. Soon, you will meet a good American person."

Walking home that late afternoon, I thought to myself, *I think I just met a good American family.*

The Doyles were a typical middle-class Irish American family. Pictures of Mary, Jesus, and the Pope graced the walls of their home. A piano sat in the dining room hall. They had dinner together every evening around five-thirty, six at the latest. Before they ate, they prayed and thanked the Lord for such bounty. On Sunday, they attended Mass. Pro-life stickers and quotes from Mother Teresa and Ted Kennedy adorned their car bumpers.

And they always had houseguests, usually priests from other parts of the world, places like Kenya, Argentina, Việt Nam, Ecuador, and the Philippines. Since they were against abortion, they often took in foster children. Mr. and Mrs. Doyle tried their best to help these children, some of whom were about Jeff's age and had crushes on Sarah. I was always taken aback to see another teenager living at the Doyles' even though I should have grown used to it. They believed in leading a life of service to humanity, in being kind and generous to strangers in need. And they were always kind and generous to me. They invited me to their dinners and barbecues. They showed me what Thanksgiving, Christmas, New Year's Eve, the Fourth of July, and other American holidays were like. They even celebrated my birthday, something that my own family never did. My uncles and aunts were too busy working, trying to pay off the mortgage, still trying to pay the U.S. government back for the plane tickets that brought us to America. They also had their own children to care for; they didn't have time to care and worry about me. I told myself that it didn't matter, that it shouldn't matter, that I was "Samnang," lucky to be alive and living in America with my Lok-Yeay, my Pu, Ming, and Oum.

With their good Catholic hearts, the Doyles were kind and generous to me. They took me deep-sea fishing, apple picking, skiing in Vermont and New Hampshire, ice skating on the frozen duck pond in Fellsmere Park, sledding down Mount Hood—all those American activities that I'd seen on TV. But deep down, I felt that something was wrong. They paid for my skiing and deep-sea fishing tickets, for lunches and dinners, for a winter jacket; they paid for everything, everywhere we went. I felt uncomfortable about all of this. They were not family, but they treated me as though I was family. And the more the Doyles showed kindness to me, the more I realized what was missing in my life at home. The more they showed me love, the more I realized what my home life lacked. The more they welcomed me with open arms into their home, the more I realized how different my family was. The more they tried to get close to me, the more I felt this pain, and so I began pushing them away. It hurt me to see how much love and kindness the Doyles showed to family, friends, and strangers alike and after a while, I began rejecting their kind offers outright, slowly pulling away from them.

A February Evening

One afternoon, I was in the living room watching *Thundercats* on the TV with my cousin Raksmei when we heard a loud crash from upstairs. It sounded like someone or something had fallen against the wooden floor. Then the door banged, slammed, and someone screamed. Raksmei and I looked at each other. I got up, and he followed. We went to the kitchen and asked our grandmother, "Lok-Yeay, did you hear that?" She had. She climbed up the stairs to the third floor, where Pu Ly and Ming Narin slept. I heard my aunt crying. We could hear heated exchanges between Lok-Yeay and Pu Ly. Finally, Lok-Yeay said, "That's enough. You stop hitting my daughter. Whatever she did, she doesn't deserve a beating. She's your wife and the mother of your children." Pu Ly began yelling in reply, but I couldn't make out what he was saying.

Then Lok-Yeay came back down the stairs.

Since Pu Ly quit his job, our home had become unbearable. When he worked, I only saw him when he came home in the evening and had dinner with his wife and children. By that time, I could stay in my bedroom and do homework. Now that he was home all day, I couldn't escape him. No one could. He was constantly criticizing everyone—his wife, his children, me. Apparently no one was as intelligent as he was. Before he quit his job, Pu Ly criticized his boss, made fun of him in Khmer with other Cambodian workers, calling him lazy and inept at his job. My uncle left before getting fired. At home, he threatened us with unimaginable beatings, reminding us that "in Cambodia, you don't look at your elders unless you want to be hung upside down and beaten with coconut leaves. Back there, you kids had no rights. Here, you have these so-called rights, children's rights, women's rights, and no one has the right to discipline you. Well, not in my house, not under my roof. What I say here goes, understand? This is a Khmer house, not an American house!"

I went to the kitchen and asked Lok-Yeay, "Is Ming Narin OK?"

"She's fine. He is her husband."

I told my grandmother, "I hate him."

"Don't say that, Samnang. He's your uncle. He knows things."

"He knows nothing but how to hit people who are weaker than he is."

"He went through a lot during the Khmer Rouge times."

"And so did everyone else. But he's the only one who hits people."

"He's your elder. You need to respect him."

"I have no respect for him. He needs to earn my respect with his actions and words. Respect doesn't come automatically just because he's my elder."

"Samnang, you're sounding more and more American."

"Lok-Yeay, he turns his anger at the world toward those of us who are weak and vulnerable. Just because he has what the doctor calls PTSD doesn't make it right for him to do that. I won't respect him. Do you remember how he beat Bopha?"

"That's how he shows his love. He wanted her to be a proper Khmer woman. If he didn't care, he wouldn't say those things or beat her."

"When I have children, I will never hit them to show my love and affection," I told her. "I'm getting out of here."

"Where are you going? You need to stay home and study," Lok-Yeay said.

"I'm going to take a walk; I just need to be away from here. I can't stand being around him." I walked out the kitchen door and ran down the steps.

It was a cold and quiet January evening. Patches of ice cemented the sidewalks. Christmas decorations were left hanging at some of the houses; red and green lights flashed, blinking against my face as I strolled about the neighborhood, hands in my pockets, looking at houses with the curtains open. I saw families seated around dining tables eating, drinking, and chatting, hands gesticulating, faces smiling and laughing, couples sitting on sofas and watching television, husbands chatting with their wives in the kitchen. I saw what I imagined familial happiness to be, a happiness that always seemed foreign to me. I wondered what it would be like to experience such love against the anger and violence of refugee life, against the meanness of the world, against the coldness of this January winter. I wondered what it would be like to be inside the warmth of such togetherness.

I thought about my own family. We never once sat down around a dining table, had dinner, and asked each other how our days went. Ming Narin and Vutha worked the graveyard shift at a hotel in Boston. Oum Seyha and now Pu Vaesnar worked at a lumber company up in New Hampshire and left the house at five in the morning, returning at six in the evening. Lok-Yeay did most of the cooking for the three branches of her family and took care of all the grandchildren. Because of Lok-Yeay, there was always food on the table when I got home from school. Weekends, each family had its own kitchen to make food and eat together. I never sat down and ate with any of them. Sometimes Oum Seyha looked up and, seeing me coming in from outside, asked, "Samnang, sit down and join us for lunch." I refused such kind gestures. It felt wrong, like I was intruding on his family, so I said, "No thanks, Oum. I already ate a while ago." I walked upstairs to the living room, plopped myself down on the couch, and turned on the TV.

That evening, as I watched American families in their dining rooms eating and talking to each other, I thought about my family's situation. I couldn't help how my mind worked. When the Doyles invited me over to dinner, I'd quickly say, "No, thank you," and lie to them about Lok-Yeay making some Khmer beef stew at home. As I thought about Pu Ly hitting Ming Narin, rage engulfed me. I imagined walking back home, running up the steps, and taking my aunt out of the house. If Pu Ly said anything, I would swing around and sock him in his face. Of course, I weighed about one hundred pounds and was skinny as a tree branch. I began hatching up different plans, fantasizing crazy scenes in my head. In one, I went back home, told Lok-Yeay, Ming Narin, Raksmei and anybody else who would be interested to pack up their belongings and run away with me. There was a field a few blocks from where we lived called the "Rat Trail," and we could put up a tent and live there. I could get a job at the local grocery store and we could use money from that job for food and clothes. We would stay there until the rest of the family missed us, until Pu Ly felt lonely and sad and, realizing how important we were in his life, came to us, got down on his knees and begged us to come back home, apologizing for the way he had acted and treated us. In another fantasy, I bought a gun from B.K. (whom I had never met in real life), shot Pu Ly when he hit Ming Narin—not to kill him, but to wound him, maybe in the leg, to teach him a lesson. When I got out of juvie, Pu Ly would change, become nicer to Ming Narin and his children, smile and show us kindness and understanding. I walked and walked with these ridiculous, wild dreams tossing about in my teenage head as snow began to fall, swirling around me, until it got so cold that I had to walk back home.

The Keys

I had very few friends at Browne Junior High School. And since Jeff was in the eighth grade and I was in the seventh, we had separate lunches. I hung out with Jeff after school, when I dropped by the Doyles' on my way home. Mrs. Doyle always had snacks and drinks for us. She made the best brownies and banana bread in the world. Even now, when I think of the Doyles' home, I think of the rich, sweet, and nutty smell of warm banana bread coming out of that hot oven. But at school, I was often alone.

To keep myself occupied, I doodled. Creating art gave me the kind of control I didn't have in the real world. I was creating worlds that were different from the world of junior high, which was cruel, absurd, seemingly without much sense. The world I created was mine, with events and circumstances dictated by my desires and sense of justice. The geeks, nerds, and outsiders became heroes, battling fire-breathing dragons, wild beasts, and bloodthirsty monsters, rescuing beautiful maidens and winning respect from peers. The drawings were childish, looking back at it now, but I was in the seventh grade then. Like the times in church when I sang out Cambodian curse words, I felt when I was drawing the exhilaration of being free to imagine and invent other worlds that were different from my own. When I looked up from my desk, I saw my homeroom teacher, Mr. O'Brien, reading the *Malden Observer* behind his desk, saw the other kids passing notes, smiling and talking to each other—and finding nothing of interest, I returned to my drawing.

One morning, while sitting in homeroom, a pink slip arrived for me. I had to report to the principal's office. Mr. LoPresti, a bald and burly man in his fifties, introduced me to a young woman in her twenties. She worked for the Commonwealth of Massachusetts and, upon the recommendation of Mr. Galanti, she was there to administer a placement test. I was taken to a small room, where I had to answer questions as best as I could on several Scantron sheets. There were multiple questions on math, English, history, and science. I knew the answers to the math and English questions, but after a while, I got bored and started to randomly fill in the ovals on the exam sheets. I didn't understand why I was taking the test, so I didn't care how well I did. When the woman returned to check on me, I told her I was done, handed her my exam, and went back to class.

The following week, while waiting outside for the school to open, a couple of kids came up to me.

"What's up, Samnang?"

"Hi."

"So, how come you don't ever change at the gym? Are you a homo or something? Maybe you don't have hair on your little balls." They laughed.

I was embarrassed. There were girls standing in line in front of us. But for some stupid reason, I played along and asked, "Do girls have hair down there?"

"Yeah, they call it a bush. You know, they also bleed down there every month."

"That's gross." Then we noticed Wanda farther up in line. Wanda was one of the more popular girls at Browne. She was tall, taller than most of the boys, with long dark hair and large brown eyes. Of course, what made Wanda Watson intriguing for us teenage boys was her rapidly maturing body. She was also dating someone in high school. Her unreachability made us teenage boys dream about her before falling asleep each night, waking up spent the next morning.

"Samnang, why don't you ask Wanda if she has hair down there?"

Still playing along, I walked up to Wanda and asked if she had hair "down there." Wanda stood stunned. I repeated, "You know, do you have a bush, like a beard, except that it's down there?" Then I felt it: her slap left a burning sensation on my left cheek. The boys in the back of the line laughed and clapped each other on the back. One fell and rolled on the cold wet grass, hollering, his legs jutting and kicking in the air.

In English class that day, I received another note from the principal's office. As I packed up my things, I felt the eyes of my fellow students and the teacher following me. I've always hated the feeling of being watched, of being made visible; it reinforced the fact that I was an outsider, different from everyone around me.

In the principal's office, Mr. LoPresti explained the results of the test I took a few weeks ago. He told me that I had excelled in mathematics, surpassing other children in the school. Upon Mr. Galanti's recommendation and based on the test scores, I was to skip the eighth grade and go straight to high school. He said he hated to see me leave Browne, but that I was better off being challenged. He handed me some papers and asked me to return them to the school's main office with my legal guardians' signatures. He rose from his desk and shook my hand firmly.

At home, Lok-Yeay was ecstatic after Oum Seyha explained the good news. She said that she wished Lok-Ta was with us. "He was always proud of you, Samnang. You were his first grandchild. He believed you will become someone important someday, and this is the first step on that path." She went to the kitchen and started to prepare one of my favorite Khmer dishes, somlor curry with plenty of potatoes and beef. My uncles and aunts were also pleased. But to me, the whole thing seemed off somehow. I took note of my family's jubilation, and slowly but surely I became suspicious of their affections. Questions began swirling in my head: *If my success has inspired this love and affection, what will happen if I don't succeed? If*

I fail, will they still care about me with the same enthusiasm? Is their love conditioned upon my success?

No one asked me how I felt about skipping the eighth grade and jumping straight into high school. I was tiny, still appearing malnourished after years of living in refugee camps and starving under the Khmer Rouge rule. To make matters worse, I hadn't reached puberty yet. I was frightened at the thought of going to high school and, more than that, confused and angry at the situation in which I found myself. In my young mind, I was someone worth showering affections upon only when I did well in school. If I didn't, I was a nobody. I wished to be loved unconditionally, wanted my family to love me for who I was and not for what I had done. But no one took notice of how I felt. No one had bothered to ask, *Do you want to go to high school, Samnang? Are you happy about skipping the eighth grade?* My uncles and aunts had their own children to worry about. Here I was, doing well at school, and they were proud of me and wanted to be encouraging. Instead of being excited, I felt like I was a secondary citizen in that family of uncles, aunts, and cousins. I was resentful of them. I couldn't help it; I was the lonely orphan.

But they couldn't help it either. No one was really at fault. Pol Pot took over Cambodia and the country fell into chaos. People were killed, starved, overworked; families separated; children turned on parents; many disappeared. Then Việt Nam invaded Cambodia and we made our escape. We lived in limbo in the refugee camps in Thailand until we were sponsored by Richard Langer and then found ourselves on the East Coast. My uncles and aunts were in their twenties and thirties when we arrived in America; I was nine years old, at least according to my green card. My uncles and aunts were learning the language, the culture, the customs, about the way things were done in the States, just as I was learning about what kids my age were doing. I had no right to expect them to be like the Doyles—to celebrate Christmas, Thanksgiving, and birthdays, to take me out to restaurants and ball games at Fenway Park. I had no right to my resentment. They were just happy that I did well at school. I could have looked at it that way, but I didn't. I was a kid stuck in his own mind.

That early spring evening, I walked out of the house and wandered the streets under the lamplight. I stood listening to the warm domestic sounds coming from a neighbor's house. I looked at the bright living room and kitchen. I imagined what it would be like to live under that roof, live that life. I wiped away tears and mumbled to myself, "Damn it, it's freezing cold tonight. I hate New England weather."

Walking alone in the quiet streets of Malden that night, I was reminded of a time before we moved to Malden, when I did something utterly stupid to test the nature and limit of my family's love.

The incident with the keys took place outside a healthcare clinic. It was done innocently, with no malicious intent. I was ten years old and I'd simply wanted to know what love was. I'd wanted to know if my uncles and aunts would love me no matter what I did—if their love for me was unconditional, like a mother loves her own child.

We were at a clinic in Revere. I was there for a regular checkup, and Ming Narin was pregnant with Chanda. As we were getting ready to leave, Pu Ly told me to warm up the car he had borrowed from a neighbor. My uncle and aunt were inside the clinic reminiscing with the Cambodian interpreter about life in a refugee camp in Thailand. Pu Ly trusted me with the keys for some reason. Maybe he was too focused on the little baby girl growing in his wife's belly.

Then it happened. I found myself standing in the parking lot between the used Oldsmobile and the storm drain, my eyes moving between the car and the drain, my heart pounding. If I opened the car door, I told myself, I would never find out. I wanted to test the love my uncle and aunt had for me.

I also wanted to know if my mother would come to rescue me. Ever since I'd seen the mermaid in the waves, I felt she or some benevolent spirit had been looking out for me. I wanted to know that other world was still there, accessible when I needed it.

So much was at stake in that moment. Everything began to spin, and I felt dizzy. "It's now or never," I muttered to myself. I would find out once and for all if I was truly loved.

I looked at the clinic. My uncle and aunt were still inside. Elsewhere, the world went on. My heart banged against my chest, and my hands shook. I dropped to my knees and suspended the keys over the storm drain. As Pu Ly and Ming Narin slowly emerged from the clinic, I loosened my grip on the key chain and, in a moment which seemed to stretch into eternity, I heard the keys clink against the drain and then rattle into the sewer. I closed my eyes and clouds parted. The sky became unbearably bright. The keys did their magic. My mother was smiling from above, her arms reached out to me. I then found myself back in Cambodia, where my father was waiting for me. He showed me his ice cream parlor, which he was able to buy after selling so much ice cream to the half-naked children running after him as he pedaled his bicycle across the village honking his horn. I sat on a stool and tasted the rainbow-flavored ice cream. It was delicious—exactly what heaven tastes like.

But that was not reality. The keys disappeared into the dark water of the sewer. Nothing spectacular happened. Seconds later, seeing my uncle and aunt walk toward the car and realizing what had happened, I clutched and shook the drain storm bars. But it was too late. The keys, obeying Newton's law of universal gravitation, fell, without remorse, without regret, without care. Nothing was going to stop the keys from falling: no flashes of lightning, no benevolent spirit, no second chance, no mermaid, no mother, no father, no Buddha, nothing. Such was reality. It was impersonal. It was indifferent to the panicked beating of my heart.

Of course, Pu Ly and Ming Narin were fuming. They called me stupid, said that they shouldn't have trusted me with anything. Pu Ly screamed, "You're in the fifth grade now but you act like you're in kindergarten! I've always known you were stupid!"

Ming Narin seemed confused, "You shouldn't have done that, Samnang. What's gotten into you?"

Pu Ly explained, "He has a big head but there's nothing inside it. His head is just an empty coconut shell. His head is hard but there's no brain in there!" He pointed at his own big head as he scowled at me. "I always knew that about him; this is not a surprise, no, not at all." Pu Ly, Ming Narin, and I waited in the clinic's waiting room for a couple of hours for Oum Seyha to leave work and bring the neighbor's extra car key. When he arrived, I asked if I could ride with him. He nodded with a quiet sadness and pity. We drove home without a single word exchanged between us.

The night my family knew I was to skip a grade, I walked around the neighborhood looking for answers. I couldn't believe it: I was going to skip the eighth grade and go right into high school. Me, the kid who'd dropped the car keys down the drain. The kid who was always scared and alone. The kid who lived in his own head most of the time. The kid who still believed in fairy tales and mermaids.

Where Is Samnang?

When I began my freshman year at Malden High School, Bopha was already a senior. During lunch, she came over to my table and asked how I was doing. I hated it when the guys looked at her. With long, shiny black hair down to her waist, large brown eyes and olive skin, she looked like a woman from one of those Polynesian islands that you see dancing in old World War II movies. I knew what those high school guys were thinking and, to my surprise, I felt an urge to protect her. Although we usually fought at home, Bopha was more than a cousin. She was the closest thing I had to an older sister.

I told Bopha in Khmer, "I'm fine. Go back to your table and be with your friends. I don't need your protection." Then I said, "I don't like it when those dudes are staring at you."

Bopha glanced around, saw the guys looking at her, and frowned. "I don't care if they're looking. I just want to make sure you're OK. How are you?"

"I said I'm fine," I replied, annoyed. She looked dismayed, so I reassured her, "Really, I'm good." Bopha gave up and returned to her table. I saw how the guys watched her walk away, and anger rose in me once again.

During homeroom, I sat at my desk, feet barely touching the ground. A few girls took notice, looked at each other, and giggled.

I kept my eyes glued to the book in front of me, turning the pages and trying to read, afraid to look up and catch the girls staring at me and whispering. I moved to the edge of my seat and placed my feet squarely on the floor.

There wasn't much difference between Browne Junior High School and Malden High School. But, as a basic rule, it seemed that everyone in high school was required to be miserable and unsure of themselves. The social divide between the "popular" and "unpopular" that had existed in middle school persisted. The so-called cool kids stuck to their kind: the jocks, cheerleaders, and party people were the center of high school life. Like everyone else, they had their misery: the pressures of being popular, maintaining good grades, and getting into college. Then you had kids who lived in the projects, whose parents were from different racial and economic backgrounds; they too stuck together. They collected comics, read graphic novels and science fiction, and listened to Metallica and Iron Maiden. Their jean jackets had Guns N' Roses, Megadeth, and Led Zeppelin insignias stitched onto them. They smelled of cigarettes and dope. They wore their hair long and greasy; the mullet was in full force then. They didn't care about homework, or grades, or college. After school, they hung out in the cemetery, smoked pot, and listened to heavy metal.

Where did I belong in this trite, class-based, and oversimplified representation of high school culture in the mid-1980s? I found myself in the second group—the kids were seemingly less petty, somewhat less territorial than the cool kids. They were sure of their lot, accepted it, and even found pride in it. They were outsiders who felt they'd never amount to anything, and they were fine with that. They took in loners like me easily. But, in all honesty, I didn't belong to any group.

I didn't have close friends in high school. I had people I hung out with during lunch or walked home with when we didn't feel like taking the bus, which was always crowded with kids from other schools in the area. There was James Mertz, who had dark greasy hair that hung over his shoulders, with glasses and pimples decorating his face. Standing about five-eight, Jimmy had all the DC and

Marvel comics neatly piled in his room. He was a fan of Axel Rose and was always telling us about the latest Guns N' Roses concerts that he'd read about in *Rolling Stone* and *Circus* magazines. Then there was Thomas Norr. He was over six feet, big and flabby, and he slurred his words when he talked. He wasn't bright, more of a follower than a thinker, and he ate with his mouth open. I was about five feet and one hundred and ten pounds. I saw Jimmy and Tom sitting together one day in the cafeteria, walked up to them, and sat down. I smiled. Jimmy looked at me and didn't say anything. Tom turned and smiled. Then Jimmy returned to his tale of going to a nightclub to check out some local metal band. And that was how I started hanging out with Jimmy and Tom. They did most of the talking. I listened, asked a question or two, then listened to them talk some more.

There weren't many Asians in Malden then. There were a handful of Vietnamese and Chinese kids in the high school, a few Filipinos, and one Thai kid whose uncle and aunt owned a restaurant somewhere in New Hampshire. Bopha and I were just about the only Cambodians at the high school. By this time, Vutha was already working as a receptionist at a hotel in Boston. When my younger cousins started school seven or eight years later, they had each other; there was a group of them going to the local elementary school together, seeing each other in the hallway, during recess and lunch, and walking home together. By the time they started third and fourth grades, more Cambodian families began trickling into Malden from Revere, Chelsea, and Lynn. More Cambodians filled the classrooms and hallways, saw each other at lunch and recess, at the playground. As a result, there was a self-assuredness in the way my younger cousins held themselves, a confidence in the way they talked and asked questions, a centeredness in the way they interacted with non-Asian kids.

As for Vutha, Bopha, and me, we were anxious, nervous, and quiet; we kept to ourselves, afraid to speak up and have others notice us. We felt the sharp edge of visibility in classrooms and hallways, every time a teacher asked us a question, every time we caught someone looking at us. Such visibility came from an

awareness that we were a blemish in the sea of whiteness. Ultimately, we were a minority. We didn't have the numbers. And like
other minorities, we were absent in the books, stories, and lessons
our teachers taught in our classrooms. When others looked at us,
what they saw was something superficial, a generalization. We were
Asians. We were *refugees.* Our home country was *ravaged by war.*
We were to be pitied, of course, but there was no initiative to make
sure we were doing all right. No system in place where someone
reached out and asked, "Hey, how are you feeling today? What's on
your mind? Do you want to talk about it?"

Some teachers tried to reach out to me, but I pushed them
away like I did the Doyles. There was Mr. Stephenson, my English
teacher. He was in his late twenties, a recent graduate from Suffolk
University, married to his college sweetheart, with a child on the
way. He asked about our summer on the first day of English class.
Allison Thompson, with long curly brown hair, raised her hand
and said she visited her mother's family in Portland, Oregon. Then
they flew to California, where they went to Disneyland and Hollywood. Mike Warren, who was in my homeroom, said he went up
to Maine to spend time with his mother's family. Even Jimmy and
Tom had something to share. They said they saw Guns N' Roses in
Worcester. When it was my turn, I didn't know what to say because
I hadn't done anything that summer that was worth sharing. I rode
BMX with Anthony Doyle, Jeff's little brother, and some kids in
the neighborhood, while my uncles and aunts slaved at factories
and lumber mills. When Mr. Stephenson asked, "What did you do
this summer, Samnang?" I told the truth: "I rode my bike around
the neighborhood while my uncles and aunts worked."

A couple of kids in the back of the classroom laughed. Allison
looked down at her desk. Jimmy and Tom pretended they didn't
hear what I'd said. Mr. Stephenson had the best of intentions; he
wanted to let me know that my voice and stories were important,
that I was a part of the community of mainly white students and
teachers at the high school. But my circumstances were different
from my peers'. My history, culture, and people were different
from Mike Warren's, Allison Thompson's, even Jimmy's and Tom's.

I knew it; they knew it too. Maybe I should have lied and pretended I'd done something exciting and worthy of sharing with the rest of the class. But I didn't. I didn't learn how to lie until I was a junior in high school and my grades were dropping away like they too were embarrassed of me.

During gym, I sat on the bleachers because I didn't bring gym clothes. I was the smallest kid at the school and, whatever sport we were tasked with playing, I was the weakest link. I couldn't follow the rules of the game. I was always picked last or second to last, which was worse because I hated to be pitied. I was the handicap to whatever team that chose me. It was best for me to be on the bleachers, watching the others play. I watched other kids play basketball and volleyball. I watched the bigger kids go with Mr. Robinson to the weight room down the hall. I watched some boys flirt with some girls. I watched Rachael Stein talk to Mike Warren and my heart sank a little because Rachel sat in front of me in algebra class and I liked the perfumed smell of her and the warmth of her dimpled smile.

But I liked sitting on the bleachers. I felt safe at the top of those steps, watching high school dramas unfold before my eyes. A quiet observer, I wasn't a threat to anyone, and no one was a threat to me from such a distance. It was a good gig while it lasted, before Mr. Robinson began threatening me with detention if I didn't bring in gym clothes.

I felt a similar comfort and safety in art class. When I drew the Cambodian countryside with lush green rice paddies under a blue sky, I felt its serene beauty calming my body and mind. The world of my immediate surroundings slowly disappeared: the students, the teachers, the principal, the cafeteria. A new world was being built from the scratching of my No. 2 pencil and in this world, there wouldn't be any name-callings.

China boy, Gook boy, Chink boy.
Why-don't-you-go-back-to-where-you-come-from boy!
Don't-they-eat-dogs-where-you-come-from boy!
What-are-you-looking-at boy!
You-remind-me-of-those-African-pygmies boy!

You-are-so-skinny-you-must-always-be-hungry boy!
If-you-know-kung-fu-why-don't-you-beat-us-up boy!
If-you-know-kung-fu-why-don't-you-beat-your-parents-up boy!
Where-you-come-from-they-use-sticks-as-toilet-paper boy!
Where-you-come-from-they-must-not-have-soap boy!
Hey everybody, it's the Prince of Siam!

On the white space of the drawing paper, I created my own world where things turned out right for me. I made up my own laws of physics, logic, and time. We didn't actually leave Cambodia. My mother didn't die. My parents were still together. I even had a brother and sister; their names were Akara and Rithy. "If you don't believe me, look at the drawings." The evidence was in the art!

During those lonely years, I spent a lot of time people-watching, staying in my own head, and solving the problems of my world with my drawing and daydreaming. Art and the imagination became powerful forces in my life then, where the unreal world took precedence over the real world, where imagination, desire, and creativity had more sway over the real world, where art provided solace, protection, and comfort.

Academically speaking, I didn't perform poorly that first year of high school. I pulled a couple of As in algebra and art, Bs in English and history, and some Cs in biology and computer science. I didn't have any real friends, so I had all the time in the world to open up my textbooks, look up answers, and memorize vocabulary and formulas for algebra.

Near the end of the year, Bopha brought home her senior yearbook and showed it to the family. Lok-Yeay, Oum Seyha, Ming Narin, and Ming Bonavy sat around our small dining table and looked at the pages of the blue and gold yearbook.

Ming Bonavy asked, "Where's Samnang?"

"He's right there. Look at how small he is in comparison to the other students!" Oum Seyha answered.

"Where? I don't see him. Where is my grandson?" Lok-Yeay asked.

"There! He's getting off the bus. That's him. That's his head! That's Samnang!" It was a black-and-white picture of kids getting off the school bus on the first day of classes. I was still sitting in my seat while others were getting off the bus.

My aunts, uncle, and grandmother laughed. They started counting pictures with me in the background. "Two, three . . . seven, eight, nine pictures. They have nine pictures of Samnang in this book!" They couldn't help it; they were happy and proud of me.

Exposed

At the beginning of my second year in high school our gym teacher, Mr. Robinson, was nervous, unusually fidgety. He had little patience for us stragglers sitting on the bleachers, so he ordered us to walk around the basketball court even with our school clothes on. After a visit from our high school principal, Mr. Robinson started giving detentions to those of us who didn't bring gym clothes to class. My days of sitting on the bleachers and people-watching were over.

That first September weekend, I went to the Doyles to ride BMX with Anthony and Kai, a Chinese kid from the neighborhood. Kai's parents owned a restaurant around the corner on Beach Street. Every time we saw him after his shift at the restaurant, he told us how much he hated the smell of American Chinese food, the sweet and sour taste of breaded chicken and pork. But Kai had money, so it didn't surprise us when Kai showed up with a new skateboard instead of the GT Pro that he had been riding that summer. The bottom deck of Kai's board had a picture of a skull with red glowing eyes and white teeth biting a snake that wrapped its serpentine body around the head. Kai was learning to power-slide and carve the curb with it. Anthony and I thought it was the coolest thing we had ever seen. Anthony told his parents he wanted one for his birthday. Mr. Doyle drove him to a skate shop in Melrose, a city on the other side of Malden, where Anthony bought a Steve Caballero board, the one with the ancient Chinese dragon on it. At the time, I was working as a paperboy delivering newspapers in our neighborhood. Most people turned off their porch lights and hid behind curtains when I came by to collect money. With my paperboy money, I bought a used Tony Hawk board for thirty dollars from another kid in the neighborhood and learned to skate.

Skateboarding became therapy for me. I transferred all my energy from drawing to skateboarding. Unlike the high school world that I'd been thrown into, this seven-layered plywood didn't discriminate. It didn't have preconceived notions about me. Its movement was a true reflection of who I was—if I was calm and collected, you could see that tranquility in the way the board moved, the way it slid, ollied, and flipped. If I was angry or upset, the board grinded and slashed the curb, destroying the man-made world. During those skateboarding years, I was able to express joy and sorrow and release my anger, hurt, and confusion on the ten-by-thirty-one-inch board. Skateboarding became my way of engaging with the world: the streets, curbs, and walls were my canvas, and the board was my brush. It sustained me.

After a long day of street skating, Anthony and I went back to his house. My friend got a can of Coke from the fridge. His mother came over and asked, "Anthony Michael Doyle, aren't you going to offer Samnang and Kai drinks?"

Annoyed, Anthony returned to the fridge and asked, "Samnang, Kai, what do you guys want?"

"Coke, please." I answered.

"Same thing, dude," was Kai's answer. We stood in the kitchen and gulped down our cola. Mrs. Doyle came up, "Don't you boys have manners? Sit down at the table."

"Mom, what do you want?" Anthony asked.

"Nothing." Then she looked over to me, "Samnang, how's high school this year? Any girlfriend?"

"Things are fine. I don't really like anyone at the school."

"No Cambodian girl? No Asian girl?"

"No." I looked down at my half-empty cola can and mumbled, "There's this thing. Mr. Robinson wants us to buy clothes for gym. If I don't have them by Monday, I will get detention."

"Well, I can take you to Target this afternoon. I need to drop off Father Augustino at St. Anthony before four, then we'll go, OK?"

"I didn't bring enough money with me. Just a couple of dollars for soda and beef jerky."

"Forget about it," she said in her Bostonian accent.

I looked at Anthony, who shrugged his shoulders, and said, "Whatever! Let's get out of here, man."

Later that day, I skated with Anthony back to his house. Mrs. Doyle was waiting for me. I got in her station wagon and she drove me to Target on Route 1. We went to the men's section, but most of the clothes were too big for me. I found Adidas sweatpants and some blue T-shirts in the kids' section. "Got it, Mrs. Doyle. All set. Let's get out of here."

Mrs. Doyle asked, "Aren't you going to try them on first?"

The thought of taking off my clothes in the changing room of a public store terrified me. I had this fear of somebody getting down on the floor, sticking his head under the door, and peering at my nakedness. I remembered taking off my clothes at a changing room in K-Mart once and hearing people walking by and talking loudly. They were only a foot away from me as I stood half-naked in the changing room. I said, "No, I'm good. This is the same size as the jeans I have at home."

Mrs. Doyle shook her head. "OK, Samnang. They're your clothes. But let me keep the receipt just in case we need to return them."

In gym class that Monday, I went through the doors to the boys' locker room, passing the bathroom stalls and showers, keeping my eyes straight ahead. I've never understood America's lack of modesty. My peers were standing under showerheads that stuck out of one main wall. There were no doors or curtains to protect one's privacy. Some of the guys were washing their arms and chests, telling stories and laughing, and they were completely naked. Avoiding making eye contact with anyone, I walked as fast as I could to the lockers. I looked at the locker numbers, found mine, and opened it. I took out my towel, wrapped it around my waist, and began changing. I'd started putting my school clothes away in the locker when this big football jock named Jerry Coleman walked over and stood completely naked in front of me. I turned and saw his penis, exposed, staring angrily at me. I looked up and maintained eye contact with Jerry. "Aren't you the kid who did well in Mr. Roth's algebra class? You Asian guys are always good in math. What's your secret?"

Without missing a beat I said, "I just study. That's all. Sorry, no ancient Asian secret." I closed my locker, got up, and walked out of the boys' locker room as fast as my legs could carry me.

The Letter

I don't know when the letter arrived. I only know that Lok-Yeay decided to let me know about the letter during winter break of my sophomore year. I knew that something was up because Pu Ly didn't say anything disparaging to me at dinner and Lok-Yeay had made my favorite dish, somlor curry with beef and peanuts.

While I was eating, Lok-Yeay sat down at the kitchen table and said, "Samnang, your father is gone." She then took out a tattered envelope with numerous stamps on it from her heavy black purse. "This is a letter from your stepmother."

I pushed a spoonful of rice into my mouth and followed it with a spoonful of beef curry. Putting the letter on the kitchen table, Lok-Yeay kept her eyes steady on me. Between spoonfuls I said, "This somlor curry is delicious, Lok-Yeay. Thank you. What did you put in it to make it so good?"

She wiped her eyes and tried to smile.

"I'm not joking. It's truly delicious. And don't worry, I'm fine."

I got up from the table and went to the sink to wash my dish. Afterward, I went to the living room, flopped myself on the sofa, and turned on the television. It was late. My cousins and their parents were in their bedrooms. I finally had the TV to myself.

On the sofa, I watched the Christmas tree blinking next to the television. My cousins begged their parents about getting one for months, and so we finally had a heavily decorated plastic Christmas tree that they'd bought from K-Mart in early December. Wrapped presents sat underneath the tree.

It was late, and I was exhausted. I had spent the whole day snowboarding with Anthony and Kai; I was surprised that no one had yelled at me for being out all day. There was nothing good on television, and the lights from the tree kept blinking loudly.

I hadn't really known my father. I was surprised and ashamed that I didn't know how to feel about the news of his death. Lying on the living room sofa, I tried to evoke the feelings of loss and sadness that one was supposed to feel when someone had died, especially when that someone was one's father. Remembering a story Oum Seyha told about my father riding a bicycle into the city to sell ice cream, I closed my eyes and imagined my father on his bike. I didn't know what kind of bike it was; I just knew it wasn't a Mongoose or GT racing bike. It was probably one of those old twenty-six-inch bicycles with a mudguard, horn, and kickstand. I imagined him pedaling this bicycle, honking its horn and calling out to city folks and tourists alike about his ice cream and soda. I started creating memories, spinning stories about my father from my imagination—how his competition was a young gentleman from another village, how they had honked and shouted, each proclaiming that their ice cream and soda were the better ones. In the end, my father and his competitor became friends, recognizing their shared love for family in each other's hard work.

That night, I lay awake, tossing and turning in bed. My blanket irritated me, felt heavy on top of my thin body. I listened to my grandmother's breathing on the other side of the room. Outside, the snow fell silently against the window. I felt both loss and nothingness then. My father had never been a big part of my life. How could I lose a father that I'd never really had? All that I remembered of my father was that day he'd taken me for ice cream, and the memory had been slowly fading, eroding through the passage of time and the treacheries of migration. Truth be told, both of my parents had been figments of my imagination for most of my life, spurred on by the stories my uncles, aunts, and grandmother told me. But that night, with my father now gone, I felt more alone. I felt that my dream of becoming normal had gone up in smoke.

I got up to use the bathroom and I caught a young face staring at me in the mirror. I reached out and touched the glass, my fingers tracing the face in the glass mirror. *Do I look like either of my parents? Whom do I resemble more, my mother or my father? Which aspects of my personality did I inherit from them? Am I as gentle as my mother and as extroverted as my father? I'm definitely not a social person. What aspects of my father live in me? Is it better this way—that is, to know the truth? I don't have to hope anymore; I am free from my dreaming. Unlike my cousins, I don't have anyone looking over my shoulder, telling me what to do. I'm free!*

I turned off the faucet and left the bathroom feeling sadly triumphant. I returned to the bedroom I shared with Lok-Yeay.

"Come and sleep with me, dear," Lok-Yeay said.

"It's OK." I said, "I'm OK. I really am."

The Letter, No. 2

It was simple. All I had to do was follow the basic format of letter-writing, making sure to include the return date, the salutation, the complimentary closing, and the signature. The toughest part was forging Lok-Yeay's signature. I felt like I had committed blasphemy. All that she had done for me—how she'd carried me on her back as we trekked across jungles, had fed and clothed me, had provided a constant and warm presence in my life—and this was how I repaid her. I didn't believe in heaven and hell, but if there were a hell, I had now reserved myself a special place there.

I handwrote the letter, folded it in half, and put it inside one of the textbooks in my backpack. I had done it many times before and hadn't yet gotten caught. No one called our home, and if they did, they would speak to a Cambodian grandmother who couldn't speak much English beyond "Thank you" and "I no talk English." I took out my letter and read it one more time:

Nov. 9, 1988

To whom it may concern

Please excuse my grandson Sok Samnang for his absences on Nov. 5 and Nov. 6. He was terribly sick and was unable to attend school last Thursday and Friday.

Thank you for understanding,

Sok Sakana

P.S. If you have any questions, please contact me at this number: 377-2992.

I wrote our last name first because that was how Lok-Yeay signed her name in the old country. Looking at the postscript, I closed my eyes and hoped the school wouldn't call. If they did call, I hoped that Pu Ly, who mostly stayed in the house watching television all day, would be out drinking with his buddies in Lowell, leaving Lok-Yeay and my cousins home alone.

The next morning, I handed the letter to Mr. O'Brien, my homeroom teacher, who placed it in a tray for the main office. I went to geometry class after homeroom and tried to concentrate on the mathematical symbols and equations written on the blackboard for us to memorize that morning. By the time I got to biology, our seventh and last class of the day, I'd relaxed a bit. I watched my lab partner dissect a sour-smelling worm on a glass plate. And when the final bell rang, I walked out of the hallway, threw my books in my locker, got my jacket and skateboard, and skated to the arcade.

Mrs. Doyle called that evening and spoke with Oum Seyha, who then talked to Lok-Yeay. Lok-Yeay approached me while I was eating supper in the living room, watching a rerun of *Three's Company* with Pu Vaesnar.

"Jeff's mother called. She said the principal called and told her you haven't been going to classes. I'm so embarrassed, Samnang. What's going on with you?" She looked more hurt than embarrassed. "Why are you doing this? I don't understand. Please let me know what's going on with you."

I set my bowl of rice on the glass coffee table. "I don't know why I do what I do, Lok-Yeay. I just don't know," I said. And it was the truth—I'd begun skipping classes, not doing homework, not studying, not caring about anything. I just didn't have any motivation, any desire to engage with the world, and I didn't know why.

Everything seemed pointless. We were all going to die eventually. Why bother trying? Like Lok-Yeay, I wanted to understand what was going on with me. But seeing Lok-Yeay's sad face, I made a promise that I couldn't keep: "I'll go to school from now on. I'll get the As that you want for me, just like before. Everything will be fine."

Pu Vaesnar sat quietly, looking disappointed. Anger boiled inside me. I wished I could tell them both that I hated being here, that this place was never and would never be ours: *The school was never mine. I can't connect with the teachers. I can't relate to my fellow classmates. I'm all alone, Lok-Yeay. I don't belong here. I'm a true alien.*

Unsatisfied with my promise, Lok-Yeay continued with her questions. "Why do you keep doing this to me? Why are you pushing me away? Don't you know how lucky we are to be here?" she begged.

"You're not listening to me. It's nothing. There's nothing to talk about. Just forget it, OK? I said that I will go to class. Isn't that enough?" I barked at her.

I wished I could explain to her how I hated being who I was, how I hated the constant awareness of being different. How death was the only thing that seemed real now. *I wish I could leave this world*, I wanted to tell her. *Like my parents.*

But instead, I said, "Just leave me alone. You wouldn't understand. All of you, just leave me alone, please." I got up from the couch, dropped my dish in the sink, and walked out of the room.

The following morning, Mrs. Doyle came with her station wagon to pick me up for school. She asked, "What's the matter with you? Don't you know you're hurting your grandmother? All that she's done for you, you should be ashamed of yourself, Samnang."

"Sorry," I said.

"Don't you *sorry* me. Tell your grandmother you're sorry for what you did. It's her name you forged, not mine." We stopped at a traffic light. Mrs. Doyle turned to me, "What's gotten into you, Samnang? You were always such a good kid."

"I don't know," I answered.

"*I don't know, I don't know.* Lately, everything you say is *I don't know.*" She clutched the steering wheel, shaking her head in frustration.

I didn't say anything. She kept her eyes on the road, both hands on the wheel, and told me I had to shape up, had to begin thinking about college and making something of my life.

I sat in "the hot seat" directly across from Principal Willis, a bulky man in his early fifties. He was a former Marine who'd spent time in Việt Nam, a fact that struck fear in the hearts and minds of us students, even though he now sported a receding hairline and a growing beer gut. Sitting in front of him, I looked up and noticed some gray in his mustache. His teeth were yellowing. But his voice was deep and booming, the kind of voice that shook windows, that woke you up from daydreaming and made you listen. Although it was called "the hot seat," I felt cold and sleepy sitting there. I'd been out skateboarding past midnight the night before. It was 9 A.M. now, and the kids out in the hallway were heading to their second-period classes, but all I wanted to do was crawl into my bed and disappear into sleep forever.

Mr. Willis switched off his walkie-talkie. "If you skip school again, you will be given a two-day suspension. Do I make myself clear?" He glared at me.

I nodded my head.

Mrs. Doyle chimed in, "Go ahead, Samnang. Tell Principal Willis."

"Yes, Mr. Willis, sir. You've made yourself very clear. I will not skip school again, sir." I knew what they wanted to hear, and I spoke the words with conviction. They both seemed pleased. Mrs. Doyle told me to acknowledge my wrongdoings and promise Mr. Willis that I would never skip school or forge my grandmother's signature again. I did as I was told.

Satisfied, Mr. Willis changed the subject, "Are you planning to go to college, Samnang?"

I looked away. "I don't know."

"What do you mean you don't know?" Mr. Willis's nostrils flared up once again. "What are you going to do with your life if you don't go to college?"

I sat in silence. My hands on my lap and my head shaking, again I said, "I don't know."

Mrs. Doyle chimed in. "He's been Mr. Negative lately. Everything that comes out of his mouth is 'I don't know.' 'I don't know why I did this. I don't know why I did that. I don't know if I'm going to college!'"

"What are you going to be when you grow up, a monback?" Asked Mr. Willis.

I looked up at Mr. Willis. I had no idea what he was talking about.

"Do you know what a monback is?" Mr. Willis asked.

I played along. "What's a monback?"

"A monback is someone who picks up trash and when the truck misses some garbage, the monback hollers, 'C'mon back! C'mon back!'"

Mrs. Doyle and Mr. Willis laughed. It was obvious that the joke was funny—to them. I sat and watched them shake their heads with laughter.

I heard the Orange Line train rumbling toward Malden Station and resisted the urge to look out the window. In my head, I could see the main library across the street. Last week, skipping school, I rode the train back and forth between Oak Grove Station and Forest Hills Station. I didn't have enough money to hang out in Boston, so I just sat on the train for several hours until it was time to go back home. I watched people get off and on at each stop. Unlike me, these people were serious. They had convictions, guiding principles that kept their lives on the right side of the tracks. They knew where they were going, at which station they needed to board and at which station they needed to exit. Their lives meant something; their futures were hopeful and clear. I didn't have much hope for my future. The train was heading toward Forest Hills. I checked my wristwatch. It was one in the afternoon, and I should be in biology class. I had one more hour of riding until it was time to take the bus back home.

A young woman got on the train and took a seat across from me. Dressed in blue jeans, a crimson Harvard shirt peeking out underneath her gray jacket, she sat reading a romance novel. Her pink lips puckered as she read. I marveled at the contrast between her white creamy skin and dark wavy hair. My mind started to wonder. What would it be like to be with someone like her? To talk to her? To interact with her? But I knew better than to think about such things. We came from different worlds. We were of different species: she was a white American woman and I was this weird Asian kid. I was forever a foreigner, a refugee, the ultimate outsider.

Conscious that she was being watched, the woman looked up and smiled uncomfortably. I turned and looked out the window. When the train approached the State Street station, she put her book in her purse and stood up. I watched her walk off the train and climb the platform stairs.

"C'mon back! Samnang." Mr. Willis said. I was slumping in the hot seat in the principal's office. Mrs. Doyle, in a chair next to mine, rolled her eyes in disbelief. I was daydreaming again. I looked at the clock on Mr. Willis's wall. Only half an hour had passed.

I was tempted to say, "Time flies when you're having fun." Instead, I said, "I'm sorry," and looked down at the floor. Of course, I didn't mean it. I had always loved daydreaming. In that moment, dreaming myself away was what I needed. But I knew what they wanted to hear; it was the key to my freedom. I thus said I was sorry, but I didn't stop there. As if compelled by the force of my own fake apology, I went on and on about feeling alone and unhappy with my life. Somehow, in the act of lying, I circled back around to the truth.

But Mr. Willis said feeling sad was not an excuse. "You must know this about me, Samnang. I'm a no-nonsense kind of guy," he said. "Emotions don't hold water here in this office; it's your actions that matter." To prove his point, he concluded our meeting by giving me a two-day suspension. I guess he was angry that I had dozed off and daydreamed while he was trying to save me from becoming a monback. I spent those two fabulous days skating in Boston, ollieing down the steps at Government Center and cruising in Harvard Square looking for that attractive Harvard student. I never did find her.

Rage

Looking back, I remember my anger and, worse, my appetite for destruction during those painful years. I was hurt, and in retaliation I wanted to hurt someone or something back, just like Pu Ly did with his family. Luckily, I had my skateboard to take out those feelings on. I skated with aggression, jumping over stairs with reckless abandon. I remember being chased by a security guard for skating in the mall. As I sped away, I turned and gave him the finger. I laughed about it on the bus home with Anthony and Kai.

One afternoon I skated the parking lot of Pioneer Bank, which was next to the convenience store across the street from our house. I was with Anthony, Kai, and my young cousin Raksmei. I attacked the red brick wall that snaked around the bank's parking lot, ollieing up and kick-flipping off it, grinding along its rough edge. I skated faster and harder, striking the red lip of the brick wall with my board, taking more risks, hoping to hurt myself. Then I went over to the patch of flowers at the side of the building's entrance and tried to ollie over it. My back wheels hit the soil and I flew off my board, my body thrown against the cement walkway. My palms and knees torn and trickling blood, I picked up my skateboard, held it high over my head, and swung it wildly against the garden plot, destroying the yellow and red flowers. Anthony came over and said, "What the fuck is wrong with you?"

"What? You like flowers now? Are you a homo, Ant?" I went off on Anthony, whose life was so different from mine. He had siblings, two loving parents, a future that was clear and bright. He was a part of that world that I felt excluded from. "You know what, man? You're a part of this capitalist bureaucratic system! You're a goddamn poseur. Don't worry. It's Sunday, little poseur. No one's gonna see you skate here. Your bank job is safe."

"Fuck you, man. Fuck you!" Anthony skated away. Kai and my cousin watched us; knowing my temper, they didn't intervene. Soon they too left for home. I wanted to destroy the world, to wreak havoc and create anarchy. The board must destroy anything representing the world I couldn't be part of. I returned to the bank's wall with anger and frustration, sliding and grinding its perfect angles, chipping its expensive red paint.

Later that day, I skated home to get some money from the envelope of bills that I had saved up from working at the local movie theater. I went in through the kitchen and came back out the back door, which is when Lok-Yeay saw me from her garden. She started barking questions at me: "Why aren't you studying? Why do you skate all the time? What are you doing with your life? Why are you always so angry? Do you know how lucky we are to be here?"

I popped an ollie and purposely fell.

"Good trick. Why don't you do that again?"

Lok-Yeay's sarcasm didn't go unnoticed. "I will. This time I'm going to crack my head wide open on this driveway. You will love this new trick," I told her. I got up, ollied again, and rode away.

I went to the convenience store and got myself a slice of pepperoni pizza and a Coke. I sat on the curb shoveling the fat pizza slice into my mouth while strangers looked at me in disgust. I didn't care what they thought of me. After the pizza and Coke, I skated to Central Avenue, walked up the hill where rich people lived in Granada Highlands, and cruised around the apartment complex parking lot in an attempt to annoy its rich tenants. But even rich people were too busy with their lives to notice me. The kids were out in the street, riding their bikes and playing hopscotch together while their parents lounged around at the gated community pool.

The Eagles' "Hotel California" was playing on the radio. I hated the damned Eagles!

Annoyed, I pushed my board faster and harder, crouching low and staying on as I bombed Kennedy Drive, the road that snaked around the hill. My board shook from speed wobbles, but I stayed focused and held on to the board. At the end of the hill was a T-junction, and I saw a station wagon coming from the right and a delivery truck speeding from the left. I was going to be hit by the truck or the station wagon, or worse, get sandwiched by both. As I approached the end of Kennedy Drive, I closed my eyes and screamed. There was a flashing light and then silence. I felt the warmth of the sun and the cool of the wind. I felt myself floating away. And I heard my mother's soothing voice telling me that I was going to be OK. And I felt the warmth of the last day I spent with my father, recalled how tasty the ice cream and soda pop were and how joyful I'd felt that day, more than any day before or since. I was my father's special boy. I'd felt loved.

Suddenly, I heard honking and screeching. I opened my eyes. Somehow, I found myself already on the other side of the road that intersected Kennedy Drive. The suburban mom behind the wheel of the station wagon was honking at me. I'd somehow managed to pass in front of the truck without getting hit and, with the help of some mysterious force, had managed to turn left ahead of the station wagon. Terrified, I ollied over the curb and did a power slide to stop the board. Sweat dripping from my forehead, I caught my breath. Standing on the curb, trying to understand what happened, I felt the sun burning my scalp. As I pushed the board forward in search of some shade, I let go of the mysterious presence that had watched over me.

Later that afternoon, I rode to a local church overlooking Route 1. In the parking lot, I attempted a 360 shove-it and landed on my ass. I tried a kick-flip to a 50/50 grind on the curb and, again, fell on my ass. My body was hurting, bruised and bleeding, but I felt good.

That's how it was with skateboarding for me. It was a way for me to deal with my anger and take control over certain aspects of my life. The board listened to me, even if the world wouldn't. The world was one of cruelty and ignorance, full of go-back-to-your-country people. It was full of people who made fun of those who picked up trash. And it was full of children orphaned by the ravages of war and relocated to places where they felt different and inferior.

The board, on the other hand, was objective. It carried no prejudice for or against its rider. It had no agenda. In its very nature, the board was real and true. If you could master the board, then the board listened to you. It was as simple as that. Skateboarding became both art and therapy for me, and the board was the medium through which I expressed myself. On a good day, I skated smoothly, without aggression, without fear, without negativity. I was one with the concrete, sliding smoothly along the pavement like a surfer riding a wave. Gravity was my only true friend. When pissed off, like earlier that day, I skated with destruction in mind. I chipped paint off walls and destroyed beautiful flowers. I cursed at friends and family. Without a helmet and pads, I sped down a hill without care. Closing my eyes, I was ready to accept the consequences of my actions.

In the church's parking lot that afternoon, I skated like nothing mattered. Not my skin color, not my refugee status. Not Mrs. Doyle or Principal Willis. Not Alan Webb, the foul-mouthed red-headed kid. Not Jerry Coleman, the naked guy asking for my help with his math homework in the locker room. Not Pu Ly, my wife-beating uncle. Nothing mattered but the board. The setting sun was the only witness to my solitary art. Sweat oozed down my forehead, brow, the tip of my nose. Below was the world of Route 1, of traffic and accidents, of rush hour and the suburban curses of speeding tickets and traffic violations, of cutting lanes and road rage. I skated until that world disappeared. Nothing mattered but the skateboard's silver trucks grinding out sparks.

Rat Boy

In my senior year of high school, I had a crush on Allison Thompson. She was tall, with long brown hair and a natural smile that showed her perfect white teeth. She sat three rows to my right in Mr. Stephenson's class. She seemed to enjoy literature. She actually read the books we were assigned for class, books by Chaucer, Shakespeare, and Milton. She raised her hand and participated in discussions. She laughed comfortably and unselfconsciously, which I found fascinating. There was a natural fluidity and joyfulness to her very being, as if life had only ever been good to her. I wondered if Allison had ever known suffering, the kind of suffering that changed one's identity and outlook on life. Had she ever felt alone, alienated, and different? Had she ever been naked in the locker room, wishing she had a different body?

Allison frequently wore dresses to school: maxidresses and sundresses during the spring, and sweater dresses in the fall and winter. She seemed to me the epitome of culture and class, everything that I was not; it was probably why I was so attracted to her. I wore dirty jeans with holes around the knees and sneakers busted from skateboarding. My hair was unkempt. I didn't understand Chaucer, Shakespeare, and Milton and even if I did, I didn't have the confidence to raise my hand and share my thoughts aloud. But it was more than an issue of self-esteem, though that was very much a part of it; it was that the world of these poets and playwright was too different from mine. I couldn't understand why I had to read such rubbish. With a combination of pride and frustration, I refused them. After classes were over, I threw my books into my locker and took my board to go cruising at city hall.

The only book I finished in high school was *Ordinary People* by Judith Guest, a novel about a rich white kid who attempts suicide by slashing his wrists with a razor but survives. I related to the hopelessness that the novel's protagonist, Conrad Jarrett, felt. I wanted to reach out to Conrad, to hug him. I was looking for answers to my own life, why I was alive and my parents were not, what I was doing in Malden, the purpose and meaning of my existence. I wanted to have a trusted friend like Conrad had in Dr. Berger, someone to tell all about my fears and anxieties. But I had no one whom I could trust; I rejected everything, even the persistently kind Mrs. Doyle, and built a wall around me, a safe haven to protect myself from the world.

Fantasy was safe, and so I fantasized about Allison. Allison, the upper-middle-class girl from the other side of Malden, the girl who dug Shakespeare and Milton, the girl whom I never dared talk to—the girl of my dreams. Allison, the girl who smiled her healthy and happy smile, showing off her perfectly white teeth, her eyes squinting as she reads a sonnet in class, her American ears picking up on the musicality and rhythm of Shakespeare's poetry. It wasn't anything sexual that I wanted from Allison; it was entry into that other world, a world so foreign and fantastic that I had only seen glimpses of it in John Hughes movies. A world that had excluded me and that, deep down, I wanted so much to be a part of.

As I sat in the back of my senior English class, spaced out and thinking about Allison and where I would skate later that afternoon, I heard Mr. Stephenson's faint voice: "Samnang, can I speak with you after class?"

I came to and said, "Yeah, sure, Mr. Stephenson."

Soon as everyone left, Mr. Stephenson turned to me, "Why haven't you turned in your previous writing assignments?"

"I don't know."

He was quiet for a moment, trying to find the right thing to say that would get through to me. Finally, he asked, "What's wrong, Samnang?"

I said nothing.

As he stood behind his teacher's desk and I in front, there was Kafka's frozen sea between us. Students were walking into the classroom. He said he would give me another extension on those papers. But he knew as well as I did that offering me extensions wouldn't change anything. It didn't matter to me whether I submitted my English essays or not. Either way, it amounted to the same thing. Nothing.

By the end of senior year, everyone was excited for prom and graduation. Mr. Stephenson went around the class and asked about the prom and what our plans were after high school. The cool kids said they would go to the prom in style, since it was their last big social event in high school—limos, chauffeurs, as Mike Warren said, "the whole shabam!" My peers couldn't wait to graduate, it seemed. Some said they would be attending local colleges and universities like Boston College, Tufts University, Holy Cross College, and even Harvard. Some said they wanted to be away from their parents and planned to go as far as Amherst College, Smith College, and Williams College. Some planned to join the military—those who did were aiming for the Marines but were willing to settle for the army. When it was my turn, I didn't know what to say but the truth.

"You're not going to the prom?" Mr. Stephenson asked.

"No."

"You should go, Samnang. It's to celebrate the end of one stage in one's life and the beginning of a new one."

I couldn't imagine what this new stage of life would look like for me. I learned later that you were supposed to be thinking about college and taking your SAT in your junior year and starting the application process early in your senior year. Like most things, I was in the dark, with little direction. When I met with my guidance counselor, all we talked about was me passing my classes and graduating on time. That was his immediate concern. Once I graduated, I'd no longer be of concern to anyone at the school

"You're not going to college?" Mr. Stephenson asked.

"No."

Someone to my right whispered something and I thought I heard laughter. Rage consumed me and I wished them all hell, even Allison. She was no different. She was one of them—those who knew where they came from and where they would be going in life. Life, for Allison and her ilk, had a clear meaning and very defined purpose. There were real goals to accomplish and exciting life experiences to unlock. Everything was mapped out.

In response to their collective excitement about the future, I did what came naturally. I withdrew inward and fell into a dream.

I was living in a sewer, only crawling out at night, emerging from the darkness, from the stench that was my home, in search of food. Yes, I was Rat Boy! I laughed at the world above me. I ruled the subterranean; I was king of the underworld, ruler of rancidity and filth. From my throne of underground darkness, I was amused at the follies of the people above me, those who went to college and had nine-to-five jobs, who lived their lives in a vicious circle of hurt and loss, of desire and despair, of success and failure, of love and hate, of power, politics, and greed, of green lawns and white picket fences. Since the American dream didn't belong to me, I spat at it. I was free to wallow in my own filth.

"I hope you consider it." Mr. Stephenson said, bringing me back into the classroom. The year was 1990, and I was about to graduate from Malden High School. I was scared and angry at the world. I felt everyone had failed me.

"Consider what?"

"Consider going to college, Samnang, if the prom is too much to ask."

And then it was no longer my turn. Someone behind me said she got accepted to Amherst College and Smith College. She didn't know what to do. Amherst was ranked higher than Smith, but she liked the idea of being at a women's college. She wanted to know what the class thought about her dilemma. In my head, I snickered at the absurdity of this young girl, at her life where prom and college were the be-all and end-all after high school graduation. I tilted my head back and shrieked and shrieked and shrieked some more. I was, after all, Rat Boy.

Graduation

Suicide seemed like a logical conclusion. It was Mr. Stephenson who'd said graduation was the end of one life stage and the start of a new one. I took that to mean leaving this world and being born again in another world. A week before graduation, I skated to the local CVS and bought myself a bottle of aspirin. For a couple of years, I had been fantasizing about my own death: where my body would be discovered; how people would cry over me, wishing they'd been nicer to me; how Pu Ly might realize how awful he had been and change his ways for the better (even though it would be too late for me); Allison and Mr. Stephenson attending the funeral with Jimmy and Tom; Lok-Yeay making beef curry and bringing it to the temple on Pchum Ben, so that I could receive such an offering in the afterlife. It would be a wonderful death, one that would bring about change in the world. People would be nicer to the quiet kid, the child without parents, the one without friends. The loner, the weirdo, the outsider. Mine would be a good sacrifice.

I went down to one of the two bedrooms that Oum Seyha had built in our basement for friends who needed a place to crash. No one was staying there at the time. I plopped down on the mattress, lay there for some time, and listened to the footsteps above. My little cousins were running around. Lok-Yeay was making some dish for the entire family. I didn't want to hurt her. After my father died, she was all I had left. She had tried her best raising all of us. Every day, she took care of us grandchildren, made food for the family, and, with whatever time she had left, tended her garden. I couldn't remember a time she'd put herself first; every minute of her life was devoted to our family. Lok-Yeay did not fail me; she did the best she could under the circumstances. She was the hardest thing to leave behind.

Lying on the mattress, I realized my mistake. It was foolish of me to want my family to be like the Doyles. There were no birthday parties, no Thanksgivings, Christmases, or New Year's celebrations, no summer house in Cape Cod, no ski trips in New Hampshire, no Hulk Hogan and G.I. Joe toys, no PTA, no going out to restaurants, no money to buy clothes for the new school year. How could they provide all of this? They were busy working for their American bosses, learning the culture and customs of American life, raising children of their own in this place that had been just as unwelcoming, hostile, alienating to them as it had been to me. They'd known hunger and seen death in ways that I hadn't, because they'd saved me from it. They understood the necessity of being frugal, of sacrificing today's comfort for tomorrow's prosperity. *Why go to dinner at a restaurant when we can stay home and eat, Samnang? Lok-Yeay made better food than the chefs at any restaurants could! Why spend money on frivolous things? You have to take this wonderful opportunity of free education and make something of your life! Don't be lazy! Don't be foolish! And above all, don't skateboard!* They would tell me again and again, *Don't waste what America has given us. We must be thrifty! We must be smart! Don't be like those Americans, Samnang!* Even if we'd ever gone out to a restaurant, I wondered if they'd have known what to make of the food choices on the menu, what to say to the waiter taking our order, how much tip to give. They were farmers. They had never set foot in cities like Phnom Penh and Siem Reap. They needed more time to adjust, and the East Coast needed more diversity, more Asians, more time to adjust to the newly arrived refugees from Southeast Asia. Of all people, I should've known what my uncles and aunts were going through, but such deep and full knowledge only came in hindsight, when I became an adult, when I became a parent myself. Even if I did have an inkling of it at that time, the awful feelings of being different, so foreign, so other, were too much.

I wept as I sat on the bed, thinking about all these things. There was no one to blame. We were the dust that remained after the civil war and genocide had left a trail of ruins and destruction, of tears and carnage, of homelessness and parentlessness, in our former home. One can blame the American War in Việt Nam, when Nixon and company decided to bomb Cambodia's countryside, giving rise to the Khmer Rouge and its supporters. But how could such understanding help me then? I was a lonely kid absorbed in my own suicidal ideation.

I opened the aspirin bottle, grabbed a handful of pills, and shoved them into my mouth. I gulped down the dark liquid of a soda can and waited for it to happen. I lay there, thoughts running wild in my head, listening to Lok-Yeay's footsteps above in the kitchen. I counted the seconds and then the minutes. Then, everything went black. It was cold and quiet, and the coldness was deep, chill at the bone, yet comforting. I heard soothing voices that I imagined to be my mother's and father's; they were calling to me. And I felt their voices grew louder and closer, "We have been watching you, Koan. We miss you, too. You are our only son, and we love you." The voices were everywhere, calling my name "Samnang! Samnang! Samnang!" and I felt them on my flesh, as if I were being soothed and kissed. There was joy in my heart, and I felt at peace.

Then I heard a bang. One of my younger cousins must have dropped a toy on the upstairs floor. I opened my eyes and heard Lok-Yeay calling my name "Samnang! Samnang! Samnang!" Footsteps like thunder ran across the basement ceiling. I got up and the room spun like a drunken clown at a freakshow. I felt nauseated and fell back on the bed, my stomach about to erupt. I turned to the side of the bed and vomited onto the rug. I lay on my stomach and again vomited, hurling out all the pills I had swallowed. When I was finished, I held my knees to my chest and cried. I still felt the warm presence vibrating all around, watching me. I knew that all of this sadness, this heaviness, would pass. In a fetal position, I cried myself to sleep.

I told no one about my suicide attempt. It was early June, and days later we had our graduation ceremony at a football stadium a couple of blocks from the high school. I didn't want to be a part of any of it, but Mrs. Doyle had persuaded me to go. "It's good for you to mark this new stage in your life." She added, "It's the reward for all of your hard work." I had no idea what she was talking about, but I decided to go because I didn't want to disappoint her. She was so excited for me. But there really was nothing eventful about graduation. The ceremony for the class of 1990 took place, like it always had, at McDonald Stadium, the Orange Line right next to it. The speeches were interspersed with the noise that the train made as it approached and left Malden Station.

The band played the songs that it had been practicing for the past year. Speeches were made by teachers, students, vice principals, and the principal, and they all told similar stories. *How much we had grown, how our teachers, friends, and families encouraged and supported us, and the world was ours now. So go out with the skills learned in Malden High School and build a better world. But remember that Malden is your home, and no matter where you find yourself it will always be in your heart.*

I stood listening, not knowing whether to laugh or cry. It made no sense to me.

Someone walked across the green turf in the direction of the train tracks and urinated at the fence. Everyone laughed. The principal, vice principals, trustees, and staff pretended not to notice. The speeches continued without interruption. The band played a couple more tunes.

Then our names were called alphabetically, homeroom by homeroom, to receive our "well-earned" diplomas. When my name was called, I walked up to the podium and was handed the diploma. Someone shook my hand and congratulated me. An older gentleman whom I had never seen before stood up and shook my hand as I walked down the platform where the ceremony was taking place. He was smiling in my direction.

But I felt nothing. I walked back to my row and quietly sat in my section. The afternoon sun was hot and I was sweating under my graduation gown. I couldn't wait to take it off and go skating at City Hall.

After the names were called, everyone clapped and cheered. A beach ball was thrown in the air and passed around until one of the vice principals confiscated the colorful ball. There were groans coming from the graduates and laughter from the bleachers where our parents and friends sat. Then I noticed the students started to yell and scream. Bull horns, bells, and whistles sounded all around me, a cacophony that made me want to vomit up everything I hated about this world. My classmates started throwing their caps into the air. Feeling weak, I surrendered and did the same with my cap. It flew up, up, and away. I didn't know where it landed and I didn't care.

Amid the jubilation, I found my way to the bleachers, where the Doyles were. Mrs. Doyle and Sarah gave me a big hug. Anthony and Jeff shook my hand. Mr. Doyle took some pictures of me and his family. They congratulated me wholeheartedly.

I guessed I was ready to conquer the world now.

PART III

A Portrait of the Artist as a Young Cambodian American

What Are You Doing with Your Life?

7:30 A.M. The train was crammed with passengers for whom life seemed to have a purpose. I sat in the back of the car, headphones clamped on my ears, my eyes scanning the train. Men were dressed in crisp black pants, ties underneath their suit jackets, one hand holding the railing while the other clutched a newspaper, a briefcase between shiny polished shoes. Women wore skirts, their faces made up, hair tied at the back. These were serious people. Focused and determined, they all seemed to know what they were doing with their lives.

After graduating from high school, I had nothing to anchor me. I lacked motivation and purpose. I was adrift. I skated through that first summer with a desperate blaze until, in mid-October, I twisted my right ankle after popping an ollie, again speeding down the hill at Kennedy Drive with no care for my safety. It was a stupid but painful accident.

On the living room couch, I nursed my swollen ankle with a grocery bag filled with ice cubes. Pu Vaesnar was lying on the sofa watching *Looney Tunes*. A few weeks prior, he was laid off from a lumber company where he had been working for more than a decade. He looked up, saw the ice bag on my foot, shook his head, and returned to the television screen. Lok-Yeay came from the kitchen to say that Jeffrey's mother called, and noticing my home-made ice pack, asked, "What happened to you?"

"It's nothing. I'm fine. Good thing I didn't crack my head on the cement, huh?"

She paused, and then asked a question that she knew would get me fired up. "What are you doing with your life, Samnang?"

I got up, limped away to the bedroom that we shared, and slammed the door shut behind me.

Mrs. Doyle called again that evening. She told me she was picking me up the next morning to drive me to Bunker Hill Community College, where I was to register for a few classes. And so, the following day, I enrolled in Introduction to Psychology. I chose the course because I wanted to know what was wrong with me, why I'd turned out the way I did, why I couldn't get my act together like everybody else and become something more than a monback. I also signed up for a sociology class; I wanted to learn about other societies and cultures too. Maybe there were places more accepting of outsiders; maybe the United States was not the only country where I could live. I took Algebra 2 and Drawing I because I assumed they'd be easy. Next to "Major" on the form, I checked the "Undeclared" box.

I attended classes regularly for the first month of the spring semester, doing homework and paying attention, even though I sat as far away from my professors as possible, with my back against the wall. But by the second month, I started to lose interest. Looking back, I wasn't prepared for college. I didn't have the tools I needed to tackle the information presented in our reading assignments and then participate in class discussions. A few weeks into the semester, I fell behind in my reading. I couldn't follow the conversations between my classmates and professors, let alone join them. By March, just before spring break, I stopped attending classes altogether and rode the train back and forth on the Orange Line instead, just like the good old days.

No one knew. And I didn't care.

Lok-Yeay said, in her matter-of-fact voice, "It's a quarter to seven. You should get up now. Your first class starts at nine."

On the train I sat, with my backpack between my legs, looking at people, studying their faces and body language, thinking about how happy their lives must be and then becoming critical of them: *Look at this guy with his suit and tie. His hair all gelled, his hands clenching the rail. Every other minute, he checks his wristwatch. It must be awful to be a slave to a company! What a drag to be this dude. A cog in the machine! What a waste. No freedom. Chicken shit!*

One evening, Ming Bonavy and Pu Vaesnar were talking excitedly in the kitchen. Ming Bonavy had been on the phone with her brother, Pu Dara, who'd by then been living in Southern California with his wife and three children for nearly a decade. After working as a baker for several years, Pu Dara bought the donut shop where he was employed. He now owned the shop on Market Street in Long Beach, where he made donuts at night and his wife worked the cash register during the day.

Pu Vaesnar said to his wife, "I don't know anything about making donuts."

Ming Bonavy replied, "Your brother-in-law will teach you." Pu Vaesnar sat smoking in the kitchen chair while his wife was cleaning the tabletop. Ming Bonavy turned to him, "Bong, you don't even have a job here. In California, we can be our own boss. No one will tell us what to do. We will make money, then sell the shop and return to Massachusetts with enough money to send our kids to college."

That night, I thought about what my aunt had said—how California was a place where our dreams resided, a place where we could achieve success. I thought about Hollywood and the skateboarding scene. Christian Hosoi, who was part Japanese, was living in Venice Beach at the time, and Ray Barbee, a Black skater, had roots in Long Beach. I wasn't doing anything with my life in Massachusetts. The more I thought about California, the more right it felt to make the move west. I tossed and turned in bed that night. The next morning, I told Ming Bonavy that I hoped to join her and her husband.

"What about college?" she asked.

"I don't know what's wrong with me, Ming. I have a hard time focusing," I said. "Anyhow, there are plenty of colleges in California. Maybe a change in the scenery will help." I was trying to convince both her and myself that this move could save me. Whether or not she was convinced, my aunt began making arrangements for our cross-country drive the following week. I think now that she was scared to make such a big journey with only her husband. Having me along made her feel less alone. After the Khmer Rouge, she had never been away from her family. As for Pu Vaesnar, I never knew what he was thinking; he usually kept to himself. I only knew I needed an excuse to leave behind this place that made me feel like a nobody—what Mrs. Doyle, in her chiding if caring tone, accurately called "Mr. Negative."

Going West

As we drove westward across the United States, Sin Sisamuth was crooning from the tape deck over a girl he met in the countryside. Pu Vaesnar sat in the driver's seat, a cigarette dangling from his mouth. Puffs of smoke rose into the air and crept into every crevice of the Toyota 4-Runner. I began coughing in the back seat. Reclining in the passenger's seat, Ming Bonavy said to her husband, "Bong, roll down your window when you smoke." Pu Vaesnar looked in his rearview mirror, saw me tearing up from his cigarette smoke, and rolled down his window.

Earlier in the week, I told my friends I was leaving for California. "Who knows? I might meet Ray Barbee in Long Beach and skate with him. Or even Christian Hosoi!"

Anthony asked, "Doesn't Hosoi live in Venice Beach?"

"That's not far from where I'll be, Ant. It's going to be friggin' awesome!"

But sitting in the smoky SUV with my uncle and aunt, I wasn't feeling particularly stoked about the trip. I didn't know anyone in California. But I knew I had to leave Massachusetts. I could see where my life was heading: after dropping out of college, I imagined how Mrs. Doyle would eventually find out and take me to the newly opened mall on Route 1, where I'd apply for a job. Working at a mall was just about the last thing I wanted to do with my life. I thought about the security guard I'd flicked off, the one who'd chased me and my friends for skateboarding. It just wasn't punk to be stuck working behind a cash register in a department store or reprimanding high school kids in a mall overlooking the highway.

In the back seat, I flipped through a *Thrasher* magazine and tried to fall asleep. We'd left Massachusetts early in the morning, my uncle determined to drive through all the states between Massachusetts and California without stopping. He drove that first night while my aunt slept. Every time her head banged against the passenger side window, Ming Bonavy woke up and asked Pu Vaesnar what had happened, and he mumbled something in return. Satisfied with his answers, she'd fall back to sleep. I only slept a couple of hours that first night. In the SUV, we ate salted fish, marinated meat, and rice that Lok-Yeay packed for us. We stopped at rest stops to stretch our feet and use the restroom.

On the second day, we stopped at a Burger King because our home-cooked food ran out. We didn't say much to each other while eating our burgers and fries. Pu Vaesnar looked like he didn't enjoy the taste of the food his wife ordered for him. I watched families around us; parents were talking to their children and sharing each other's fries. When a bearded man in a green John Deere hat noticed me looking at his family, I looked away and out the window.

Later that afternoon, our truck kept veering to the left, crossing into the center lane toward oncoming cars. Someone honked, waking my aunt from her nap. Ming Bonavy studied her husband, then touched his arm and gently said, "Bong, maybe you're tired from driving. Let's get dinner and find a hotel nearby, OK?" We took the next exit and found ourselves in an endless stretch of nowhere, no buildings to be seen, only telephone poles connecting us with civilization. I stuck my head out the window. The air was hot and dry. The sun was still beating down on us even though it was six in the evening.

Ming Bonavy studied the map. We were somewhere in Texas. An hour later, we found what looked like a restaurant with lights blinking around a pair of cowboy boots on the entrance. We could hear country music playing as we approached the roadhouse. Once inside, everyone stared at us. A woman with dirty blonde hair who looked to be in her forties approached us, smiled, and led us to a table in the back near the restroom. She explained the day's specials and said, "Let me know if you have any questions, OK?" before returning to the bar.

Ming Bonavy turned to me and said, "Thanks for coming with us, Samnang. It would have been tough for me and your uncle to do this by ourselves."

"No problem," I said as I watched the waitress chat at the bar with a gentleman sporting a rancher's hat.

My aunt continued, "Don't worry. As soon as we are settled in Long Beach, Lok-Yeay will join us."

"Really?" I asked, surprised but happy at this news.

"Well, with Lok-Ta gone and the grandkids now all in school, she wants to join us."

I hadn't wanted to leave Lok-Yeay at all; like Ming Bonavy, I had never been away from my grandmother. We didn't see eye-to-eye on many things, and she didn't like the direction my life was taking, but she was too busy taking care of my young cousins to do anything more than chide me about it. Like the rest of us, Lok-Yeay had been unprepared for what America was like, and she was doing her best for her family. I was more than just a grandchild to her; I was what was left of her daughter. She loved me like a son, but this realization didn't occur to me until years later, when I was in graduate school and finally asking my aunts and uncles questions about our family history, learning about how Lok-Yeay carried me on her back as we crossed the Cambodian jungle. Decades later, I would write a book of poems about my family's journey and dedicate it to her.

When the waitress returned, she looked at me first and asked, "What do you want, young man?"

"A bacon cheeseburger and sweet potato fries, please," I said. My aunt ordered steak and potatoes for her husband but nothing for herself. She said she wasn't hungry. When the food arrived, I chowed down on it, shoving the sweet fries into my mouth, while my aunt looked on. Her husband ate the steak quietly. He didn't touch the baked potato with melted cheddar and bacon on top. Ming Bonavy ate the leftover food from her husband's plate.

After our roadhouse dinner, we were back on the highway for a couple of hours before we finally saw a motel sign. We pulled into the parking lot, grabbed our suitcases from the truck, and headed toward the main entrance. No one was at the desk. We waited for a few minutes until I suggested we ring the bell. A young man appeared from a closed door behind the counter. He was rubbing his eyes and yawning. My aunt said we needed a room for the night. She signed her name on a clipboard and handed him a handful of bills.

The room had twin beds. I had a bed to myself, and my aunt took the other twin bed. My uncle slept on the floor. He was snoring before we turned off the lights, but I couldn't sleep that night. I kept thinking about going back to Malden. Maybe it wouldn't be so bad to work at the mall, or even to return to my job as an usher at the movie theater. After several years, I could become a supervisor or manager. I didn't need much money, just enough for a bed to sleep on, food on the table, and skateboarding equipment. I opened my eyes in the darkness. My aunt was snoring now too. I listened as my aunt and uncle began a snoring dance; as soon as one stopped snoring, the other picked up the strange melody. They went on like that all night.

We woke up at six, checked out at six thirty, and immediately got back on the highway. We paused only for gas and food at rest stops along the way but we didn't stay at a motel that third night. We were outside of Las Vegas the next morning. My aunt was singing along to a Cambodian song coming from the tape deck, my uncle smoking his Marlboro cigarette out the open window. We were getting there. I felt both excitement and anxiety overtaking me. California was the promised land, the place of dreams, and we were heading straight for it.

Several hours later, smoke started flying out of the hood of the SUV. Ming Bonavy screamed, "Pull the car over, Bong! Pull the car over, Bong!" I rubbed my tired eyes.

Pu Vaesnar stopped the car on the side of the highway and we climbed out. We were just outside Barstow, California. The heat was dry and oppressive. The wind was hot and grainy on my face. I felt the sun burning through my scalp, cooking my brain. My uncle opened the hood, remained quiet for a few minutes, then walked over to us sitting on the side of the road. He said that the engine had overheated. He went to the trunk, grabbed a bottle of green liquid, and went back to the hood. I looked around. There was no sign of life anywhere. We were in an endless stretch of desert. This was not the California of palm trees, fancy cars, and movie stars that I'd seen on TV. This was a wasteland. And the sun was relentless; the heat went inside you and made you want to lie down, close your eyes, and go to sleep forever.

I looked at Ming Bonavy. If she felt terror, my aunt fanned it away with the map she was using to keep her cool. We heard the hood slam and looked up. Pu Vaesnar went to the driver's seat, got the engine started again after several tries, and told us to get back in the car. The emergency light was no longer flashing. We kept the air conditioning off as we inched cautiously back onto the highway. The music was off. No one said anything. I looked out the window as other cars sped past us. The SUV felt like a metal sauna as we crawled toward Southern California in search of our Cambodian American dream.

"Ana-herm" Street

We ended up living in Long Beach for the decade I was in Southern California. What I immediately noticed about this part of the country was its diversity. Each neighborhood in Long Beach contained its own world. One minute you were driving in a Cambodian neighborhood, the next in a Mexican neighborhood. The border shifted, and you found yourself in a completely different culture and having to deal with a completely different language, listen to a completely different kind of music, eat completely different food, but you were still in the same city in America. After living on the East Coast for more than ten years, I had never imagined that such an experience could be found in the United States. I felt more at ease, at home, in this new America. In this world of immigrants and refugees, of foreigners and migrant workers, of yellow, brown, and black skin, the periphery became the center, and the center, the white world, was relegated to the periphery. To have white people experience, even for a split second, the feelings of being different, estranged, alienated, and insignificant that I'd so long felt, was a certain kind of beauty, a miraculous thing, a kind of poetic justice, to my young refugee mind.

When I walked down the streets in this strange new world, I didn't feel so out of place. I didn't instinctively crave invisibility. I was still awkward, shy, and uncomfortable around people, still plagued with a paralyzing self-consciousness, but I also felt that, here in Southern California, I had a chance of belonging. I was not alone in looking different, in speaking a language other than English, in eating foods other than meatloaf and potato salad and bread. I was not alone in practicing a religion that was not Christianity. Of course, there is absolutely nothing wrong with being a Christian who eats meat, potatoes, bread, and cheese. The point had to do with diversity and inclusion, of having other options available and accepted—not just food but other ways of speaking and acting, other ways of raising children, other ways of treating one's parents and grandparents, other ways of expressing love, other ways of being in the world. This was a world, I hoped, of openness, of empathy and compassion, where differences were recognized, valued, and embraced.

Our first few weeks in Long Beach, I walked everywhere, paying particular attention to the bigger roads like Cherry Avenue, Orange Avenue, and Atlantic Avenue that intersected with Pacific Coast Highway and Anaheim Street. When I had money I went to Cambodian restaurants, shopped at food markets, and perused music and video stores adorning what the Khmer people called "Ana-herm" Street. It was an area of Long Beach that, later, would be officially named "Cambodia Town." It felt surreal to step inside a restaurant, speak Khmer and order Khmer food from a bilingual menu, listen to Khmer music playing in the background, and momentarily forget that I was in America. The young woman at the register took my order, smiled, then disappeared into the kitchen. I sat listening to the political gossip of older Khmer men seated a few tables over from mine. The men were passionate. Their hair slicked back, some wore black-rimmed glasses. Most smoked. They were talking about Hun Sen, how he had been a Khmer Rouge member and now he was a puppet for the Vietnamese government. Someone at the table said he used to go to school with Hun Sen. I had no idea who Hun Sen was, as I hadn't kept up with Cambodian politics. I was too busy trying to survive America to pay attention to American politics, let alone Cambodian politics. The waitress came back with a bowl of rice and two plates of Khmer food—one was beef marinated with lemongrass and the other was papaya salad topped with dried shrimp. I tuned out the old Cambodian men smoking and politicizing a few tables from me—and ate. I felt really good about Long Beach. I thought to myself, *This is a Cambodian America I have never thought possible. California, you embody the true spirit of America. You open your arms to welcome us immigrants and refugees. You let us be who we are without the pressure to assimilate. I am home at last!*

I also discovered Mexican food around the block from where we were living. The restaurant was basically a concrete square with a small window in the front and a kitchen in the back. Around noon, I waited in a long line of people, some I recognized as neighbors and others who, I assumed, were professionals on their lunch break. When it was my turn, I stepped up and ordered one of only two items on the handwritten menu taped to a glass window: burrito or taco. It was the meat options that got me excited. There was the usual shredded meat: chicken, beef, and pork. Then there were cow tongue, tripe, cow brains, and other staples for the peasant, the laborer, and migrant worker, those without much visibility and voice except in the service industry. The guy taking my order spoke limited English. I pointed to the items on the window menu; he nodded his head and yelled something in Spanish to the cook in the back. He then wiped his sweaty forehead with a white apron and nodded at the customer behind me. I moved to the side and waited for my food. Somehow, I felt at ease with all of this. Here was a guy speaking English with an accent, doing his best to make a living. He was short like me, and his skin color was close to mine, and I felt an imagined affinity with this stranger in this little concrete box. A few minutes later, he raised a white paper bag to show me that my order had arrived. I went to the window, smiled, and awkwardly said, "Gracias" as I took my food.

Sitting at one of the tables that were chained together in the parking lot of this establishment, I took out a taco from the greasy white paper bag. On top of the slices of cow tongue was cilantro and minced white onion. I poured red chili sauce and squeezed a bit of lime over the meat; then I gulped down my delicious cow tongue taco. The food was spicy and limey, hitting all the right spots on my Cambodian tongue. No one was talking politics or smoking cigarettes. I was by myself with my tacos. The sun felt warm on my skin. My tongue started to burn. I was happy.

Lok-Yeay arrived one month later. And the world felt right again. My aunt and uncle finally felt good about the move. After learning the trade from Pu Dara, who'd had a donut shop in Long Beach for almost a decade, Ming Bonavy and Pu Vaesnar bought a shop in the city of Bell, in Los Angeles County. Pu Vaesnar left the house at 11 P.M. each night for his new shop, made the dough, and waited for it to rise before deep frying it. Lok-Yeay and Ming Bonavy left the house at four in the morning to open the donut shop for the late-night truck drivers. Ming Bonavy worked at the cash register and Lok-Yeay cleaned the tables and smiled at customers. Since Lok-Yeay couldn't work the register, I helped out once things got busy. I arrived around seven to help Ming Bonavy with the wave of students stopping by for donuts on their way to school. My uncle went to the bathroom, opened a cot, and slept. I sometimes had to hold my pee until Pu Vaesnar woke up from his nap.

During those few weeks at the donut shop, I did what I could to help with the family business. Forcing a smile, I said to the elementary and middle school students, "Hi, how may I help you?" After a while, I found repeating the same question tedious and lacking in authenticity, so I varied my welcome with "Help you?" or "Hi" and "Hey." Sometime between nine and ten each morning, the rush died down and I found myself completely bored. I took several quarters and went to the two video games in the front part of the shop and played Ms. Pacman, a game I used to play when I was a kid in Revere. The next and final rush occurred during lunchtime; this was followed by a small stream of students coming back from school around 2:30 P.M. We usually ended up with a tray or two of donuts by the end of the day. Ming Bonavy sold these donuts at a discount price around four and threw the rest out when we closed shop.

I was never good at the business side of things. Maybe I didn't understand how the donut business worked or simply refused to accept its laws. When a kid didn't have enough money for a donut, I took whatever he had and gave him a donut anyway. I figured that, since we were going to throw the donuts in the trash bin in the late afternoon, I might as well give them to someone. Why waste food, I reasoned. One time a family came to the donut shop at two o'clock. The father was a stout man, maybe in his late twenties, and his wife was probably a bit younger, with beautiful olive skin. They had a little girl, around six or seven years old, and a toddler with them. The father, dressed in blue jeans and black boots and a white shirt with stains on the cuff, pointed to two donuts and gave me a worn-out dollar bill. The father returned to the table where his family sat; he and his wife shared a donut, and the girl shared the other with her little brother. They ate quietly, sometimes the father tearing a piece of his old-fashioned donut to give to his son. The family then began showing up regularly every Friday between two and three in the afternoon: the same order, the same sharing of donuts, the same quiet meal together as a family. Each time I saw the father, I was reminded of the Mexican guy I bought lunch from at the taco shop in my Long Beach neighborhood. Finally, I told him to come later in the afternoon. "You can get a dozen donuts for two dollars," I told him. He smiled at me with such gratitude and nodded his head. Every Friday afternoon from then on, he showed up at 4 P.M. I gave him a box of donuts, and he gave me two wrinkled dollar bills.

Eventually, Ming Bonavy caught on. "What are you doing?" she asked.

"Nothing," I shrugged my shoulders. "Selling donuts."

"You know we're in business to make money, not give it away, right?" she asked accusingly.

"Ming, we were going to throw those donuts away anyway," I replied. "What does it matter?"

"Each dollar you give away, you're taking it from our savings. Savings to go back east, savings to be with family once again, savings for my children's future."

"It's just that the family is so poor. They remind me of us. We were like that once. The dad can't even speak English!"

"We are like that now."

"Fine, I'll find a job somewhere and pay you back with interest." My aunt didn't say anything. I had little work experience. The next few days, I borrowed Pu Vaesnar's 4-Runner, drove to an unemployment center in downtown Long Beach, filled out a few dozen job application forms, and waited for someone to call. No one did. I continued to work at the donut shop, with my aunt watching over me. Weeks later, I finally got a call. There was an opening at a maintenance company. I went that afternoon and was hired on the spot.

A Dream

Like most jobs that didn't require a college education, working for the maintenance company was physically demanding. I was like a traveling janitor. And I had the graveyard shift. I showed up at six in the evening, waited for my coworker Luis Hernández to arrive, and together we drove the company van to private schools, synagogues, people's homes, and the Long Beach Naval Shipyard to clean, sweep floors, empty trash bins, scrub toilets, and mop until five in the morning. Anything that needed to be cleaned, we cleaned. We drove from city to city with our white van full of buckets, mops, brooms, brushes, gloves, and masks. I made small talk with Luis. He was in his thirties and came from a town in Puebla, Mexico. He and his wife lived in one of the roughest neighborhoods in Long Beach, where a Cambodian gang was at war with a Mexican gang. Luis wanted to save enough money to move his three children to North Long Beach. Listening to Luis tell of an incident where one of his daughters saw someone get killed in a gang shootout, I knew I had no right to complain about my lot.

I kept my mouth shut, kept my head down, and worked hard, sweeping, scrubbing, and mopping. By five in the morning, the sun came back up and we drove the van from Santa Ana back to Long Beach. I returned home and tried to catch some sleep. With this work schedule, I felt like a zombie, mechanically mopping, scrubbing, and vacuuming and not really thinking about the future. While scrubbing a young couple's bathtub one evening, I saw my life flashing in reverse: shoveling rice and pork into my mouth before my shift; cleaning people's dirty toilets and mopping floors of factories at the Long Beach shipyard while others slept; returning home in the early morning, eyelids heavy with sweat and exhaustion, falling into dreamless sleep while normal people woke up to begin their day. I knew I was going nowhere fast with this kind of life, but I didn't have the energy to imagine a way to escape the cycle of work, sleep, eat, and work.

Then it happened. One summer morning, I woke up from a dream. It was the kind of dream that had no story—no beginning, no middle, no end. In the dream it felt like I was back in Cambodia, in some distant past, and there was this man on a white horse. He had a golden crown atop his head, like he was a king or prince, some kind of royalty, and he was riding toward a village. Then the perspective changed. The man on the white horse was riding toward me. But I couldn't see his face. All I could see was the golden crown and the sun glaring behind it. I felt warm and bright all over. As he came closer, I winced from the glare and woke up. My heart racing, sweat running down my forehead, I went to the kitchen, had a glass of water, and looked out the window. Kids were playing and parents were sitting on porches, listening to the radio, smoking, and chatting with neighbors. A middle-aged woman was walking her dog. Without explanation, a heavy loneliness overwhelmed me, and an unexpected urge took over. Of all places, I felt a sudden desire to go to the library, a place that I avoided in high school, where I scoffed at those who frequented it. I had hated books all my young life. In high school, I read a few books—well, that wasn't true. I finished only one book, *Ordinary People*. It was the only book I was presented with that I could relate to. Like its protagonist Conrad Jarrett, I too had tasted loss, felt its psychic marks imprinted on my soul, how it made an outsider out of me, an orphan in my own extended family.

So, on that strange Sunday morning, I first set foot inside the Dana Branch of the Long Beach Public Library. People were sitting quietly at tables and in private corners reading or scribbling in their notebooks. Some looked up from their work, saw whatever they saw in me, and then returned to their reading. Feeling embarrassed and naked, I made a beeline for the stacks of books in the back and hid among the shelves. I was determined to go through the poetry section alphabetically in search of answers to my life. I started with the "A" authors and then found my way to the "B" authors where I stood, suddenly captivated, paralyzed by the titles of the books by this one author, titles like *Poems Written Before Jumping Out of an 8 Story Window* and *Burning in Water, Drowning in Flames* and *Flower, Fist, and Bestial Wail* and *You Get So Alone at Times That It Just Makes Sense.*

What was this? It all felt eerily familiar, like someone on the verge of suicide, speaking directly to me from a past that was my present. It was like meeting an old friend, a familiar self, who was telling me to pick up these books and find the answers to the questions I had been asking for most of my life.

I stopped and listened. My hands shook. I took one off the shelf and turned the book over, studying its cover. There was a picture of an old white man grinning. His eyes squinting, his pockmarked face had this warm smile all over it. What was remarkable about the photo was how ordinary the old man looked.

The author was none other than German American poet and writer Charles Bukowski. I found a quiet corner and began reading. The book was *Play the Piano Drunk Like a Percussion Instrument Until the Fingers Begin to Bleed a Bit.*

There were no gimmicks, no fancy tricks, no metaphors and similes. I didn't need to have read Shakespeare, Milton, or Pope, in order to "get it." I didn't need to be part of an inner circle, a member of the elite and the cultured, to understand that suffering was suffering.

Bukowski was deceptively simple and accessible to those who, like me, didn't have a proper education. He was Shakespeare for the illiterate, a patron saint of the poor and the downtrodden, an idol of aspiring writers and poets who felt like they didn't belong to any elite circle of writers and artists or in the ivory tower of academia.

I found a home in the ordinary madness of Bukowski's drunks and whores, gamblers and criminals, poets and writers down on their luck, working in factories and betting on horses, mistaking barflies for angels, living in rooming houses of wailing landladies and crawling cockroaches. Bukowski, the German child immigrant, the outsider, the stranger in his own home and in his America, was no different from me. His father was like Uncle Ly. His high school experience was an alienating one, like mine. I didn't suffer heavy acne, but my skin made me feel different from my peers just the same.

At night the cockroaches in our Long Beach apartment crawled out of their dark crevices, gathering together in a strange communion, serving as witness to this bond I was forging with Bukowski. I went through his books of poems as if they contained promises of salvation. The poems were easy to consume. I was a child who hadn't read much. I was not accustomed to the critical and sustained attention that most poems and novels demanded. After the poetry books ran out, the itch still burned. Bukowski had entered my bloodstream and irrevocably infected me. I craved more, wanted to read anything and everything he'd written. I got ambitious, then. I finally turned to his semi-autobiographical novels: *Post Office*, *Ham on Rye*, *Factotum*, and the rest—I read them all, one by one.

When I found that the local branch of the library didn't carry some of the titles that were listed on the back of his books, I mustered up enough courage to walk up to one of the desk librarians and place an order through the library's interlibrary loan system. As was the case with Bukowski, his books were frequently missing or found in some corner with pages torn, scribbled upon, smeared with lipstick, or stained with frightening and exciting fluids.

A sweet elderly white lady was working at the front desk when I walked up to the poor soul and asked if she could help me locate a certain book.

"What is the author's name?" she asked in her sweet soft voice.

"Charles Bukowski."

"What is the title of the book you're looking for?"

I scribbled the title *Erections, Ejaculations, Exhibition and General Tales of Ordinary Madness* on a scrap of paper and handed it to her.

An uncomfortable silence fell between us. If she had formed any judgment, she didn't show it. She returned to her computer. "B-U-K-O-W-S-K-I, you say? Let me take a look at this here."

"Yes," I said. Then I added, "Thank you."

A few minutes later, she emerged from the computer screen. "No, I'm sorry. We don't carry that book."

When I'd read through Bukowski's fiction and poetry, I turned to his letters to editor John Martin, to writer friends and readers from around the world. After reading his letters, I was introduced by Bukowski to other poets and writers—Robinson Jeffers, Henry Miller, Ernest Hemingway, Carson McCullers, John Fante, and Fyodor Dostoevsky. With Miller's *Tropics* and *Sextet*, I stayed under the cover and masturbated the night away. Miller found the cosmic force, the Infinite Consciousness, in the physical act of copulation and the beautiful filth of the human body. But it was Dostoevsky who made more sense to me. The Russian writer showed me another side of madness. Not necessarily the physical madness of drunks, prostitutes, and aspiring writers, although they were all connected somehow, but the madness of fear and desire, of love and passion, of religion and irrationality, of the human psyche.

For Dostoevsky, this inner world leaks, breaks through, and infects the rational daylight of the Apollonian world. Not only was this a return to Dionysus, the god of wine and drunkenness, but for me, it was an honest celebration of that which was my life, where logic sometimes failed and failed miserably, where meaning had often become meaningless, where two and two became five, where strange events took place and no rational explanation sufficed. The mysterious and violent worlds of Prince Myshkin, the Idiot, the Ridiculous Man, the Underground Man, and, of course, the Brothers Karamazov spoke to me.

I gobbled it all up and thought about my own life. There was never order and structure in it. There had never been a good explanation for why my mother had to die from sickness and hunger. Why I was separated from my father, why I grew up without parents. Oh, my life. It began with chaos and destruction wreaked by the Khmer Rouge and continued with more pain and confusion when I arrived in America with my aunts, uncles, and grandparents. The suffering never stopped. Dostoevsky was right. The Buddha was right. Life was suffering. The answers were in the books, and I was no longer alone. I wept late into the night, in the darkness of my room, a darkness that was real and true and honest.

At dawn, I finished *Crime and Punishment* and wept for Raskolnikov, who walked away from the prison building. The light hurt his eyes. He strained to see Sonia waiting for him. His knees trembled and collapsed, his lips touching the ground. I too trembled and collapsed.

I saw that he suffered like I had suffered, even though he played a central role in his suffering, in his punishment, in a way I had not in my own. His suffering was nonetheless my suffering. And in seeing my suffering reflected back to me, somehow, I felt released from it.

Unlike Raskolnikov, I didn't want redemption because, to the best of my knowledge, I had committed no crime. In the night, I wanted to scream, yell, beat my chest, and scream some more. There was so much I needed to say but I lacked the tools necessary to express and empower myself. I couldn't even write a complete, grammatically sound sentence. I needed an education. I needed to go back to school.

It had been a few years since I dropped out of Bunker Hill Community College. Seeing college students playing frisbee on the green lawn, listening to music, and hanging out in small groups, I felt nervous, intimidated, as I walked across the Long Beach City College campus toward the administration building that housed the Office of Enrollment. I filled out the required forms and took a class schedule. I submitted my college application to the lady behind the counter. She was of African descent, slightly over-weight, with a friendly smile. She listened to the questions I had about registration.

"How many classes can I take?" I asked.

"That depends on your major," she said. "What are you inter-ested in?"

"Everything. Philosophy. History. English. Anthropology. You name it." The woman looked baffled. There and then, I felt the compulsion to tell her everything about my life, the forces that led me to this exact moment of babbling in front of her window, how I really didn't have a proper education and now I was hungry for it. My soul was starving. I wanted to tell her that I was going to be a famous writer someday. But the woman was losing patience, as there were other students waiting in line after me. I simply told her, "I don't care about the degree. I just want to learn how to read and write. I'm going to be a writer someday. You will see! I'm going to be the first great Cambodian American novelist!"

"That's nice," the woman smiled. "Well, here's the paperwork. Please fill out these forms and bring them to Window 8." She pointed to the window on the far right.

I didn't tell Ming Bonavy or Lok-Yeay about my new dream of becoming a writer. The idea was too foreign to them. Until recently, it was foreign to me too. Instead, I chose this lady, this stranger who sat behind a glass window, to make my confession to. She sat in her chair smiling, puzzled by my rambling yet nevertheless remaining professional. I returned her smile and thanked her for her patience.

Sitting on a bench at the bus stop on Carson Street, I browsed the college catalogue. Fulfilling the requirements for an Associate Degree was the last thing on my mind. I simply wanted an educa-tion, the tools necessary to rebuild my life and lead a thoughtful and meaningful life. I wanted to receive what should have been given to me in high school.

Br_ndon Lieu

In my first year back at college, I took all sorts of classes in history, sociology, anthropology, and philosophy. I particularly enjoyed courses on ethics, logic, and comparative religion, finding pleasure in the speculative thinking that such courses encouraged me to do. These classes asked students to question their cultural assumptions of what was right and wrong, good and evil, reality and dream. I stayed up late at night reading the philosophies of Chuang-Tzu, Confucius, the Buddha, Socrates, and Plato, and I couldn't go to sleep from the excitement of playing out the passionate discussions I would have with the professor and my classmates. I dreamed of engaging in a lively debate on the true nature of reality with the professor as we discussed Chuang-Tzu's parable of the butterfly.

The next morning, I sat in the back of the class, not far from one of the windows, and watched most of the students try to stay awake as the professor, Dr. Applebaum, did his best to engage the class in a discussion on the nature of reality. He asked, "So, class. Is Chuang-Tzu dreaming of being a butterfly or the butterfly dreaming of being Chuang-Tzu? What do you think? What evidence from the reading do you have to support your claim?"

No one raised their hand. At the awkwardness of it all, I squirmed in my seat, wanting so much to engage with Dr. Applebaum, to rescue him from the slumber and general malaise of my peers, but feeling anxious and shy, uncomfortable about speaking in class.

I feared everyone would turn around in their seats and stare at me. Whether or not Chuang-Tzu was the dreamer was no longer relevant. I was now a butterfly pinned and pressed on a glass slide. No one could hear my screams but they could see me, see what I looked like and how I dressed, see the maddening fear in my eyes.

After class, I made sure everyone had left the room before I went up to Dr. Applebaum and asked if I could talk to him during office hours. His face lit up. "Of course, drop by this afternoon." He smiled, "I look forward to our conversation." Not knowing what to say, I forced a smile and left the classroom.

Dr. Applebaum's office was cluttered with bookshelves, postcards of places in Italy and France where I assumed he had visited or had even lived with his family, and printouts of quotes from famous philosophers. Books and papers lay scattered across his coffee-stained desk. I waited for him to signal me to sit down in the seat across from him. "Yes, yes, how are you?" he asked.

I nodded.

"So, what do you want to talk about?"

Once again, I found myself mute, nervous that I was in a room with this great man who, as far as I was concerned, was the epitome of knowledge and wisdom. I mumbled a question about the historical circumstances surrounding Chuang-Tzu, something about how did we know which poems and parables were written by the great Tao master himself and which were told by his students? It was a question that, I hope, didn't require follow-up questions. *Let Dr. Applebaum do the talking, I'll just listen. When he's done, I'll go my merry way.*

I left the office unsatisfied with the visit and more unhappy with myself. The question about authorship wasn't part of the deep conversation that I had dreamed about exploring when I was in the comfort of my own apartment reading the night before.

On the bus home, I cursed myself for not being able to simply talk, to be heard and thus to articulate myself into being.

Since I didn't have transcripts from Bunker Hill Community College, I had to take and pass an E.S.L. class before I could enroll in college-level English classes. The professor was once a respected scholar in the field of Renaissance studies. He'd taught at U.S.C. for over a decade before coming to the community college. Recently divorced from his wife of twenty years, he was now a drunk and an adjunct. Often, he came to class late, rambled about the day's mishaps, and confided in us about his relationship with his children, who were now in their teens and, like most teenagers, wanted nothing to do with their parents. We sat uncomfortably in our seats as he continued his tirade. He capped off his list of complaints with a story designed to showcase the deliberate cruelty of his ex-wife.

After twenty minutes of sitting on top of the desk explaining to us why his ex-wife deserved our hate, he walked around the desk, reached into his brown satchel, and took out an old grammar text. He returned to his previous spot and, perched on the edge of the desk, legs dangling, he began to read out loud the directions from the textbook, as if he were reading them for the first time. Then he asked us to form groups of four or five. We were lucky if we went through two exercises in one meeting (and the class only met once a week). Since we didn't grow up in America, someone inevitably asked a question about life in America. In his attempt to answer such questions, the professor returned to his favorite subject to illustrate "life in America": his ex-wife, her insidious cruelty, and the many reasons why he was relieved they were divorced. After an unsettling joke about his ex-wife, he turned to a group of Vietnamese female students sitting in front, smiling at them, and they in turn giggled.

I sat, arms folded, lips pursed. *This is a waste of my time and everybody else's too. I don't care about the first time this guy was suspicious of his wife's infidelity. I wanted to learn how to write, goddamnit! This lunatic's rambling is not helping at all. I want to write about suffering and madness—not those of King Lear, Hamlet, or Henry V of England, but the suffering and madness that I am familiar with, my memories of war and Khmer Rouge atrocities, of the loss of home and loved ones, of the shame and embarrassment of being a refugee and racial other. All of this suffering which manifests in my inability to speak.*

After class ended, I watched as the professor walked over to another group of female students. Frustrated, I left the room and marched across campus. I reminded myself why I must endure this humiliation, this parody of an education, in order to learn how to write, so that I could speak about the invisibility and silent rage, the shame and self-hatred, the powerlessness and inertia that came from being an ethnic minority in this country. I must write about and against this feeling of not being at home in America.

While waiting at the bus stop, I repeated the following phrases: *I know what I want. I know what I need. I must keep going no matter what. I must be patient.* I took a book out of my black backpack and began reading. It was Huxley's *1984*, a book I was supposed to read in high school.

After completing the E.S.L. class, I was finally allowed to take a literature course. I browsed the college catalogue, looking over the names of English professors. One name in particular caught my attention: Lieu. He was teaching an introduction to literature course early in the morning, and if his name was any indication, he was Asian. I immediately signed up.

I sat in the back corner of the room, as usual, pretending to look out the window and paying no one any attention. My heart was pounding, and I began to sweat. Everyone in the room was white. It was a class for English majors. Not only was I the only Asian, I was also the only person of color. Sitting in the front row were two girls talking about the classes they had enrolled in for the spring semester. They were talking about these writers and poets whose names sounded familiar; they were ghosts from half a decade earlier, back in high school, when Mr. Stephenson asked us to open an anthology of British literature. I felt nervous, intimidated, scared. I began to question myself once again. *Do I belong here? What do I know of literature? Do I know the right way to find meaning in literature? What is literature, anyway? It has something to do with Shakespeare, Chaucer, Milton, Pope, Queen Elizabeth, Spenser, those people, right? Mr. Stephenson talked about them in high school, but I paid him no attention. What will happen if studying literature is still not for me? Maybe I just should drop out and be a janitor for the rest of my life. Damn it. Why did I even come back to college?*

Then the professor walked in and introduced himself. He told us not to call him "Professor Lieu" or "Dr. Lieu." "Instead, call me by my first name," he smiled. "Br_ndon." His hair was black, like mine, and he parted it to the right. I parted mine down the middle. His skin was lighter than mine. He wore blue jeans and a gray long-sleeve dress shirt. And he had an accent. He was an English professor with an Asian accent!

Br_ndon was from Malaysia but, he told us passionately, if someone were to cut open his wrists, Chinese characters would dance out of them. He passed around the syllabus, went over the course description, and explained his grading rubric. "I don't usually give out As," he warned us. "This is why the A is missing in my first name. You have to surprise me, delight me with your writing, your insights, to earn that A." Everyone sat quietly in his or her seat. I looked around and wondered how many students would be dropping this class by the end of the week. Br_ndon took out the course roster and began taking attendance. He made a couple of jokes as he went down the list of names. I dreaded this part of the first day of classes, as my name would inevitably be mispronounced by the professor and I would keep quiet about it, enduring my name being butchered throughout the semester. Once, I'd just told a professor to call me "Sam."

"Sam?" he'd asked.

I nodded.

"Sam, like *Sam-I-Am*, from Dr. Seuss?" the professor asked again.

Again, I nodded. And the class laughed.

But when Br_ndon came to my name, he enunciated each syllable slowly and clearly: Sam-Nang Sok. He pronounced my name as close to the Khmer as I had ever heard a non-Khmer utter it. I raised my hand to indicate my presence in his class.

I felt good about my first literature class. And I felt good about Br_ndon, who was the only other Asian in the classroom. Immediately, I looked up to him. I worked hard in his class, and it wasn't

185

for the grade. I wanted to show Br_ndon my respect. I also wanted to be like him. If someone who looked like me could do it, then why not me? With my face, skin, and Asian name, I dreamed of standing in front of a group of American students and teaching them how to write and read literature. There was a strange kind of beauty to it. I wanted to teach them about Milton and Shakespeare, John Donne and Alexander Pope. I wanted to master their literary canon, shake things up a bit with my name and accent, and inject my Asian blood into it, troubling and transforming their expectations about literature in the process.

I stayed up late reading the short stories, novels, and poems that Br_ndon assigned to us. I sat on the couch in our living room reading Kafka's *The Metamorphosis*. Pu Vaesnar was at the donut shop. Ming Bonavy was sleeping alone in their bedroom. Lok-Yeay woke up to use the restroom and saw me reading from the *Norton Anthology of World Masterpieces*. A bowl of ramen noodles sat on a milk crate next to the couch

"It's three in the morning. You should get some sleep, Samnang."

"I just need to finish reading this story about a guy who turned into an insect and how his family rejects him." Lok-Yeay stood quietly still in the dark hallway. I said, "I know it's late; I'll go to bed soon. Good night, Lok-Yeay."

"You have changed so much these past few months. Lok-Ta was always proud of you. I'm proud of you now, Jeow."

I picked up the bowl of noodles, which had been left unattended for thirty minutes, and slurped them up.

I devoured those assigned texts late into the night like I devoured the noodles. The night was quiet except for the rain falling against the windowpane. The cockroaches came out from their crevices. I felt less lonely when they came out, less lonely when I read about Kafka's life and work, less lonely with these voices and stories circling around me. It was a strange communion, and I felt I finally belonged to something good and important, that I was at long last a part of humanity. Br_ndon said that Kafka was the complete outsider. He was Jewish in Christian-majority Austria. He was alienated from his father, who had wanted a healthy and robust son, not a shy, awkward, pale child suffering from tuberculosis. Kafka prayed to God for help but God didn't answer. His alienation and despair resonated with my entire being. I was Kafka. I was Gregor. I was the nobody. I was the outsider. The loner. The reject. I was the insect. The cockroach. The identification was quick and simple for someone like me, someone who'd so long felt desperate to be a part of some imagined community of outsiders.

Lok-Yeay thought I was studying to become an engineer. When you are a child of immigrants, you have several options laid out for you: first, become a doctor; and if that doesn't work out, then a lawyer; the smart, quiet, socially awkward Asian is a future engineer. Since I couldn't stand the sight of blood and I was too shy to argue my way out of a problem, an engineer I must be. I remember after graduating from high school, Oum Seyha handed me a box of architecture tools. Seeing what was inside the box, I smiled and politely thanked him for the gift. I don't remember him saying anything to me. The box of tools was the only gift I ever received from any of my uncles and aunts, and it sat in a drawer, never touched again. A reminder of my failure to meet my elders' expectations.

At city college, I read mostly Western writers and poets of the twentieth century. Eliot and his Wasteland. Fitzgerald and his Great American Novel. Hemingway and his marlin. Salinger and the problems of the Manhattan upper class. But it was Raymond Carver whom I admired most. He was the epitome of the blue-collar writer. He had this beautiful obsession with everything ordinary and mundane. He was also an alcoholic, a smoker, and a perfectionist. A "good workhorse," as Br_ndon called him. Carver spent hours taking out and putting back a comma. A master of minimalism, he pushed Hemingway's iceberg deeper in the cold literary water of America. If I could write a fraction as well as Carver did, I told myself, I could die with my eyes closed.

Carver wrote about ordinary people, the kind you'd meet in certain places in America, those who lost jobs due to the economy, who took up drinking, who fought with their wives, who felt lonely as they looked up at the night sky. If he could write about his people, I could write about mine: the immigrants and refugees who left war-torn Southeast Asia and found refuge in America; the uncles, aunts, and grandparents who had quietly rebuilt their lives in a new country from broken memories; the child who was torn between the world of his parents and the world of his peers, feeling lost and confused, looking for a home, picking up a pen or some kind of instrument to tell his stories.

The Writers' Club

The black-and-white poster hung in the hallway of the English department, announcing "The Writers' Club" in a bold Century Gothic font. In smaller type, "Writers at all levels are welcome. Meet us in the Alphonso Room this Wednesday at 4 P.M. Bring your work to share!" Sitting in his office, I asked Br_ndon about the Writers' Club. "It's an open forum where writers come together, share their stories, and comment on each other's work," he said. "It might be good for your writing, and you have nothing to lose. You should check it out, Samnang."

I wasn't sure I was a writer. I had yet to write anything substantial, let alone publish. I wrote mostly songs and poems inspired by the music I had been listening to at the time. Jim Morrison was a big influence on me then, especially his writings in *Wilderness*, *The American Night*, and *The Lords and The New Creatures*. My early attempts at writing were juvenile in both style and theme. I hadn't found my subject matter. But I was also keeping a journal, jotting down my daily thoughts and observations on the Khmer community, and taking notes on the relationship between Ming Bonavy and Pu Vaesnar. I had the urge to share these personal observations with others.

I arrived ten minutes early for the first Writers' Club meeting and sat at the conference table in the center of the Alphonso Room. A few people trickled in. A guy with black-rimmed glasses sat next to me. He wore gray pants, a white collared shirt, and heavy black-rimmed glasses. His hair was parted to the right. I thought he'd taken a time machine and come right out of the 1950s. There was a blonde woman with cute freckles sitting on the other side of the table. A lanky kid in plaid shorts and a Nirvana T-shirt arrived a few minutes later, followed by an older woman, in her mid-thirties, wearing a police uniform. The president of the club arrived a few minutes after four and apologized.

We smiled anxiously as we waited for our leader to officially begin the meeting. "Welcome, everyone, to the first meeting of the Writers' Club. My name is Chris. This is a club for those of us interested in writing. It doesn't matter if you are a published writer or if you are just starting out. This club is for everyone at all levels. We are here to support and encourage one another. Let's go around the room and introduce ourselves. Tell us your name, what you like to write and read." I was relieved when the blonde surfer girl went first, because she sat on the other side of the table from me.

"Hi, everyone. My name is Callie. I like to read and write poetry." Callie's voice was soft and breathy, barely a whisper, and it put everyone at ease.

The next person up was the kid in the Nirvana T-shirt. "Name is Gil. My father's a Hollywood producer. I write screenplays. And, oh, Samuel Fuller kicks ass!" We laughed after Gil's entertaining introduction.

The woman in a police uniform introduced herself. "My name is Janet. I work for the L.A.P.D. I don't read and write literature. I'm here because I've seen a lot of stuff in my line of work and it helps me to put it down in words and share them with others." We nodded our heads as if we understood what Janet had gone through.

Chris's turn came up. "I'm a father to a six-year-old boy and a four-year-old girl. My ex-wife and I share custody. I write mostly short stories. Raymond Carver is my favorite writer."

The guy who dressed like an FBI agent took his turn. "My name is Robert J. Williamson. I write science fiction." He then opened a small black briefcase, took out a binder, and said, "This is my latest novel. I'm looking for an agent."

I sat frozen, smiling at Robert, sweat oozing down my face. It was now my turn. I had been going over various introductions in my head while the others took turns introducing themselves. Now that I was up at bat, I forgot what I wanted to say. I mumbled, "My name is Samnang. I don't know if I'm a writer. I'm here to learn from you about writing."

Chris said, "If you write, then you're a writer." Everyone nodded in agreement. Chris said we should go around the room and share our work.

Callie read a love poem about a guy who'd broken her heart the previous summer. It was a standard love poem, with an AABB rhyme scheme and images of waves crashing and seagulls flying in the blue sky as the two young lovers said their goodbyes under a Santa Monica pier. Gil read a scene from his screenplay about two buddies surviving the American War in Việt Nam and falling in love with each other. Janet read her police report. Some kid got shot the other night and she held him as he lay dying. She read as if she were reporting, with little emotion shown, just the facts. Somehow it worked on me, on all of us in that room. We were moved by the list of brutal facts: a burglary in process at a liquor store in Florence, a pit bull mauling a neighbor's child, a husband shooting his wife on the suspicion of infidelity, a kid dying from a gunshot to his stomach. Her reporting stunned us into silence.

Then it was Chris's turn. He read a short story about a boy fishing with his best friend. The story didn't have much of a plot. But it had a good setting: a small, quiet town somewhere in the Pacific Northwest, with trout jumping out of still water and the adults busy working, drinking, or cheating on their spouses. Chris had a great ear for dialogue. I could hear the two boys talking about things that matter to boys at that age: curiosity and anxiety about sex, attraction to girls, and fear of death and dying. Chris's style was clear, simple, and intimate. It was something I wanted to do in my own writing. I thought to myself that if he could do it, maybe I could write like that someday. Maybe I could be friends with Chris and we could talk about writing and Carver.

When it was Robert's turn, he gripped the binder in his hands and began reading from his unpublished novel. He read without pause, without looking up at us, his eyes moving left to right, like an old typewriter. He was absorbed in his own world of invading aliens and of inter-species love. When Robert was done, he looked up and turned to me. Chris said, "Well, I guess it's your turn, Samnang. Thanks, Robert, for sharing your story. What a wild roller coaster ride you had us on."

I felt everyone in the room looking at me. I squeezed my knees below the table and pinched my right thigh hard, trying to hold myself together. I told the group that I had been keeping a journal and I wanted to share some of the entries. Chris made a *Star Trek* joke about Kirk's captain log. A few of us laughed uncomfortably. My hands were shaking as I held on to the white papers in front of me. My lips quivered as I began to read. I caught myself, looked up, saw everyone looking at me, and began again, determined to read in a louder voice. I read about Ming Bonavy and Pu Vaesnar, how they had left their children in Massachusetts and come to California in search of the American dream, how much they missed their children. I read about how I missed my parents, how much I wanted to understand myself, and how that was the reason I'd gone back to college.

When I was done reading, I shook in my seat. I brought my hands down underneath the table, squeezed my still-shaking knees, and didn't look up. The room was quiet. Chris didn't say anything. It was Janet who finally said something, about how she admired my courage, honesty, and emotion. Everyone else nodded.

We had three more Writers' Club meetings that semester. It was a supportive group while it lasted. Knowing we were all different, misfits in our own ways, we encouraged and supported each other, tolerating one another's idiosyncrasies. I never sensed any jealousy or competition among us. We were beginning writers, and except for Robert, we knew and accepted this fact. And so, we lifted each other up. But when Chris transferred to the University of California, Davis, in the spring semester, it was the end of the Writers' Club.

That April, the Los Angeles riots broke out. Three of the four white officers were acquitted for beating Rodney King, a Black motorist. The all-white jury couldn't reach a verdict for the fourth officer. The vicious beating was caught on video, in which King was tasered to the ground and swarmed by police officers who took turns hitting him with their batons. When King tried to get up, they kicked him back down and kept swinging. The video and verdicts were both horrifying and horrifyingly familiar. This was the America I had known and seen in Revere, when the police came to our neighborhood and didn't do anything about the crimes we reported. But when one of us was under suspicion, they came immediately and responded with excessive force. It was terrifying to see my uncle's friends or a friend's father living next door being kicked to the ground and then dragged into a patrol car. I was taught at a young age by what I witnessed and heard to be careful and not trust the police, but what I didn't know then was the depth and breadth of America's racial violence.

That April afternoon I sat on the living room couch glued to our thirty-inch color television watching the live coverage of the chaos unfold. A group of reporters were discussing the Rodney King trial and how the Black community was outraged by the verdict. The television then switched to an aerial view of the streets of Los Angeles. I saw people running wild in the streets. Cars were stopped, drivers pulled out, beaten. Stores were kicked in, broken into, looted, then set on fire. A church leader appeared on the screen pleading with people to remain calm and stay united as a community. Then something exploded. Smoke everywhere. "That's too loud to be a gun shot, folks," said one of the reporters.

"I can't believe what I'm seeing," a news anchorman told the viewers. "I feel so helpless. There's a man being beaten, and people are cheering on the attackers. I feel so sorry for this truck driver and his family. What's happening to America?" The camera zoomed in on the man lying on the pavement.

I sat on the living room couch horrified. I had never witnessed such collective violence, such public outage. I said to myself, *Los Angeles is on fire and the police are never around when you need them most!*

The report switched to Koreatown, a neighborhood in Los Angeles, with a similar scene of pandemonium: people running, looting, and setting fire to trash bins, dumpsters, and buildings. Smoke was everywhere. Korean store owners were seen standing on rooftops with riot gear and rifles. "They are protecting their businesses," a reporter said. "There's a long history of tension between Koreans and African Americans in Los Angeles. There's jealousy and mistrust between Korean store owners and Black shoppers."

I thought about my aunt and uncle. Pu Vaesnar was still sleeping in his bedroom after a night of making donuts. I called Ming Bonavy. "Are you seeing what I'm seeing? Turn on your TV, Ming."

"Don't worry, Samnang," she tried to reassure me. "It's between Black people and Korean people."

"Rioters can't tell the difference between Koreans and Cambodians. And you own a store, that's where they go. It's crazy out there, Ming. You should close your shop now!"

"But there are still donuts left."

"Forget the donuts. Your life is more important. Come home, please."

"OK, OK." She said goodbye and hung up.

I couldn't stay put. I got up, paced around the living room, sat back down on the couch, and got up again. I was worried about my aunt. I had to get out of the apartment. And this was historic. If I was to become a writer, I had to be out there, experiencing the world. Like Hemingway, an ambulance driver and correspondent during the First World War, I had to get out to where the scene was. "Los Angeles is at war," I muttered. Taking my uncle's truck, I drove to Anaheim Street, where Khmer stores, restaurants, and supermarkets lined the road. Long Beach was eerily quiet. A few people walked hurriedly on the sidewalk. The big Khmer supermarkets hired security officers, while the smaller ones closed shop. Security guards stood at entrances of supermarkets, wearing shades and carrying rifles. I parked my uncle's Toyota 4-Runner, got out, and approached one of the guards. I asked him what was going on in Long Beach.

"It's crazy out here. Black people are angry. They are angry because the police beat up Rodney King. White people should be punished, not the Koreans, not the Asians, not us Cambodians. But white people are smart. They live in suburbs with gates surrounding their communities. They have money. Those of us who don't, Blacks, Asians, Mexicans, we fight each other. We've seen enough war and killings in Cambodia. That's why we are here, to escape the violence and deaths. I hate what I'm seeing on the streets."

I spent a few more minutes with the security guard before heading back to the car. I didn't want Ming Bonavy to return home and find me missing. And the guard certainly didn't want to be bothered further with my questions. He had a job to do.

Back at the apartment, I sat down and turned on the television. Police in riot gear. Molotov cocktails flew at them, bounced on the ground, and exploded. Cars were on fire, buildings were burning. People went mad, screaming and crying, breaking windows and kicking down store doors. No one was winning. Los Angeles was burning. The poor were hurting.

Later that night, I sat behind my electric typewriter and wrote the following poem:

A City on Fire

I am at home studying with the television on.
A regularly scheduled program is interrupted by live coverage of
    mayhem.
Four white officers get a slap on their wrists for beating a black
    motorist.
The city cries for justice. The city cries for blood.

People run wild on the streets. Looting, burning, hunting.
There is an explosion, and no one seems to care.
Smoke climbs the horizon and the world is in darkness.
The city cries for justice. The city cries for blood.

A helicopter looms over the corner of Florence and Normandie.
A white driver is pulled out of his truck. And kicked and hit.
His offenders laugh, point, dance, and spit.
The city cries for justice. The city cries for blood.

But the reporters get it all wrong.
It shouldn't be about Blacks versus Asians,
African Americans against Koreans. White people are to blame.
We cry for justice. We cry for peace.

A looter beat up a Khmer woman so bad
she couldn't speak. Everything valuable in her purse is gone.
He carries her to an ambulance, but the woman couldn't speak.
I cry and cry. This is all wrong. This is all wrong.

Another Beginning

I had been at Long Beach City College for four years when I was told by an advisor that I had too many credits and that I should apply for an Associate of Arts Degree and transfer to a four-year college or university. I considered my options: the California State University or the University of California schools. With the meager income I earned at the maintenance company, I didn't think I could afford the tuition of a U.C. school. The state university was the only option. So, with the help of a staff person in the Advising Office, I filled out the transfer form, signed it, put it in an envelope, and dropped it in the mailbox.

Near the end of that summer, I had another panic attack. As was always the case for me, every new path came with self-doubt and anxiety. I'd done just fine at city college: a few Bs and As in my English classes. I wasn't a terrible student, but neither was I an exceptional student. To begin with, I wasn't interested in grades. All I wanted was an opportunity to learn, to think about the world, and to apply what I had learned to my life. But city college said I had to leave. I was throwing money away taking classes that didn't count toward anything. I would transfer to a four-year university in the fall. *Me at a university? That is something that smart, rich people do. Not this refugee kid who is still trying to figure things out.*

I was afraid that I wouldn't fit in, afraid of how other English majors might see me, afraid that I didn't have a certain understanding and knowledge of literature privy only to those in the know. With my skin color and Cambodian name, I didn't look or sound like an English major or what I imagined an English major should look and sound like. To prepare myself, I did what I had done in the past: I went to the library and borrowed poetry and short story anthologies. I began photocopying poems and stories and placed them in a binder I titled "Poems and Stories to Live By." I wanted to expand my understanding of literature and have more experience reading and thinking about books. I wanted to be ready for what was to come at the university.

Studying the university catalogue, I didn't know what Comparative Literature was but I found the course name intriguing. It sounded simple enough: one compares literature, like what one does when writing comparative essays, which I had done for classes at city college. The intriguing part had to do with the courses being offered by a department separated from the English Department. It sounded more global and inclusive. Since its focus was on international contexts and global perspectives in literature, I naively thought I wouldn't have to master grammar and grasp the English language with precision. And since Comparative Literature was worldly and I was part of the world, I thought I would have a better chance finding a home in this discipline. I thus enrolled in a couple of classes that the Comparative Literature Department offered that semester.

I took an immediate liking to Professor Schwartz. To me, she was the underdog, the outsider, the stranger—right up my alley. She was a woman in academia. She was Jewish. She was passionate about the books she taught, and she spoke as if she were one of us, because she was. She'd grown up in nearby Echo Park, went to high school there, and still had family there. She became an inspiration for me, as Br_ndon had. If she'd made it, maybe I could too.

The stuff we read in Professor Schwartz's classes fell under a category of literature called "emerging literature." This was a new concept to me. Sitting on her desk, back turned to the blackboard, Professor Schwartz told us that this was literature as political protest. It was writing by and about those on the literary and cultural margins. These texts operated against the reading tradition of Aristotelian identification, the very foundation of Western aesthetics. We were reading works outside the literary canon and studying writers and filmmakers in Latin America, Africa, and the Middle East. I didn't understand most of the reading assignments. I stayed up all night reading and thinking about writings that were unfamiliar, foreign to me. It seemed as though the literary world I once knew and loved had imploded. I found myself feeling anxious and uncertain, infected by this newness, this strangeness. But I was also excited by it.

Once I stayed after class and told Professor Schwartz about my recent literary "infection." She smiled, "I knew you would be receptive to this kind of literature, Samnang. America needs someone like you, with your history, experience, and perspective. It needs to be seen from the outside and reinvent itself to accommodate differences." She then told me to follow her. We walked past the campus food court, went inside the Humanities building, and took the elevator up several floors, where she introduced me to the Comparative Literature faculty. I had never felt this welcomed before but, being so nervous, I couldn't listen to what the professors were saying to me, let alone respond to their kind greetings. I had always imagined professors to be of a different species altogether. They seemed to me like demi-gods. There was an air of importance in the way they sat behind their computers or talked busily on the phone. It must be the best job in the world: teaching, reading, and writing about literature. But I noticed that the faculty were mostly white males in their late fifties and sixties. There were three women professors and one Black professor, a man. I counted each one of them in my head when I was introduced by Professor Schwartz.

I wondered if there were other Asian American professors like Br_ndon Lieu in academia. What about Cambodian American professors? Not the Cambodian professors who left Cambodia to study in the U.S. or France before the Khmer Rouge takeover because they were rich and had connections. No, I was thinking about those who were child survivors of the Cambodian genocide, who had lived through refugee camps in Thailand and faced discrimination growing up in America, yet they still made it.

It was a late Saturday evening, and I was in bed struggling to get through Thomas Mann's *Doctor Faustus*. I put down the book and rested my head on my arm listening to the traffic outside our apartment complex. Some tenants were still awake. Babies were crying. Someone was singing Khmer karaoke in the apartment below us. I didn't know the apartment complex's official name. I told friends that I lived in "that green apartment on Cherry Avenue." In the Khmer community, it was known as the "Khmer Village on Cherry" since most of the tenants were Cambodian refugees. Like our family, they were farmers back in the old country, and some were even from the Battambang province. And like any good village, there were lok-kru living in the apartment complex. In fact, we had two lok-kru competing with one another for the business of local tenants and other Cambodians in the area. They conducted exorcisms, performed blessing rituals to protect clients from evil spirits, and led ceremonies at funerals and weddings. They concocted love potions for wives who were afraid that their husbands would leave them for someone younger and more beautiful. Lok-kru were known to communicate with the spirit world. Lok-Yeay went to them to seek news of her eldest son, Oum Piseth. Ming Bonavy went to the lok-kru to help with her donut business. She brought plates of fruits and money and a bottle of Hennessy. The lok-kru lit incense and prayed, asking the spirits for help to bring in more customers for my aunt and uncle.

There were also two video stores in this Khmer Village in north Long Beach. One store was in an apartment on one side of the building complex and the other in another apartment on the other side. These stores carried bootleg VHS tapes of Thai, Chinese, Indian, and Khmer movies, as well as cheap candy bars, homemade Khmer beef jerky, and homemade Khmer desserts. The videos were popular among the older Khmers as these movies helped them get their minds off the reality of living in a foreign country, the difficulty of speaking English and understanding American culture, the arguments they had with their children and grandchildren about maintaining Khmer culture and customs, and the heartache of seeing their young ones turn to gang violence and drugs.

Every evening, these older Khmer women went from one video store to the other asking whether the latest video in a popular series had arrived. They smelled of tiger balm and their foreheads had red circles on them from being rubbed with coins. They wore faded sarongs and slippers as they knocked on an apartment door. They asked the store owner, "Me-teow (Little One), has part 26 of *Love Never Dies* arrived yet?"

"Not yet, Oum. They should be here by tomorrow. Come by in the morning and I'll have a copy for you."

"Orkoeun (*thank you*), Me-teow." They walked away slowly, their heads full of worries about their children and grandchildren.

I kept thinking about what Professor Schwartz had said about emerging literature, and I thought about my neighbors, those Khmer people living in this village in north Long Beach. Their stories were absent in the novels, plays, and poems I studied in class. I needed to write about them, to share their stories with the world. I wanted American literature to be *infected* by our Cambodian American presence. We had been here in America for some time now and the reasons we were here primarily had to do with the war in Việt Nam and the American bombings of the Cambodian countryside. Oh, how I ached for my people, for our voices to be heard. I needed to study harder, absorb the art of storytelling, so I could tell our stories.

I tossed and turned with these thoughts running in my head. I was giving up on Thomas Mann and his high European culture. His sentences were too long, and the atmosphere was thick, dense. It was three in the morning, and I found myself reading the same sentence over and over again. I yawned and put the heavy book down on the floor. I stared at the ceiling. All was quiet, finally, at the green apartment complex. Even the traffic had died down. I was too comfortable to get up from bed to turn off the light. I closed my eyes and fell asleep with the light still blazing.

A Dream on Fire

Coming back from working the graveyard shift at the cleaning company, I needed food more than sleep. I fried a couple of eggs and placed them over a dish of steamed rice, the yolks warm and gooey. I splashed soy sauce and sriracha over the eggs and rice and headed to the living room for the TV. Nothing interesting was on, just daily soap operas and *The Jerry Springer Show*. It didn't matter. I was starving.

Minutes later, Ming Bonavy came out of her room. Her eyes were red, her face ashen, her hair a mess. It was ten thirty in the morning. *Shouldn't she be at the donut shop?*

I stopped shoveling rice and fried eggs into my mouth, looked up, and asked, "What happened to you?"

"I was robbed this morning." She started to cry. "Please don't tell Lok-Yeay. I don't want her to find out. You know how she is. She worries too much already. I don't want her to worry about me. Keep this quiet, OK?"

I turned off the TV. "Where's Pu Vaesnar?"

"He's in the bedroom. He doesn't know what to do."

"Did the police come?"

"You know how the police are. They came, but it was too late to do anything by then."

I put the spoon down and said to her, "Please tell me what happened."

In between sobs she said, "Two Black women came to the shop. They ordered donuts and coffee. When my regular customers left, one of them came up to the counter and pointed a gun at my head. The other went outside to be a lookout. I thought I would never see my children again. The gun was pointed right here—at my temple, Samnang. Do you understand?"

I couldn't imagine what she had gone through in that moment. I nodded in acquiescence of my own ignorance and helplessness.

Ming Bonavy continued, "She yelled, 'Give me all your money! Give me all your money!' When I opened the register and gave her the money, she yelled at me again, 'Where do you keep the rest of the money? Give it to me now, make it quick!' I opened the refrigerator and handed her the money I keep for change. Then she left. My Mexican customers came inside the store and called the police."

Ming Bonavy collapsed on the couch and sobbed. I'd never felt this helpless before. I said, "Don't worry, Ming. They will be captured by the police. I'm glad you are safe. Everything will be OK."

Ming Bonavy went back to her room and gently closed the door.

The donut shop was closed for several days. Ming Bonavy couldn't leave the apartment. Every time she reached the door, her body shook and she broke down crying. Pu Vaesnar carried her to their bedroom.

I heard Pu Vaesnar say to his wife, "Neang, don't cry. It's all right. Don't cry, Neang."

"I miss my children. I miss them so much. I want to go back home. I want to go back to Massachusetts, Bong. I want to go back home and see my kids."

When Lok-Yeay came back from one of the video stores in the apartment complex, she asked Pu Vaesnar and me what was going on and we told her that Ming Bonavy wasn't feeling well. Lok-Yeay looked sad and worried, but she didn't press the issue further. In the back of my mind, I knew that Lok-Yeay realized something terrible had happened to her youngest daughter but she, like the rest of us, felt helpless to do anything. So she accepted what we told her.

I'd never thought something like this could happen to us when we first moved to California seven years ago. I remembered all of us in Pu Vaesnar's 4-Runner crossing the Nevada desert and listening to Khmer songs from the cassette deck. It was the last stretch before we reached California, and my aunt was talking excitedly about the donut shop, how she would strike it rich and send her children to college, then take a fancy airplane ride back to Massachusetts in style. We were all smiling, and I was happy to leave Massachusetts and start anew in this land of donut dreams.

Still feeling helpless, I took my uncle's truck and drove downtown. I stopped at a video store and picked up *Men in Black*, thinking that the comedy would help cheer my aunt up. In the living room, I put the tape into the VHS player. I wanted to make sure that the movie was good and that it would take her mind off what had happened to her. Will Smith was funny as always, and the movie was slick, cool, and fun.

The next morning, I went to Ming Bonavy and Pu Vaesnar's room and told my aunt to be strong. She needed to take steps, no matter how trivial they seemed, to regain a sense of normalcy. "This is no good, staying in your room all day and all night," I said as if I knew what I was talking about. I then told her that I had rented a good comedy that was guaranteed to make her laugh and feel better.

"It's a funny movie, I promise. You will laugh until Lok-Yeay comes in and asks what's the matter with you."

I put the tape into the VCR player, pushed the play button, and turned on the television.

The opening credits rolled. She sat on the sofa surrounded by pillows. As soon as she saw Will Smith's face, she hid under the blanket, sobbing and whimpering.

"It's them! It's them, again. They're all trying to get me. Help me, help me, somebody, help me."

"Ming! Ming! That's Will Smith. He's an actor in a movie. Just because he's Black doesn't mean he's going to hurt you. He has nothing to do with the two people who robbed you," I was upset and tried to reason with her.

"Go away, Samnang." Ming Bonavy sobbed under the blanket. "Please go away."

Pu Vaesnar yelled at me to turn off the TV and throw the damn tape away.

The next day two detectives visited our apartment. They informed Pu Vaesnar that the suspects were in custody and that they needed Ming Bonavy to confirm that the suspects were indeed the two individuals who had committed the robbery. Pu Vaesnar went to their bedroom and, holding his wife's hand, brought Ming Bonavy out. As soon as she saw that one of the detectives was a Black woman, she cried, "It's them. They're here to finish the job! Why are you all doing this to me? Somebody, please help me. Somebody, please." She ran back to her bedroom and slammed the door.

I walked over to their bedroom and stood outside the door. "They're not here to get you, Ming. In fact, they're the good guys. They caught the people who did this to you and now they need your help to put them away," I explained calmly to my aunt. "You have to be strong and help them so that they can help you get through this. Others will benefit from what you do."

Ming Bonavy screamed from her room, "No, no. I won't help them. They're lying to all of you. They're all here to get me. Why doesn't anyone listen to me? Help me, somebody. Please help me."

The other detective, a bulky white man with a mustache, asked if they could come back at another time. I asked if they needed Ming Bonavy's testimony to keep the suspects in custody. He told me, "It's not necessary. Her customers' testimonies will suffice. And we found illegal drugs in the suspects' car."

I turned to his partner, "I feel really awful about what my aunt said. I'm so sorry."

She said, "Please know I take no offense. What your aunt is experiencing is common after what she's been through. Unfortunately, I've seen it too many times. Here's a card of a psychiatrist who specializes in PTSD."

I took the card and, again, apologized for my aunt's actions. I then thanked the two detectives and wished them a good afternoon.

I went back into the apartment and all I heard coming from Ming Bonavy's bedroom was her repeating, "I want to go home and be with my children. I don't want to be in California anymore.

I want to go back to Massachusetts and be with my kids. Please, I need to see my boy and girl."

I was reminded of the time my aunt asked me to help her write a Christmas letter to her two children back in Massachusetts. She'd said, "I talk, you write, OK?"

I'd nodded.

Then she'd told me, "Write everything down, OK?"

"OK, I will." And I had. I still remembered the letter:

To my dear children:

Hi, guys! How are you over there? I miss you all—in my head, in my heart, in my soul—I miss you very, very much. Every day, my mind is with you guys. And every night, you guys become so real that I wake up crying. Your dad, annoyed by my crying, he asks me with his sleepy eyes about this crying thing. "What's the matter?" he asks. And I, pretending to smile, say to him that the night is just too cold. He then goes back to sleep.

"Oh, my dear children, you know how things are! I don't have anything to give you for Christmas, and that's why I let your dad and Grandma go visit you guys and the family over there. It is all I can do—all that I can give— for now. This is my only present. And I work hard for you guys. Please, remember Mommy. Remember that I love you guys, always.

Let me tell you one thing before I go: Education is the key to freedom. Freedom means you have opportunities, more choices, in this world. So, study hard and don't be imprisoned by ignorance, like Mommy stuck here in this donut shop. Please also remember this ancient Cambodian saying: No one can take away your knowledge. This means that no knives, no guns, can take away what you have already learned, what you have already put inside of you. Please, remember me, Mommy loves you and remember what I just told you. It is important, and I tell you this because I love you. Keep good work at your study. My darling sweethearts, Mommy have to go now. Mommy wishes you guys a Merry Christmas and a Happy New Year!

Love You So Much,

Your Mommy

P.S. Please be kind to all your oum over there. They are my brothers and sisters; love them like you love your Dad and Mommy.

A New Family

The rent was affordable: two hundred dollars a month. I had my own bedroom but had to share the kitchen and bathroom with a family of four. The landlord and his family lived in the front part of the duplex; I was going to move into a room in the back of the duplex with another Cambodian family. I scanned the neighborhood: trash littered the street and sidewalk. I could hear children playing but I couldn't see them. Some of the walls and driveways were tagged with gang signs. "The neighborhood is getting better," the landlord reassured me. "Now, there are police everywhere. Don't worry about your car. Since I live in the front part of the house, I will keep an eye on it. We Khmers take care of each other."

After the robbery, Lok-Yeay, Ming Bonavy, and Pu Vaesnar decided it was best to move back to Massachusetts. A couple of weeks before Lok-Yeay and Ming Bonavy flew back to Boston, Pu Vaesnar drove his truck back across the States. From Long Beach, California, to Malden, Massachusetts, it took him four days and three nights. When he reached Malden, he had an accident not far from the house. He veered off the road and hit the guardrail. Once home, he collapsed on the couch in the living room and slept for two days and two nights straight.

I couldn't go with them, as I needed to complete my studies at Long Beach State. Lok-Yeay said she wouldn't leave until she found a good place for me. She talked to her friends at the Khmer temple on Willow Street, and one of them recommended this place near Orange and Pacific Coast Highway. Lok-Yeay and I drove over to her friend's place, a few houses down the block from the house that we were interested in. The friend said, "It's better than before. Now, the police are everywhere. Besides, he'll be living with a Khmer family. They will take care of him." Then she looked at me and said, "Koan, if you run into any problems, come to me. I'll take care of you like you were my own grandson."

I nodded, clasped my hands together, and said, "Orkoeun, Yeay."

On our way back home, I said to my grandmother, "Really, it's a good place to start. For one thing, the rent is only two hundred dollars a month. I certainly can afford that. Don't worry, Lok-Yeay. I know how to take care of myself. Everything will be fine. I promise I will call every weekend."

I dropped Lok-Yeay and Ming Bonavy off at the airport at five in the morning. I watched them disappear slowly into the boarding gate. Ming Bonavy held Lok-Yeay's hand. I sat in the airport lobby for a while, thinking about my new life.

I was alone for the first time in my life, without my family. I was scared. I worked three days a week at the maintenance company. As long as I held onto that job, I would not be living on the street. I just needed to finish college and then I could decide what to do next: stay in California or return to Massachusetts to be with Lok-Yeay.

I drove back from the airport and had pancakes and sausage links at Denny's on Long Beach Boulevard. The waitress kept coming over to refill my coffee cup and ask if I was OK. I said I was fine and looked away, out the window. Traffic was unusually light for morning rush hour. I was in no hurry to get back to my new home.

The family that I lived with had two children: ten-year-old Sandra and eight-year-old Billy. Sandra kept to herself most of the time. She knew about her parents' situation. In the bedroom she shared with her brother, she sat on top of their bunk bed and stared at the television all day. Billy, her young brother, couldn't sit still. He jumped, screamed, and yelled, while Sandra sat motionless, lost to the bright screen.

Their father played soccer for a Cambodian team in Southern California. His team competed at the local and state levels with other Cambodian teams. He was a short, dark, and fit man. He was also a singer. When his team won a match, he had his soccer buddies over for dinner. They drank, got wasted, and sang karaoke all night. It didn't bother him that my bedroom was next to the living room where these parties took place. Women often showed up at these parties. Sandra's and Billy's parents argued about one of the women.

"I saw the way you two looked at each other. Do you think I'm blind?" the wife asked her husband the next morning.

"She's a friend of Tevy's, that's all. She likes soccer."

"Do you think I'm stupid? You humiliated me in front of your friends last night and now you're humiliating me with your lies." The wife was a tall and slender woman, standing an inch or two above her husband.

"If you don't believe me, I'm leaving." He went to the TV stand and grabbed the car keys.

"Leave! Go to her. You were going to do that anyway."

I heard the back door slam, then the engine revving. The father would be gone for a couple days, weeks even. I turned on my TV to tune out the silence in the house.

Coming back from class one evening, I heard the mother talking to someone on the phone. She was crying. She came out of her room afterward, looking embarrassed and apologetic. I tried to avoid catching her tear-stained gaze as we exchanged pleasantries. I went to my room, closed the door, and tried to forget what I heard and saw in that house.

In the end, the children were the victims in all of it. Billy cried for his father, then changed his mind and cursed him. Perched on the bed, Sandra silently watched television all day, as if nothing mattered. I couldn't stand seeing how these children suffered and knowing that the adults were responsible for such misery. Their parents were about fifteen years older than me but they behaved as if they were college students. They worked during the week and partied on the weekend, as if they were trying to make up for the time they'd lost living under the Khmer Rouge and in the Thai refugee camps. I hated the recklessness with which they led their lives; I did what I could to avoid my new home. I stayed on campus all day most days, eating lunch at the university food court. After evening classes, I stopped by 7-Eleven and had a couple of hot dogs, a bag of Doritos, and a large Coke for dinner. I'd finally return to my new home only to crash on the mattress. I couldn't study there, especially on weekends, because there was always noise—cartoon sounds coming from the television shows that Sandra watched, singing and laughing coming from the karaoke parties, and the yelling, crying, and breaking of dishes from the parents on the mornings after.

One afternoon, the landlord saw me and said, "Son, your grandmother has been trying to get a hold of you. Call her when you're not studying. She's worried sick about you."

I thanked him, called my family's home in Malden that evening, and asked for Lok-Yeay. She sounded tired over the phone. "Have you eaten rice yet?" she asked. That was the Cambodian way of saying "I love you."

"I have, Lok-Yeay."

"How is school?"

"It's all good, Lok-Yeay. I like the books I'm reading and I feel good about my own writing."

"How are the people you're living with?"

"They are fine."

"Remember: never stay alone with the wife or the daughter."

"Lok-Yeay!"

"It's their word against yours. You have to be careful."

"OK, OK, Lok-Yeay. I know," I said. "How are Ming Bonavy and Pu Vaesnar?"

"Your aunt is with her children. Pu Vaesnar is visiting friends in Lowell."

I thanked Lok-Yeay, said goodbye, and hung up the phone. It was one of the loneliest and most miserable periods in my life. I started looking for another apartment as soon as I could afford to.

Why Write?

In those days, I kept a journal where I wrote songs, poems, and short stories. But after a while, private writing was not enough. I wanted others to read my words, to know where I came from and how I came to be. I wanted to be understood. I enrolled in my first creative writing class at the university: a poetry workshop.

The professor was none other than William Mahoney, who'd met Bukowski in the 1970s, drank with him, and even invited him to read at the university. Professor Mahoney was encyclopedic in his knowledge of Western literature, co-authoring scholarly books on Shakespeare, Dante, and Hemingway. He had also edited anthologies of contemporary Southern California poetry, and he regularly gave readings and workshops all over the States and in Europe. He was the kind of professor whose classes always had wait lists. Undergraduate students clamored to work with him on independent study projects and MFA students prayed that he would serve on their thesis committees. He was kind and generous with his time and energy, and supportive of his students' work.

But on that first day of class I almost didn't recognize William Mahoney, the writer and poet whose books I had read when I was a student at city college. On his book covers, Mahoney had a solid beer belly yet was tough looking, the kind of guy you wouldn't want to bump into in a dark alley late at night. But the Mahoney sitting behind a desk in that classroom was scruffy, thin, and frail, so slight that if the Santa Ana winds were to knock him off his feet, he would have a hard time getting up. It wouldn't surprise us if Professor Mahoney, with his unusually casual attire, wind-swept hair, and graying beard, were to be mistaken for an unhoused person by campus security. All of this is to say, he was one cool dude.

That first day, he had on a faded blue T-shirt, denim jeans with holes in them, and sandals. He started the class by asking, "What's happening?" Someone said they were excited about the new Quentin Tarantino film, which led Mahoney to talk about film and television. He told us that the other night he'd watched an episode of *South Park* with his wife and kids, then cracked a joke or two before praising the show for its searing commentary on American culture and religion. Somehow he was able to steer the conversation from Tarantino and *South Park* to contemporary poetry. Mahoney gave us a preview of the poetry books and chapbooks we would be reading that semester. It seemed like he knew all the poets on his syllabus personally. Before we left, Mahoney reminded us "to read, read, read and to write, write, write. Always carry a dictionary with you to expand your vocabulary." He was a great believer in the power of exact words.

Then it was our turn to introduce ourselves. I was nervous, of course, and as usual, most of my classmates were white. In this workshop, however, there were two other students of color, and it felt good to know that I was not the only non-white student interested in poetry. Mahoney's jokes and laid-back teaching style made it easier to forget my discomfort. He was friendly and informal, as well as knowledgeable about both traditional and contemporary poetry. He didn't take himself too seriously, much like the persona I had encountered in his poems and stories. Like my other literary heroes, he found beauty in the ordinariness of life and celebrated it in his writing. With clarity, honesty, and self-deprecating humor, he wrote about his relationships with his wife and girlfriends, his love for his children; about Los Angeles, Long Beach, and Seal Beach; about his parents and grandparents, aunts and uncles; about teaching and drinking, drinking and teaching.

We were required to make copies of our formal and free-verse poems to be workshopped in class. Everyone was kind and helpful to one another. I did, however, detect an air of smugness from some classmates. Unlike the folks in the Writers' Club, some of these students thought they were the shit: cool, special, chosen to be writers and artists. They flaunted their coolness in the way they dressed and styled their hair, in the way they smoked cigarettes moodily outside the classroom and sneered at the rest of us. I discovered later that some of them were fine writers, with poems that were impressive, publishable, but I never understood why they had to be so full of themselves.

I particularly admired the writing of a red-haired student named Steve. He looked like Thom Yorke of Radiohead, except that Steve was taller and a bit more handsome, his eyes and mouth more symmetrical than Yorke's. Steve's writing style was different from mine. His tight control of language contrasted with my own "emotional" style. The first time I read a poem in class, it was my usual nerve-racking nightmarish experience: I didn't sleep much the night before. My body trembled, my hands shook as I held the poem to read. Halfway through the poem, I lost my voice and could no longer read. I looked up at Mahoney, who picked up right where I'd left off and finished reading the poem. A long and uncomfortable silence followed. Then Mahoney commented on the imagery and the voice of the poem, how they were personal and intimate. Other students followed Mahoney's cues and shared their feedback. I sat quietly clutching the bottom of my chair. Steve's style, on the other hand, was clear and distant, only a hint of emotion at the surface. And when he read, his voice was cool and collected. There was confidence in his voice. He was in control.

Later in the semester, I found the courage to walk up to Steve at the coffee shop on campus. He and his friends—mostly attractive alternative girls—were sitting around a table.

"Hi, Steve. I don't know if you remember me, but I'm in Mahoney's class with you. Anyway, I just wanted to say that I really like your poems."

"Thanks, man. I dig your stuff too. It's pretty intense, really personal."

"Thanks." After an awkward silence, his friends turned to each other and began chatting again. Then I said, "Listen, I was wondering about something. Why do you write? I mean, what makes you write? Is it something that tells you that if you don't write, you'll go crazy? You know what I mean?"

"Nah, man. I'm not into that Romantic notion of writing. It's nothing like that," Steve smiled. "It's entertainment for me. It's fun shit, you know. I write because it's fun."

I didn't know what else to say to Steve. "Alright man, I gotta go. It's nice talking to you, Steve. See you in class."

"OK, man. See you later."

The idea blew me away: writing for entertainment. I wouldn't discover the joy of writing until I wrote my third book of poetry some thirty years later, after my wife had given birth to our daughter. I wrote poems that only a father could. My subject matter was joyful, putting down exact words in their right order was pure fun. It felt great. But back then, in that workshop, I felt that I had to write. There was no other way. If I didn't write, I would fall into deep depression, possibly try to kill myself again. The truth was: writing didn't solve anything. The demons would be conjured and confronted, but there was no actual triumph. They would retreat into the recess of my subconscious, plotting to come out again, and they would, with a vengeance. Of course, I felt a little better after writing about my demons, but total exorcism was never attained from writing. Yet, like breathing, I had to write. For me, writing was survival.

Writing was ranked way up there among my hierarchy of needs—food, sleep, and writing. I looked at the MFA students in Mahoney's poetry workshop and wondered if they had the same need as I did when it came to writing. Did they lie awake at night, unable to sleep until they put down their thoughts and feelings on a piece of paper? Did they feel the moon rising inside them, hear the radio crackling, and see the cockroaches crawling on the wall? When they completed their MFA requirements and mailed out their manuscripts to publishers, did they stay up all night and hear the same cockroaches scurrying and feel the wind howling outside their window? Did the moon serve as witness to their evening ritual of hammering the keyboard and transferring heart and soul onto the page? After graduation, would they still write?

By the end of my third year at Long Beach State, I had made a small group of friends. We had taken comparative literature classes together and had seen each other at various campus readings. At a poetry reading organized by William Mahoney, a student named Cal Limon came up to me afterward and asked about the poets and writers I admired. I learned that he loved Bukowski, Carver, and Dostoevsky as much as I did; we also bonded over British bands like The Smiths, Joy Division, The Jam, and The Cure.

Music and literature were our religion then. We believed in their power to change us and the world we lived in. Most of all, we both wanted to be poets. And Cal lived the writer's hard life. He was married to an older woman with a child from another marriage; he drank and smoked as if those activities were akin to breathing. Cal also had a friend named Josh Ratner, a bookish kid who played guitar in a bubblegum shoegaze band and whom I knew from a class on literature and the avant-garde that we'd both taken with Professor Schwartz a semester earlier. Cal loved teasing Josh and his girlfriend, Ellie Hartman. They were cute together, Josh and Ellie, and they dreamed of becoming an academic power couple some-day. As soon as Cal saw Josh and Ellie walking over to us at the food court, Cal said to me, "Oh, here come Jean-Paul Sartre and Simone de Beauvoir."

Then there was Elizabeth Harmon. She and I were similar: awkward, shy, reserved. She had also had a difficult past, and that made me feel comfortable with her. We hung out, went to the movies, talked about music, books, and films. We were good friends. And there was Luna, the Cure fan. She had a poster of Robert Smith in her dorm room. She also knew The Smiths' lyrics by heart. We all did. We were comparative literature majors, and we were young, and we felt that what the world needed was the healing and transformative power of the arts and humanities. And I was this Asian kid and they were all white, but somehow that didn't matter to me like it had before. I wasn't as conscious of being different. In our own ways, we were all outsiders, and our shared love of literature, music, and the arts along with our belief in their unmistakable power to nurture and transform lives brought us together.

I was at home with friends at last.

Dear Mr. Sok

In my last year at Long Beach State, I was having so much fun with friends that I didn't want it to be over, but I knew it had to end. I feared what the future held for me after graduation. I thought about all of this and more while sitting in the tiny studio apartment that I'd recently moved into. Literature had played a significant part in the formation of my present self. It was through literature that I had experienced an intellectual, emotional, and spiritual rebirth. Books had become surrogate parents to me. They'd nourished me with their insights and wisdom. And they'd taught me about the world and my place in it, and even more importantly, how I could reimagine myself through the magic of words. That was the power of literature: to imagine things otherwise, to dream of other realities, to believe in other possibilities, to have faith in the elastic and resilient nature of the self.

Grateful for this chance at a new beginning, I knew I wanted to give the gift of literature to other young Khmer who found themselves in the same American lot that I'd found myself in some years ago. I wanted to give them what was given to me: the pain and pleasure of reading and writing, of discovering and reinventing the self and the world. It hadn't been easy for me to learn about the world, about its beauty and ugliness, and to be held accountable after such an awakening. It was a mixed bag, a double-edged sword, but it was worth it to feel the words entering my bloodstream—infecting me, awakening me to the realities of the world and its imagined possibilities. I'd never felt more alive and hopeful than I did when I first found myself in literature, and I wanted to provide that experience to young Khmer American students in search of purpose and guidance.

For these reasons, I wanted to continue with my education. I wanted to dive deep into the educational system, shake it up, turn it upside down, make something new and better, something more open and inclusive. But where would I go? Which graduate program would I apply to? Although I loved creative writing, I didn't want to get an MFA because I was afraid that I wouldn't be able to get a job after graduation. I didn't want to play the role of a starving artist. As a child I'd known hunger under Pol Pot's regime and in the refugee camps in Thailand. The starving artist was not a romantic notion to me. I considered graduate studies in literature and imagined myself returning to teach at a city college, either somewhere in California or back in Massachusetts, where I could be close to Lok-Yeay. I would introduce literature to Cambodian American students and show them its power. I would do what Br_ndon Lieu had done for me: inspire students, get them to see themselves and their possibilities in literature. As a scholar, I would translate Cambodian stories and novels, poems and plays, anything I could get my hands on. After earning tenure, I would go on to write my own poems, stories, and novels. Ultimately, I wanted my Khmer American students to be proud of their culture and heritage, and to know that if they wanted to pursue the life of an artist or scholar, then they could.

Around this time, I was hanging out with Rich Watanabe, a Hawaiian of mixed race. His father was Japanese, and his mother was a blonde surfer girl from California. I met Rich in a literary theory class taught by Professor Schwartz during my junior year at Long Beach State. Rich was ambitious. He planned to get a doctorate from Berkeley and teach at one of the Ivies on the East Coast. He wanted to develop a new theory, one that would deconstruct all other theories and become the theory of all theories that every graduate student of literature is required to read. He wanted to be the next Derrida. If not Derrida, then the next Paul de Man, without the antisemitism. He and I were having dinner at a local diner one summer evening when the subject of graduate school came up.

"Dude, you gotta apply. We gotta deconstruct the very notion of an education," Rich said excitedly as he cut into his medium-rare steak. He continued, "You and I know that the system was created and maintained by those in power, and those in power are comprised mainly of the white majority. We have to go deep into the structure of academia and rebuild the foundation to include our voices and stories."

I knew Rich was right. I had to learn the master's language before I could do anything useful toward reimagining it. I said, "Yeah, it's more effective to fight from the inside than from the outside."

"You're damned right, brother. So you gotta go to grad school."

But the idea of graduate school frightened me. To me, graduate school conjured up images of the rich and privileged, mostly white sons and daughters of foreign diplomats, exiled scholars and doctors. It was not for me: a Cambodian American, a refugee, a boy orphaned at an early age who had crossed the jungle with his Lok-Pu, Lok-Ming, Lok-Oum, and Lok-Yeay to escape the Khmer Rouge, a boy from some unknown village in Battambang.

"I don't know, Rich. It sounds crazy. I don't think I could even get in."

"Samnang, you'll never know unless you apply."

It was hard to argue with that logic.

"But you've seen me in class. I'm quiet, awkward, afraid to speak up. I have a panic attack every time the professor makes eye contact with me. I don't know how I'd fit into a PhD program." I wanted to say more to Rich, about how having gone through the public school system had left me feeling insecure, and that it was hard to shake off the shackles of my past. Would I know how to talk, dress, conduct myself at conferences and meetings, and worst of all, those dreaded department parties? Would I feel alienated from the other graduate students? Would my childhood scars be reopened, my differences exacerbated once again?

"Dude, it doesn't matter. Your problem is that you think too much. Just do it."

Again, he had a point. I picked up a french fry and tossed it into my mouth.

Looking back at my early life in America, I didn't have role models whom I could look up to and be proud of for being Cambodian. I never saw or heard about Khmer teachers, doctors, politicians, journalists, movie stars, poets, and writers. This absence had a detrimental effect on my young psyche. In a sea of whiteness, I grew ashamed of my Khmer self. And when I looked to my uncles and aunts for help, they were struggling too. This was one problem with migration and the refugee experience: entire families were emotionally scarred by the shame of seeking refuge in a country not their own. We were the walking dead. And if, like us, these refugee families came from that part of the world where American lives had been lost in a war, and if these refugee families were racially and ethnically different from the majority of Americans, then the odds were stacked against them and their children.

I didn't want other children growing up with that particular psychic scar, the one where they felt different and inferior, where they were told that they could only play a minor role on the white world's stage. I wanted to change the stage itself. Despite my shyness, I wanted to be someone who was visible in the public realm, someone young Cambodian Americans could look up to and feel proud of. In my mind, then, visibility became synonymous with power: the power to effect change and infect those around me, the power to reshape the world and make it mine. I made up my mind to apply to graduate school.

Seeing how lost I was in my own thoughts, Rich said, "You better sign up for the GRE next month, Samnang. Don't think about the future. That will only make you anxious. Focus on what you can do right now."

"Yeah, you're right." I smiled.

"Of course, I'm right," Rich chuckled. "Hey, are you going to eat the rest of those fries?"

The summer before my final year at the university, I had a recurring dream of a man riding on his horse toward a village, a dream that I'd first had eight years earlier when I discovered the work of Charles Bukowski at the public library. In this new iteration of the dream, the man still wore a golden crown, as if he was royalty, and he was riding on his white horse, now adorned with gold and silver. The villagers came out of their stilt homes, parents holding their children's hands, looking curiously at the stranger on his white horse. The stranger rode by them, his horse neighing and trotting toward me. The sun's glare made it difficult for me to see the rider's face. But this time, instead of waking up, I stayed in the dream. The man stopped in front of me, and I saw his face: his face was mine. The stranger who was me smiled; he was radiating confidence and happiness. Then he rode past me on his white horse and the villagers came to him, petting the horse and cheering him on, as if he were some kind of a hero.

I signed up for the GRE at the beginning of the fall semester and took it during midterms. Having never learned how to prepare for the entrance exam and not knowing that there were classes you could take and books you could purchase to help you prepare, I bombed. But a month later, I retook the GRE. Again, I did poorly on it. Still, I persisted. I wrote my statement of purpose and bared my soul to these strangers on the graduate school admissions committees, telling them why I wanted to attend graduate school, how I felt this obligation, this duty to myself, to my family, to my mother who'd passed away when I was too young to remember, to my father who'd taken me to that shop with the television and the rainbow ice cream, to those Khmers who lost their lives under the Khmer Rouge regime, to those Khmers who had experienced the shock of arrival and those Khmers who saw their children grow up to be strangers to the Cambodian culture and language. To those Khmer American children who were balancing on their shoulders the Cambodian world of their parents and the American world of their peers. Oh, how I loved them all, my Khmer people—especially my grandmother, Lok-Yeay, who had carried me on her back as she trekked through jungles and miraculously avoided landmines in order to get to that first refugee camp on the Thai side of the border. I had a duty to them all, because I was a part of them and they were a part of me. There was no other way of explaining it. I had to go to graduate school and make something of my life, something that would be worthy of all that suffering.

I mailed out my applications. By early April, I'd received my fair share of rejection letters from the schools I had applied to in December of the previous year. Then, in mid-April, I received a letter from the Department of Comparative Literature at a state university in Pennsylvania:

> *Dear Mr. Sok*:
>
> *We are pleased to inform you that you have been accepted into the MA/PhD track in the Department of Comparative Literature . . . Enclosed in the envelope you will find . . .*

I picked up the phone and called Lok-Yeay to tell her that I was coming home.

PART IV

Koan Khmer

Letter from Koan Khmer

Lok-Yeay was in her seventies by the time I returned to the East Coast after graduating from college in Southern California. My graduate school was in Pennsylvania, a few hours away from Massachusetts. During the holidays, I took Route 80 eastbound toward Massachusetts, where Lok-Yeay prepared Khmer dishes for me and asked how I was doing. No matter how much I struggled, I always offered the same reply, "Everything's great. I'm learning a lot, and everyone is really nice to me."

She smiled, "Your Lok-Ta always believed in you. He thought you would be a scholar someday. You made him proud, Samnang"

I shoved a spoonful of rice and fried fish into my waiting mouth. She added, "Remember, be careful with women."

"Lok-Yeay, I'm trying to eat here! It's been forever since I had rice and fish with mango salad."

Ming Bonavy laughed, "Leave him alone, Lok-Yeay. Let your grandson eat."

It was Thanksgiving break, and I was home to interview my family about their experiences under the Khmer Rouge regime and coming to America. This was for an independent project supported by a faculty member at the university. The more I asked questions and listened to the stories of survival told by Pu, Ming, and Lok-Yeay, the more I found myself in awe of what they'd experienced and recognized how much love they had for each other and for our family, and I began to realize how lucky I had been. There was no mistake in my parents naming me "Samnang." I was indeed lucky to have been rescued by my grandmother and raised by her. She did what she could. Given the circumstances, they all did what they could.

Realizing how fortunate my life had been, several times I picked up the phone in my apartment at Penn State to tell Lok-Yeay how grateful I was for her love. After we hung up, the dial tone pierced my ear. All these intense emotions came rushing out. I put down the receiver. I turned to an old photograph that Oum Seyha had given me before I'd driven back to the university at the end of Thanksgiving weekend. It was an old picture taken in one of the refugee camps. We were all standing together, with the Gulf of Thailand behind us. Lok-Yeay and Lok-Ta, Lok-Oum, Lok-Pu and Lok-Ming, Bopha, Vutha, and I, all of us stood together, our faces fatigued by war, hunger, and death, by displacement and homelessness. We barely survived the Khmer Rouge. I stood in a red T-shirt and gray shorts. Lok-Ta in his blue pants and white shirt, his gray hair parted to the right. Ming Narin was holding her naked son, Raksmei, in her arms. Behind us were the sun and the crashing waves. Our eyes stared directly at the camera. The expression on our faces was hope mixed with uncertainty. We were exhausted, but we were together. Looking at the photograph, it was clear to me what I needed to do. As a way of thanking them, I must write about them.

That first summer of graduate school, I stayed up until five in the morning working furiously at my Dell desktop computer with nothing but coffee in my bloodstream. In the introduction, I explained my reasons for writing:

> *I want to take the language that is not given to me at birth, possess it, INFECT it with my presence, my history, my voice, and hurl it back. Only when I know that I have the power to infect, to disturb and pervert the English language with my Khmerness, do I know that I am alive*

and well, a human being, with the agential power to
accept, reject, and create. Thus, I write this book!

I wrote about my aunts and uncles, Lok-Yeay and Lok-Ta, how
we left Cambodia after the fall of the Khmer Rouge regime, our
experiences in the refugee camps in Thailand, and our early years in
America. I titled the manuscript "Under a New Sky" and sent it out
for publication. I received a slew of rejection letters from various
presses. Maybe American publishers weren't ready for this kind of
project. Maybe I wasn't ready to tackle my past—to tell my story.

Ten years later, after completing my first year as an assistant professor, I returned to this story of my life. I rewrote, revised, switched
points of view, revised again. I had friends read it. I revised and edited
further based on their suggestions, and then the miraculous happened: a publisher took a chance on me; the book finally came into
being. Sadly, Lok-Yeay passed away long before its publication. And
Lok-Ta had passed away many moons ago, as though it were another
lifetime. Even if my grandparents had been alive, they couldn't have
read a word of this book. Even if they were here with me today,
I wouldn't know how to look them in the eye and tell them how
much I love them. To be direct and open is not the Cambodian way.

Please allow me, then, to carve out this space and write an imagi-
nary letter to them here.

Dearest Lok-Yeay and Lok-Ta:

We did it. I couldn't have done what I've done without you
both. Thank you.

Thank you for taking me with you to the refugee camps
in Thailand and Indonesia, for feeding and keeping me
warm in America, for taking care of all of us, for always
seeing something good in me.

Lok-Yeay, when we talked on the phone, I told you not
to worry about me and that things would turn out right.
We said our goodbyes. You hung up. I heard the dial tone
through the receiver.

But I needed to say more. I couldn't tell you how much I loved you because I didn't know how to say such things. It's not our Khmer way. I was afraid that I might break down and cry. I was afraid that if I cried, then a lot of what I'd kept inside would burst through to the surface and I wasn't ready for that. It is safer for me to write out these words than to utter them. That is why I am a writer.

Here are the words that I owe you, Lok-Yeay: I love you and I am forever grateful to you. I keep you here with me in this book, alive and well in these words. I'll let the world know how strong and fierce your love for our family was. I wouldn't be here writing these words for the world to read if it wasn't for you.

As for you, Lok-Ta, thank you for always believing in me. I will make you proud. With the Khmer that you taught me, I'll read Khmer folktales, novels, and epic poetry, and translate them into English for future generations of Cambodian Americans. Together, we will build an understanding of Khmer literature and culture in this America. Together, we will construct the foundation of a Khmer America, and make this new place a home for our people. I will write and research about the Khmer Rouge, to tell the world what happened to our people and our beloved Srok Khmer. I will tell the world about our family's strength and courage to continue to love one another, in spite of what had happened to us under Angkar.

Lok-Yeay and Lok-Ta, I never knew what it meant to have a mother and father of my own but now, when I look back at my life, I realize you were the closest to a mom and dad that I could ever have. You were both my grandparents and my parents. War does that to families. It tears apart relations and, amid the debris of war, new relations are created, hybrid ones to accommodate the hunger and needs of surviving family members.

You are both gone now, but your memories, your world, and your people will be here with us in my writings. Lok-Pok and Lok-Mak will live through me. You do not need to worry: I will tell our stories. I will translate our folktales. I will translate your memories. I will carry your bodies. Your breath. This book is for you, and it is made of you.

Everything I have done that is good is in honor of you. With songs and dances, Cambodia will be here with us.

Lok-Yeay and Lok-Ta, you need not worry. Wherever there are stories, you exist. Wherever there are readers, you will never be alone. And when the younger generations of Khmer Americans read our stories, Cambodia too will be with them, indelibly imprinted on their psyches.

Rest assured: you will never be forgotten.

With the deepest love,

Your Koan Khmer

Epilogue

It's summer 2013. I have been frantically gathering materials for my tenure file. But today I take a break. My daughter Neary, named for Lok-Yeay, runs up and down the red and yellow playset in our local park. Her hair is light brown, like her mom's, but her eyes and face, round like the moon, remind me of my grandmother's. My wife Sarah is seven months pregnant with our second child. We want to be kept in the dark regarding the sex of the baby, but no matter their sex, we both agree to give them a Cambodian name. Sarah and I met when we were graduate students at a university in Pennsylvania. After we became serious, Sarah did all she could to learn about Cambodian culture and history, consuming history books, monographs, and scholarly articles about Cambodia. She probably knows more about the country of my birth than I do. At family gatherings, she asks Oum Seyha about life under the Khmer Rouge and Ming Bonavy and Ming Narin about my mother while I play the family translator. Sarah calls herself "an American mutt," being told that she is part Pennsylvanian Dutch, Irish, Italian, and Syrian. Her ancestry comprises all these ghosts, she says, but their faces are murky, unclear. We both agree that our kids need to know about their Cambodian roots. We start with their names, then the Khmer language, and their Ming, Pu, Oum, and Khmer cousins.

From a distance, it looks like my life is the American dream realized. I have worked hard, and it shows. I have a beautiful wife, a smart three-year-old daughter and another child on the way, a job teaching college students, and a house in the suburbs, only a forty-five-minute drive to Philadelphia. Recently, I traded in my Toyota Corolla for a Subaru Forester, now that I'm going to be a parent to two children. But my American dream was more like an American nightmare, filled with the pain of losing family members, friends, and home and the trauma that came with such tremendous losses, which were then compounded with the humiliation and grief of life as a refugee and a racial other in America. Growing up Cambodian in the 1980s on the East Coast meant living with the knowledge that we were hated, inferior because of who we were: refugees from Southeast Asia, a place that had hurt America and destroyed its families.

I remember that walk with Lok-Ta some thirty years ago, in Revere. He couldn't believe how those adults allowed their children to spit and humiliate us so openly and that they seemed to teach and encourage such hate. As a Cambodian and a former monk, Lok-Ta believed that respect was one of the most important virtues and that elders should lead by example. If these American elders could not show respect, then America was a lost cause. I believe that walk, more than anything, broke Lok-Ta.

As for me, the American public school system failed me. I felt alone and insignificant, alienated from my peers, and that life had no value and meaning for someone like me. I didn't see a future in America. The pain was so unbearable that the only recourse I could see was suicide. What saved me, then, was not the American dream. It was some entity from the spirit world, protecting and guiding me back to the land of the living. Maybe it was the spirit of my mother, or maybe it was my father. Maybe it was Lok-Ta, or the mermaid. I didn't know who or what it was then, and I still don't. But I'd felt the same spirit that morning in Long Beach, when I had the unusual urge to visit the library. It was that same warm presence, mysterious yet familiar, that pulled me out of bed and made me drive to the library that Sunday.

Last night, after kissing my daughter goodnight, I read the letter I wrote to Lok-Yeay and Lok-Ta the summer of my first year as a graduate student, and I wept all over again. I wept for all those Cambodians who had lost their homeland, who were separated from families, and whose children and grandchildren spoke a language that was foreign to their ears and tongues. And I wept for their children and grandchildren, who forgot the old ways, who wished to speak to their elders but didn't know how. I wept for Lok-Yeay and Lok-Ta, and I wished they were still alive to see what I had accomplished. How their grandson had gone to graduate school, survived the bizarre world of academia, and earned his doctorate. How their little Samnang got a job as an assistant professor of English at a small college in Eastern Pennsylvania. How their orphan is now a husband and father.

That is how it goes with immigration. It ruptures history and memory, with war and displacement breaking down the cohesive narrative of family and culture. It's the reason I wrote *Under a New Sky*. Stories are my way to suture the wounds of history. They build bridges that connect the younger generation of Cambodians living in the diaspora with the older generations of parents, uncles, aunts, and grandparents.

As these thoughts of the past, present, and future swirl in my head, I hear Neary calling out to me, "Daddy, come up. Come down the slide with me." She wears her My Little Pony T-shirt and blue jeans. She smiles and waves at me from above. *Under a New Sky* is as much a book for her and her sibling as it is for Lok-Yeay, Lok-Ta, Pu, Ming, and Oum. I want my kids to know who their father was as a child, what he and his family endured, what life was like for them in the refugee camps and during the early years of surviving in America. This is part of their story, their heritage, and in that sense, it's for an entire generation of Cambodian Americans. I want them to know what life was like for their parents, the struggles and confusion, the heartaches and desperation, the hurt and loss, and yet, somehow, they have made it. They are here.

"Be careful, Neary," Sarah looks up at the slide. I run up the steps, my heart and legs racing to catch up with our daughter. The day isn't perfect. It's windy and clouds are heading toward us on the horizon. I have no idea how my tenure case will be decided but in this moment, it doesn't matter. For the first time in my life, I am truly happy. I have a smart and happy daughter, a beautiful and caring wife, and another child on the way. I find myself on top of the slide, put my daughter on my lap, wrap my arms around her, and close my eyes. For a split second, I feel the warm presence of my ancestors everywhere in this local park, their undiscernible voices whispering in the woods of Eastern Pennsylvania and in the beautiful cloudy imperfect sky. I inhale their presence and smile. I open my eyes to see Sarah waving below. I hold Neary close to me and, together, we count down in Khmer as we prepare ourselves to go down the yellow slide: muoy, pii, bei!

Acknowledgments

A book tells many stories. This one is no exception. One of the stories *Koan Khmer* tells is its own birthing, and like most births this one involves a community of family and friends, of good decent people who helped bring it to life. *Koan Khmer* may begin with the historical rupture of war and genocide in Cambodia, but it was nurtured and given voice in America. These are the people who nurtured it with support and encouragement and helped usher the book into the world.

Koan Khmer would not have existed without the stories of my aunts, uncles, and grandparents. Their memories of Cambodia, Thailand, and America are the seeds from which this book sprouted. I owe them a debt of gratitude. In particular, I am eternally grateful to Bunyonn Tuon.

I thank my wife, Nicole Calandra, for her support, patience, and understanding as I spent years cloistered in my office working on this novel only to emerge to ask for her opinion on my writing. Her patience is godliness.

I also thank Maureen and Kenneth Pawl, and their children, for their kindness, generosity, and compassion toward me—a stranger "from a different shore," to quote Ronald Takaki. They took in this refugee kid and made him feel like he belonged.

I owe a debt of gratitude to Sunaina Maira, whose graduate seminar "Documenting Asian Americans" I took at the University of Massachusetts many years ago. It was in this seminar that I began watering the seeds of *Koan Khmer* by interviewing family members and collecting their stories.

I also thank David Lenson, Peter Kahn, and Chris Michalski for reading early incarnations of this book. These versions were more experimental and fragmented than its current form. Apologies for the headaches I'm sure these earlier drafts inflicted on David, Peter, and Chris. I thank them for their early support.

Thanks also go to Jim Hicks for pointing me in new directions and for his wit, humor, and support.

I'm grateful to Anita Mannur for publishing an earlier draft of the chapter "Under the Tamarind Tree" in the *Massachusetts Review* as "Cambodia: Memory and Desire."

Hired primarily as a critic, I was hesitant to show my poems and stories to colleagues at Union College. April Selley, a lecturer in the English Department, was the first person to whom I entrusted my creative writing. She gave me comments about this manuscript before she passed away. She was more than a dear friend.

The English Department at Union College has played a crucial role in nurturing and supporting my creative endeavors. Past and current chairs Judith Lewin and Bernhard Kuhn have been instrumental. Knowing that the best way to understand a subject is through teaching, they gave me creative writing classes to help me grapple with issues of craft and style and engage in conversations with established and emergent writers. Jordan Smith, Harry Marten, Jim and Carol McCord, and Judith Lewin read various versions of this novel and provided invaluable comments and suggestions, as did former student Nicholas Soluri, who reminded me of the invaluable lesson of paying attention to only the writing and nothing else. For their support and friendship, I am in debt to Pattie and Tarik Wareh, who exemplify the best of what the humanities has to offer. The English Department on the whole is the place where I learned how to write; it is where I earned my "MFA" credentials. I will always be grateful to this department and the folks there whom I have the honor of calling friends.

Floyd Cheung served on my dissertation committee many years ago. He's been a mentor and a friend ever since. I sent him a version of this book and he got me to think about literary links to Asian American literary forebears. This was during the early stages of the pandemic when we were all scrambling to adjust our teaching and figure out Zoom, but he made time for me and my work. He's such a good, kindhearted person.

Alan Catlin is a fine poet, writer, and friend who lives a ten-minute drive away in Schenectady. His comment about framing helped me to think about ways to sharpen my story angle.

Thanks to Michelle Ross for publishing an earlier version of "The Old Woman and her Dog" in *Atticus Review*.

And thanks, also, to Douglas Glover for publishing "On Fathers, Losses, and Other Influences" in *Numéro Cinq*. This essay laid the groundwork for the chapter "A Dream."

I have never met Melissa Ostrom in person. We follow each other on Twitter. She's a fine novelist. She knows the craft and language of storytelling. I thank her for asking really smart questions about an earlier version of this book. Not only do I follow her on Twitter, I also follow her writerly advice.

A special thank you to David Kaczynski for his selfless act of combing through this manuscript, highlighting writing issues and making smart and careful suggestions. He is another dear friend.

Finally, I am in debt to the generosity and kindness of editor Marisa Siegel. An ethical, savvy, and conscientious editor, Marisa saw immediately the true vision of *Koan Khmer*. Her support and encouragement affirmed my project of normalizing Khmerness in this book. Thank you, Marisa, for championing my work. My appreciation to copy editor Anne Gendler, who sifted through my transliteration of Khmer words, making sure the spellings of those words and the word "Việt Nam" were used consistently, but who is also respectful of my linguistic choices and understands that they reflect both the aesthetic and political intentions in *Koan Khmer*. For all of this, I am grateful.

And so, these are the friends and family members who helped me usher into the world this *Koan Khmer* that you're holding in your hands. And I thank them with all my heart.